NOR ALL YOUR TEARS

NOR ALL YOUR TEARS

A Dr Lance Elliot Mystery

Keith McCarthy

This first world edition published 2012
in Great Britain and in the USA by
SEVERN HOUSE PUBLISHERS LTD of
9–15 High Street, Sutton, Surrey, England, SM1 1DF.

British Library Cataloguing in Publication Data

McCarthy, Keith, 1960–
  Nor all your tears. – (Dr Lance Elliot mystery)
  1. Physicians – Fiction. 2. Serial murder investigation –
  England – London – Fiction. 3. Detective and mystery
  stories.
  I. Title II. Series
  823.9'2-dc22

ISBN-13: 978-0-7278-8119-9 (cased)

All Severn House titles are printed on acid-free paper.

Severn House Publishers support The Forest Stewardship Council [FSC],
the leading international forest certification organisation. All our titles that
are printed on Greenpeace-approved FSC-certified paper carry the FSC logo.

Typeset by Palimpsest Book Production Ltd.,
Falkirk, Stirlingshire, Scotland.
Printed and bound in Great Britain by
MPG Books Ltd., Bodmin, Cornwall.

ONE

The journey to Bensham Manor School is not a particularly cheery one. It is a red-brick Victorian building situated in Ecclestone Road, a not particularly outstanding or memorable part of the oasis in South London that is Thornton Heath, surrounded by streets formed by houses that bear the air of an inevitable decay, so that whilst many of the householders were attempting to make the best of their castles – lawns kept mowed, flower-beds weeded, garden gnomes aplenty – there were too many that were empty and boarded up, or in a state of serious disrepair, and most of the public green spaces were ill-kept and tatty. I knew the area quite well because many of the people living there were my patients, and I knew, too, that many of these people were decent and honourable, the whole environment spoiled by a small but significant minority of undesirables. To Max, though, it was all new. Coming from an upper-middle-class background (both parents were senior doctors, she was a trained vet), areas such as this one were as alien and scary as the dark side of the moon, and I suspect she had eyes only for the less seamy views around, was blind to the positives. She kept looking around her with widened eyes and mouth ever so slightly open, as if she had heard of such places, but had never before quite believed in them.

It was somehow worse because it was hot. My God, was it hot; it seemed to have been hot for years now. The whole world now seemed desiccated and dusty, the only moisture a sort of greasy film adhering to every surface, tainting every memory.

The campus of Bensham Manor School (although that word had yet to find its way into the British English language, as we must call it) was not itself, at least at a distance, harsh on the eye. There was a three-storey main school building in red brick, a very Victorian affair but none the worse for that. In front of this was a large playground, to the right of which was a more modern two-storey building attached by an annexe to the original edifice. To the left were some single-storey 'temporary' classrooms ('temporary' as in not made of brick or stone, but going to have to last a long time anyway), whilst behind was another playground bounded by a science block, an arts centre and a gymnasium. A lot of the bare surfaces were decorated in graffiti which, to my aged eye, did nothing to make it a more pleasant environment. We were going there because it was the school's summer parents' evening; it was late July 1977, and the weather was hot.

Perhaps at this point, lest you be leaping, nay bounding, to unwarranted conclusions, neither I nor Max, either singly or in combination, was a parent of anyone attending Bensham Manor School in Thornton Heath, Surrey. Indeed, quite the reverse; we were going to see my parent, Benjamin Elliot. For those of you not familiar with my progenitor in this vale of tears that is modern existence, let me explain some things. I am a general practitioner in the fair burgh of Thornton Heath, which itself lies to the south of Streatham and north of Croydon; it is positioned on the Brighton Road, which is nice because it means that once a year the London to Brighton Old Crocks race passes through – always a treat for the entertainment-starved locals. Max, as I have said, is a vet, also residing and living in Thornton Heath, and I am lucky enough to have found that she rather likes me; my father is a retired GP, dedicated gardener and allotmenteer, and just – but only just – sane enough to have escaped permanent incarceration in a padded cell.

The reason this reprobate was present at the school that evening was because he had spent the last six months running a Horticultural Club there. This had been the idea of the headmaster, Mr Silsby, as a way of teaching some of his more troublesome pupils (he preferred the term 'high-spirited', but we all knew what he meant) some useful skills, and Dad had got the gig because he was friendly with Mrs Ada Clarke, and Mrs Ada Clarke was the head dinner lady at the school. She had heard talk of Mr Silsby's new, pet project, and had rushed to propose Elliot Senior as a potentially useful volunteer. Dad, in turn, with his customary enthusiasm for striking out in different directions whenever he could, had jumped at the chance.

'I wonder what she looks like?' asked Max. Neither of us had ever met Ada, although we had heard plenty about her. She was in her early sixties, was a good Christian woman with a penchant for bell-ringing (which she did at St Jude's Church on Thornton Road) and was, according to Dad, a real 'stunner'. From my perspective, this meant nothing; since he had become a widower some decades before, he had sought the attentions of a startling variety of womanly types – Margaret Wallcroft (who had a glass eye and a vocabulary that would have made many a hardened navvy feel faint), Annie Mallett (a very pretty, petite woman who spoke in a high-pitched lisp and giggled with such irritating regularity that an evening in her presence had left me a gibbering wreck) and Nanette LaRoche (who was French and sophisticated, played the bagpipes – I kid you not – and did so badly) to name but three. Dad had been seeing Ada for eight months now and tonight was to be the night that we would finally be allowed to cast eyes on what he assured us was pulchritudinous perfection.

'Well, on the whole, he tends to go for reasonably attractive women – although I had my doubts about Margaret, especially when she tripped on the stairs and her eye fell out – but it's the personality you've got to worry about. Like attracts like, so that, generally speaking, he only goes shopping for life companions at the fruitcake stall.'

'That's not fair. Your dad's not a fruitcake. He's just . . .' She hesitated, groping for some words that might encapsulate my father's propensities for extreme eccentricity but that did not go so far as to say he was a total, eye-rolling, frothing-at-the-mouth maniac. 'His own man.'

Well, as an epitaph, it sounded pretty good, but as an excuse it left a lot to be desired. I murmured, 'At least Ada doesn't sound as though she eats insects and sleeps hanging upside down in the understairs cupboard.' In fact, during Dad's little problems with his neighbour (Oliver Lightoller, who had once been at perpetual war with Dad), Ada had refused to join in with my father's lunatic schemes, something that had temporarily put a dampener on the relationship; clearly, though, love conquer'd all.

'She sounds as if she is a very fine and upstanding woman,' said Max.

'So what does she see in Dad?'

'You're being unfair; your father's a thoroughly decent man.'

'Seven months ago he spent two nights in a police cell, accused first of arson and then of murder. That kind of thing doesn't usually happen to "thoroughly decent" men.'

'He was innocent,' she reminded me, with more than a touch of scolding in her voice.

We had reached the gates of the school. There was a man in a red nylon tabard telling the world that he was a steward; he was short and portly, and had a moustache. He also wore rounded, NHS glasses. I knew the sort; the soubriquet 'steward' is actually code for 'little Hitler'.

'Over there,' he said, indicating a field to our left where the cars seemed to stretch to a heat-shimmered horizon that could easily have been Land's End. It wasn't so much the words as the tone that started me off; I must own that this is perhaps a trait of my father's coming out in me, but I tend to get slightly annoyed when people like this assume that authority legitimizes rudeness.

'There's space over there,' I pointed out, indicating several empty parking places behind him in the nearby outdoor basketball court.

'They're reserved,' he said, without even looking round.

'Are they?' I peered intently. 'Where does it say that?'

There was a queue building up behind us. 'Here,' he said, stamping a short, tar-stained finger down on his clipboard.

Max was shaking my arm gently as I enquired coldly, 'Who for?'

'The Mayor.'

I peered again. A horn sounded behind us. 'I can see four places free. Coming with the entire Town Council, is he?'

At last I got a reaction, in that he bothered to look at me, as he said in a nasty manner, 'Look, sir. Ordinary visitors have to park over there. You are causing an obstruction.'

And what with the increasing honking of horns and Max hissing my name in a dangerously angry voice, I decided that a point had been made and that I could move on with dignity.

TWO

'I mean, I really cannot understand what on earth possessed you . . .'

I thought that Max had forgotten it. She had given me a good ten minutes of earbashing as we bumped over the field and parked, a ticking-off that had subsided only gradually; suddenly, as we approached the main entrance to the school (feeling exhausted, hot and dusty, as if we'd been for a three-day hike in Death Valley), she had started up again. 'I don't like people like that,' I reiterated. 'They're the kind of people who run golf clubs for their own convenience, and who run for the council as if it was their own personal fiefdom . . . And who become traffic wardens.'

'They do a necessary job.'

'But they do it with such glee! It's people like him' – I indicated my friend who was still imperiously directing cars into the Outback while close behind him there were acres of available parking – 'who formed the small but essential cogs in the Nazi war machine.'

And Max did then what only Max can do, which was to deflate me with a giggle and a very accurate observation. 'You sound like your father.'

We entered the foyer of the school; or rather, Max entered it and I stalked into it. Some surly looking yobbo with a fuzzy felt moustache, a shirt with a phobia of underpants and a tie contorted into what was then popularly known as a 'Double Windsor' thrust a programme at me, his expression suggesting that he was secretly wishing that it was a Bowie knife. We moved on into the main hall. Most of what was happening tonight was of no interest to us. This was primarily an evening when the parents could talk to their offspring's teachers although, to be more accurate, it was usually the teachers who did the talking. Mr Arthur Silsby was the headmaster, and had been for as long as I could remember; he was a patient of the practice and thus I knew that he was a dedicated man, always keen to do his best for the school and the children. Tonight, he had laid on a variety of exhibitions, displays and demonstrations to show that Bensham Manor not just an upgraded secondary modern, it was a shining example of comprehensive education. Thus, in the art department, we would be able to find hundreds of pictures, sculptures, collages and pasta mosaics, in the gymnasium we could marvel at an unrivalled demonstration of backward rolls, flips, handstands and 'crabs' and in the newly constructed science wing we would be blinded by flashes, deafened by bangs and electrocuted by static electricity.

In the hall in which Max and I found ourselves, there were rows of desks alternating with rows of chairs; the teachers sat at the desks hiding behind piles of loose-leaf folders, the parents either sat in front of them like nervous applicants for a job or waited on the rows of chairs, the women gossiping, the men looking as if they were hacked off that they were missing that night's *Starsky and Hutch*, scattered pupils resembling zombies on the point of attack. All of which found me appalled and intrigued in equal measures. Wherever I looked, the faces were uniformly bored and I found myself wondering just what, precisely, was the point of this ritual? I remembered it from the point of the children, but the memory was no happier than the vista before me; it was one of ennui leavened by slight trepidation that one or more of the teachers (usually the geography teacher, I recall) was going to tell my parents exactly what he thought of me. Through this whole melange stalked the tall, slightly stooped figure of Mr Silsby, his face bearing a mask of worry, clearly terrified that something could go so easily wrong.

We pushed through the hall, heading for the small garden at the back of the gymnasium that Dad had spent the last three months preparing and planting with the help of a dozen or so of the less academically bright final year children. He had become really enthusiastic about the project, telling us over

Sunday dinners (always a joint of meat or a chicken, accompanied by roast potatoes, roast parsnips and two green veg, together with a side order of enough saturated fat to cause his drains to clog up regularly) how the sprouts were doing, that the soft fruits had blight or that the runner beans were a beauty to behold. During these eulogies, he would wave his eating implements around, depositing small flecks of gravy and minuscule servings of vegetables around the table; we had learned long ago never to wear our best when breaking bread with Dad.

In the gymnasium, children of assorted shapes and sizes performed various gymnastic manoeuvres with greater or lesser skill and success, supervised by a tall but thin woman of about forty or so with short dark brown hair, big eyes and a slight pout; she wore tracksuit bottoms and a white T-shirt. There were perhaps thirty parents looking on.

As we walked past, Max murmured, 'Bet she's a lesbian.'

I was shocked. 'Max! I didn't know you knew of such things.'

'My old PE teacher was definitely one. She used to wander around the changing rooms and the showers, pretending she was there to make sure that we weren't whipping each other with wet towels, but in reality she was perving on the naked girls. Makes my flesh crawl.'

'They all prowl the changing rooms,' I pointed out. 'They're supposed to. It's in the job description that they have to make the pupils feel inadequate, terrified and slightly sick.'

'Then they're all homosexuals and lesbians.'

It seemed that there was no arguing with her.

On the far side of the gymnasium, a side door had been opened and it was through this, at the rear of the school, that we found Dad. He was talking animatedly to a small group of parents, explaining, no doubt, the intricacies of pricking out, how to make your carrots grow straight (one of his favourites) and the evils of parsnip canker. Half a dozen youths – large boys and pubescent girls – were variously showing off some of the produce that had come from the garden; impressive looking lettuces, juicy red tomatoes, salad onions and baskets of new potatoes. Both Max and I were impressed and I felt pleased for Dad that he had made such a success of the venture;

I had the impression that this was probably something of a triumph over the odds. Certainly the location was not totally what I would have called hospitable; the vegetable plot was situated at the base of a brick wall that was five feet high and topped with broken glass; it was heavily and garishly graffitied, not something I found particularly pleasant on the eye. One good thing about the plot was that it was south-facing, although the slight problem with that was that for most of the day the sun was blocked out by the edifice of the gymnasium on the other side, about twenty yards distant, and also badly defaced by graffiti; in the intervening gap was a cinder running track, as well as areas for the long jump, the high jump and the shot put; the grass around these was browned and weed-strewn. It all had something of the air of a prison backyard.

THREE

D ad spotted us and came over as soon as he could. 'Sorry about that,' he said. 'They wouldn't let me get away. Most interested, they were, in how we get the carrots to grow straight.'

I forbore to comment that the body language had suggested that it had been a captive audience rather than a captive lecturer. Max said brightly, 'This is very impressive, Dr Elliot.'

He looked around, a man seeing success wherever his eye rested. 'I'm fairly happy with it,' he said airily, much as the bloke who built the Great Pyramid at Cheops had probably once been quoted as saying in *Ancient Egypt Today*. 'They're a good bunch of kids, too.' Max clearly had that innate survival instinct that makes you automatically afraid of large school children en masse, for her face suggested that she might need a little persuasion on that subject. Dad continued with characteristic unregard, 'Would you like to meet my star pupil?'

It was one of those questions that have only one answer. He led us over to a rather tall, clearly well-muscled lad with sandy coloured hair, light-blue eyes and high cheekbones. He was over six feet tall and his whole demeanour suggested that he thought he was the bee's knees. 'David? I'd like you to meet my son and his girlfriend.'

David turned and gave us a smile. Of its type, it was a fine example. It stretched his cheeks, it reached to his eyes and his body language opened up. 'Of course,' he said. His voice was standard South London, not ugly, not refined. He held out his hand; I was interested to see that he held it out to Max first. 'How do you do?' he asked of her with an expression that I thought was a tad too rakish for my liking. Max smiled nervously. To me, the hand was accompanied by a rather more perfunctory, 'Hi.'

All sorts of primeval mating instincts whispered in the back of my head and I told myself not to be stupid.

Dad said, 'David is Ada's grandson.'

'Oh,' I said. 'And where is she?'

'Providing refreshments in the dining room. She'll be along shortly when she's finished her shift.'

In an effort to be sociable, I said to David, 'You've done a wonderful job here, David.'

It took him a moment to respond, perhaps because he was staring rather more than I liked at Max. 'Yes, yes,' he said eventually, seeming to bring himself back from somewhere. 'Not bad.'

'David's got green fingers,' proclaimed Dad, as if David had recently had the Légion d'honneur bestowed upon him. 'I gave him the beetroots, and look how they've turned out.' He indicated two rows of dense and luxuriant green and purple foliage, neatly arrayed and impressively weedless. David bowed his head as if overcome with pleasure at this praise but, cynical old git that I am, I had the feeling that he was taking just a little bit of the urine at the same time. Dad smiled at Max. 'I know how much you like them.'

Max smiled nervously. 'Thank you so much.'

'Don't thank me, thank David.'

Whose smirk widened whilst into his eyes there came a certain gleam, one that perturbed me a tad; I was starting to have my suspicions about this metaphysical heir of Percy Thrower.

At this point, we were approached by a middle-aged couple and an adolescent girl who, it transpired, were David's family. Pater was tall, completely bald, dressed in jeans and a black shirt and extravagantly tattooed; mater was somewhat shorter, with knee-high leather over jeans that she could only have got into by oiling up first, a T-shirt that probably had the nicest job in the world and the kind of make-up job that Michelangelo would have swooned over. Between them was what I assumed was their daughter, who was also carrying a considerable weight of cosmetics; it was difficult to judge her age and could have been anything from sixteen to twenty-two. The body language – I have read *The Naked Ape*, so I'm fairly adept at this – was fascinating. The father stayed with the girl, whereas the mother split off immediately to go to David and begin cooing at the vegetables.

Dad made the introductions – Mike and Tricia Clarke were the parents, Joanna the daughter – but then there followed one of those pauses I know so well; conversation is a tender plant and, unlike the Clarke filius, I do not have green fingers. It didn't help that Mike Clarke seemed to be an angry man and Tricia Clarke a woman with little to say. Inevitably we were reduced to asking about jobs, but that didn't help because Mike, it turned out, was a Fleet Street printer – which in those days meant that he earned substantially more than I did whilst doing considerably less; I am not a bitter man, but then I am not a saint either, and I have seething resentments against members of NATSOPA, the printers' union. To make matters worse, Tricia apparently whiled away the long days by . . . well, whiling them away not doing anything much at all.

'Are you a pupil here?' I enquired of Joanna in some desperation but with little confidence that it would open a vein of dialogue rich in conversational possibility; for one thing, she seemed obsessed with her patent-leather shoes and had rarely raised her eyes from them. She was dressed in widely flared jeans and a bright yellow crop top that left little to my imagination. Her father replied for her immediately. 'Yeah.'

'What year are you in?' asked Max.

'She's in the third year.' That Mr Clarke should once again respond was strange; that he said what he said was surprising;

she was no more than fourteen. Max's surprise was as great as mine, I think, leading to yet another awkward lull in the social niceties. It lasted until Tricia asked Max if she had ever stuck her hand up a cow's bottom, and then followed it up with the inevitable corollary, 'What does it feel like?' I think we were all grateful when Dad suddenly said, 'Here comes Ada.'

I turned to see a woman of average height, greying hair and bright, sparkling eyes who, thankfully, bore little resemblance to her son. She was smartly dressed and had a smile that was, perhaps unfortunately, formed of thin lips giving it an underlying hint of cruelty; when she came up to Dad, she seemed genuinely pleased to see him, though; I am ashamed to admit that I had been starting to wonder if there was more to her affection for him than just a love of loony pensioners with beards. They held hands and it seemed that Ada's slight faux pas a few months before (when her loyalty to Christ had outweighed all else, including her passion for Dad) was a thing of the distant past. She then turned to her son. 'Hello, Michael.' She give him a peck on the cheek for which he bent down obediently, then managed to exchange smiles with her daughter-in-law that struck me as a trifle strained on both sides, then turned to David, who was enveloped in the kind of hug that only grandmothers know how to give. David's expression was difficult to read; he might have been enjoying it, might only have been enduring it. 'Gran,' he said noncommittally.

For a few moments I was dreadfully afraid that Max and I were going to be required to spend the rest of the evening making polite but entirely meaningless conversation about typesetting and fonts, hair dyes and blusher, but then Ada said to Dad, 'I've got to be going now, Benjamin. Michael said he'd give me a lift home.'

Dad looked devastated. 'But I thought . . .'

'I know, but I'm rather tired, and you're going to be here for a good hour longer, aren't you?'

Dad nodded sadly; the call of love being trumped by the call of duty is not an easy thing to swallow. 'Of course.'

A quick peck on both cheeks for Dad (I admired her fortitude and pluck in not flinching before she buried herself in the Brillo pad that is Dad's beard), a smile for Max and me, and Ada was gone with her family.

'Isn't she wonderful?' murmured Dad as he watched them go.

'She seems like a nice lady,' I said carefully and Max concurred.

It was just the rest of her family I wasn't so sure about.

FOUR

We stayed with Dad until the parents' evening began to wind down at about eight thirty. During all this time the weather had stayed fine and warm and although the numbers coming to view the efforts of the Horticultural Club had gradually dwindled, Dad had still managed to spread the word on the arcane rituals necessary to entice asparagus to grow to at least a dozen more ever-so-slightly interested parties. The pupils were well behaved and most of them helped him clear away the tools and, as a reward, had been given a selection of vegetables to take home; they even managed to look slightly delighted. The shed locked, Dad clapped his hands together and asked, 'Well? What did you think of her?'

I said with genuine honesty, 'She seems very nice.' Thankfully he didn't ask me to comment on her son, daughter-in-law or grandchildren. Max agreed enthusiastically, and Dad was satisfied. Max added, 'And you've achieved a lot here.' She indicated the neat rows of vegetables and soft-fruit bushes.

'Mr Silsby's very pleased,' admitted Dad. 'Some of the lads and lasses who've been working here were quite troublesome, but this seems to have given them a bit of focus in life.' He lowered his voice, although we were outside and unless there was a hidden microphone amongst the runner beans, it was unlikely that we would be overheard. 'Ada's grandson, particularly so.'

'Really?' I said, I think quite convincingly hiding the fact that I was not in the least bit surprised. 'How come?'

'Well . . .' Another glance around, but he failed to spot the hordes of spies and eavesdropping equipment he evidently believed might be arrayed around us. 'He's got into quite a lot of trouble over the past couple of years. Very disruptive in class, truanting, threatening behaviour; he's been caned on several occasions and once he even physically assaulted someone. Beat them up quite badly, actually. It was only because the poor chap didn't want to press charges that nothing further came of it.'

I was saved having to make further surprised noises by Max who, bless her, said, 'Gosh! I'd never have guessed.'

Dad smiled proudly. 'That's because he's changed.'

'You've changed him,' she said, a sight too gushingly for my taste.

Before Dad could perjure himself with false modesty, a figure appeared in the doorway to the gym. I recognized him vaguely, which meant almost certainly he was a patient of the practice, although not registered with me, I thought. He was an inordinately tall and broad-shouldered man with cropped dark hair, unshaven features and the merest hint of a stoop as he poked his head out the doors to the gymnasium. 'I'm locking up soon,' he pronounced in a deep voice. He spoke slowly, with care, as if words were a thing new to him.

Dad waved and smiled at him. 'OK, George.'

The figure retreated. Dad explained, 'The caretaker, George Cotterill. Nice chap. He sometimes helps out in the garden; we often have a cup of tea together.'

The evening was progressing as we trudged back towards the front of the school. Dad was apparently amongst the blessed in this life, for he had been given a parking space close to the school buildings (I noticed that the Mayor's reserved spaces were still empty, presumably because he had found something better to do with his evening – perhaps a statue to unveil or the freedom of Thornton Heath to convey upon someone), so we said goodnight to each other and Max and I began our expedition to the outer reaches of the known world where the car was parked. The sight of my BMW all alone, far from civilization, was slightly surreal; behind us, we could hear Dad turning over the engine of his bright red Hillman Avenger, the 'Red Hornet' – a sound that the denizens of Pollards Wood, where he lives, were well used to.

A further five minutes passed before we were in the car and retracing the bumpy, dusty way back to the school entrance. The Red Hornet was still there, its bonnet up, Dad daring to put his head in its maw; I drew up beside him. 'Problem?'

I made him jump so that he hit his head on the bonnet and nearly dislodged its support. 'For God's sake!' he said, rubbing his forever disordered hair. 'Do be careful, Lance.'

'Have you got a problem?' I asked again, although it was obvious that he did.

'Alternator's been misbehaving for a while now. I've been meaning to buy a new one, but kept putting it off; I thought this one would see me through a couple more journeys.' He sighed, 'Apparently not, though.'

This was typical of Dad; he wasn't about to replace a part of anything until it was not only dead, but mouldering in the ground and all but an archaeological exhibit. 'You'd better leave it here for the night, Dad. We'll give you a lift home.'

He hesitated, looking slightly shocked as if we had suggested leaving his ailing baby grandchild out on a hillside. 'I suppose . . .' he said eventually.

'It's getting dark, Dad. You can come back tomorrow and fit a replacement.'

It had probably been an easier decision when they decided where precisely to put the Iron Curtain, but he got there eventually. 'All right,' he sighed.

As we drove off, I saw him looking back at the school gates as if grieving, a man separated from his spouse for the first time in years.

FIVE

The phone by my bed rang at six the next morning. I ought to be used to this kind of thing, but I'm not; in fact, as I grow older, I resent it more and more. I do a one-in-seven on-call rota, which ought to mean that I do a corollary six-in-seven not-on-call rota, but it doesn't seem to work like that. Believe me, I love my job and I really care about my patients, but one of the golden rules about medicine is never to let any of them get hold of your home number; if you do, you may just as well set your alarm clock to go off three times a night, every night.

'Yes?'

'Lance? Didn't get you up, did I?' My father once rang me at four in the morning because he'd lost his driving gloves and he thought he might have left them at my house. And (can you believe it?), his first words on that occasion were also, 'Didn't get you up, did I?'

'Well . . .'

'Good. Look, can you give me a lift to the school? I want to pick up the car as soon as possible. I've promised to take Ada to Texas Homecare this morning and unless I get a move on, I won't make it.'

'I didn't think you had a replacement; you said that you hadn't got around to buying one.'

'I've been scouting about in the garage and found an old one. I'm sure it'll fit. No point in spending money when there's no need to.'

'Dad, I'm due in surgery at eight thirty . . .'

'Plenty of time to drive me over there, then. Can you pick me up in half an hour?'

Which was how, at just after seven, I drove again through the gates of Bensham Manor School, accompanied by a father who was so bloody cheerful, he made me want to scream. At least this time, Mr Hitler had apparently repaired to his underground bunker for a good night's rest before again imposing his will on the undisciplined masses. There was only one other car there, a Morris Minor which looked to be in almost perfect condition. Dad explained, 'That's George's car. I expect he's opening up.'

After revelling in the illicit pleasure of parking in what last night had been the Mayor's parking space, Dad and I went across to his car and for the next fifteen minutes we wrestled with his alternator. I say 'we' but in fact he quickly began to complain of a bad back (which was new to me) and made groaning noises every time he bent over the engine. Then he

said he was having trouble undoing some of the bolts, and
within a very short time it was I who was covered in grease
and who was dirty (despite the fact that I was dressed for
work), while Dad gave me oh-so-helpful advice and lots of
negative encouragement (as in, 'For God's sake, Lance, you'll
never do it like that'). I had only just succeeded in getting the
old alternator off when on the warm morning air there came
a faint cry, one that came with weak, ill-defined echoes. I
might have thought nothing of it, except that Dad said at once,
'That sounded like George.'

It had come from the back of the school. Dad said in a
worried tone, 'He sounded as if he might be hurt.' And now
I came to think about it, there had certainly been an anguished
quality to the sound. He continued, 'Perhaps we should go
and look for him.'

I was sweating profusely, had seriously scuffed and dirtied
hands, grease on my shirt sleeves and an oil spot on my tie;
all I wanted to do was to get the new alternator fitted and rush
back home to shower anew and get a change of clothes. 'I'm
sure he's all right.'

But Dad was already walking off. 'He didn't sound it to
me,' he said over his shoulder. I would have carried on with
the car, but when I went to look for the new alternator, I
discovered he had taken it with him. By the time I realized
this, he was out of sight around the main building.

'Dad?'

I hurried after him but when I rounded the corner he still
wasn't in sight; I couldn't help wondering how a man with
such a bad back could move so quickly. I heard him call out,
'George? Is that you?' and hurried onwards. Around the next
corner, I saw him stepping into the front doors of the
gymnasium.

'Dad?' He was already inside, though. I walked across the
quadrangle to follow him, feeling all too familiar feelings of
irritation.

Feelings which vanished completely as I entered the coolness of the foyer, for ahead of me, Dad was kneeling over a
body lying just in front of the opened double doors of the
main gymnasium hall. I rushed over to join him to discover

that it was George. He wasn't unconscious, but he was a long way from being totally with it; in fact, my first thought was that he was drunk. Dad was feeling for a carotid pulse and had checked his pupils.

'He seems just to have fainted,' he said.

'Is he under the influence?'

Dad looked shocked. 'George hasn't had a drink for twenty years. He's very proud of that.'

There was no obvious smell of alcohol, but I still wasn't absolutely convinced; at least not until I looked up and into the gymnasium hall.

'Oh, shit.'

Dad looked up at me, frowning. 'Please, Lance. There's never a need for language like that.'

Then he saw what I was looking at. 'Oh, fuck,' he breathed.

The gymnasium was a large square space about fifty yards a side that could be separated into areas of various shapes and sizes by drawing across curtains suspended from the ceiling high above. The floor was marked out with plastic lines of varying colours into basketball courts, badminton courts, indoor cricket nets and two five-a-side football pitches; on the wall were scattered climbing frames and in the far right corner, close to the side door that led out to Dad's gardening area, there were thick climbing ropes, most of which were tied to suspension points on the wall so that they were out of the way.

One of them wasn't, though. One of them hung down, straight and true. One of them ended in a noose, and in that noose was a dead woman.

SIX

Well, it's Thornton Heath, isn't it? I mean, to most people it's just an anonymous place in South London that you might even not notice if you were in a hurry to get from Brixton to Horley, say; it barely registers on the radar for most people, but its citizens keep getting murdered. I am sure that in the future, people will say that it is a black hole of murder, a strange rift in the space-time continuum through which homicide seeps; or something to that effect. And, what is more, they keep getting murdered when I'm around. This, of course, is fascinating in and of itself – worthy, I think, of some sort of academic treatise – but it has certain unwanted effects on my life. The most acute and painful of these is that I come into regular contact with Inspector Masson.

It would be over-egging the pudding to say that he is my nemesis, but then he isn't top of the list for my desert-island buddies; he isn't even *on* the list; he isn't even on the reject list. He's on the list that also includes Benny from Crossroads, that bloody emu and Gary Glitter. He is small and grey and, well, not happy. Not happy, not contented, nor even, apparently, even merely disgruntled; he is as far from being gruntled as it is possible to get. He comes across as a fundamental force for grumpiness; he appears to see crime as a personal insult and, of course, murder as the most profane; that would be bad enough, but he does not take kindly to people trying to help him out of his grumpiness. I know nothing about him. I do not know if he is married or single, his age, where he lives or even if he is technically alive at all. On two previous occasions, I had attempted to help smooth his path through life, only to be met with less than enthusiastic gratitude; in fact, he had tended towards the contemptuous end of the spectrum, had even some-times threatened me with prison for interfering with his enquiries.

And here we were again.

I knew enough not even to enter the gym when Dad and I had spotted its rather unpleasant exhibition, although I had had to hold Dad back, pointing out that the police would not be best pleased. 'But we need to make sure that she's dead. And you're a police surgeon now.'

Which, although true, was not the point. The police invited me when they wanted me; it didn't work the other way round. I looked across at the gym's new exhibit. The body was suspended about four feet off the ground and under her was a pool of something that was undoubtedly drying blood; she had the clothing and the general build of the PE teacher I had seen the night before, but I couldn't be sure because her face had been fairly severely battered. 'I don't think we need to worry too much about that, Dad . . .'

'You've got to make sure, Lance,' he insisted and by golly, I suddenly realized he was right; I was first and foremost a doctor and, as terrified as I might be of Inspector Masson, I had a duty to check that she, whoever she was, was not still alive. It didn't take long, though. Her flesh was cold, waxen; her eyes (or, at least, what could be made out of them) were dried; her fingers were stiff. While Dad continued to tend to George (who was clearly in shock from what he had seen), I went at once to the small office where the PE teachers did whatever paperwork PE teachers have to do (presumably returns on numbers of pupils humiliated, ankles sprained, near-drownings in the swimming pool and cases of concussion following football practice) and dialled 999. The first police car arrived eight minutes later, two more straight after that, then an ambulance (who took over George's care) and Masson after another fifteen, accompanied by a woman I had never seen before; her age was difficult to judge, because her eyes looked wise, her skin young. She had the high cheekbones of a young Afro-Caribbean woman, and, I noticed immediately, impossibly perfect eyebrows. Her demeanour suggested more than a hint of detachment; it was as if she was constantly judging what she saw.

Their arrival coincided with Mr Silsby's, which made for an interesting spectacle.

Arthur Silsby had been a patient of our practice for far longer than I had been a doctor there. He had been born in the area and never moved except for teacher training; his first job had been at Bensham Manor and he was clearly going to work there until he retired or died (whichever came first). My impression of him had been that he was a kind and gentle man – clearly a good teacher – but a bit remote; if anything something of a martinet. He was quite close to retiring – near to sixty – perhaps six feet tall, thin with greying hair and one of those small tufty moustaches under his nose that is always a mistake; pre-Nazi Germany, I can see that some men might have thought it did something for their looks, but in the modern age, anyone considering facial hair of such a design should be taken into a corner and given a good kicking. Mind you, Mr Silsby would probably be able to give as good as he got; when he arrived to find his school full not of teachers and pupils – the police had been turning them away at the gate – but the boys in blue, he was not a happy headmaster; not happy at all. He demanded to know who was in charge, was pointed in the direction of my old mucker, Inspector Masson, and set to with a purpose, Masson's new woman friend looking on. He wanted to know what was going on, why the school was being closed without his permission, what gave Masson the right to take charge of a Local Education Authority establishment and why he, Arthur Silsby, had not been at least kept informed at home.

I had not laid eyes on the Inspector for some months and I was pleased to see that he had yet to take advantage of any available anger-management classes. Dad and I were still in the office and the confrontation took place just outside, so we had a grandstand view, complete with sound (at least to start with); Sergeant Percy Bailey, who was in the office with us, decided it wise to shut the door after the preliminary exchanges, and so thereafter we could not hear what was said, but as a mime, it was second to none. Percy, too, found it fascinating; in fact he even commented that it could take off as a professional sport. At first, it did not appear to be an equal contest; Masson was shorter than Mr Silsby by a good head, and the headmaster clearly had a longer reach, which he demonstrated early on by jabbing his finger at Masson, then pointing all over the place, as if demonstrating the general geography of the school to a particularly stupid parent. Masson's face clearly showed that he did not appreciate being on the receiving end of a bony finger, because he tried a little bit of his own, preferring to wave it somewhere in the vicinity of Mr Silsby's nose, which, I noted idly, was sprouting a few stray hairs. Then Masson fronted up to him, hands on hips, mouthing something through rather tense lips, eyes aglow.

At this point, Mr Silsby's face changed and I would guess that this was the point when it was brought in upon him that the local constabulary hadn't taken over his school on a whim, and that they didn't call out multiple squad cars and senior police officers because someone had stolen a box of HB pencils. The curtains that could divide the main gym hall had been pulled across obscuring the body, so he had had no idea of the atrocity that had occurred. Apparently now fully apprised of the situation, his demeanour changed; he shrank slightly, stepped back and looked a trifle wan. Masson, never a man to let the quarry go without giving it good mauling, took advantage and apparently put Mr Silsby fully in the picture regarding who gave the orders to whom.

There was worse to come for Mr Silsby, for Masson clearly needed someone to identify the victim of the slaughter. The look on the headmaster's face was testament enough to be able to work out what he thought of that particular idea, but Masson did what Masson always did and, having established just who was the alpha male in the vicinity, Mr Silsby was prevailed upon by the good Inspector to enter the gym hall.

He emerged about five minutes later and although when diag- nosing people I generally like to take a full history and do a thorough examination before reaching a diagnosis, I was fairly sure from just looking at the headmaster's face and posture when he passed the office that he had been affected by the sight within. Masson followed him out, there was a brief exchange of words which ended with Mr Silsby nodding in a slightly bemused way and then he made his way out of the gym, presumably to find a bottle of something strong in the top drawer of his filing cabinet, or maybe to have his shoulders massaged by Mrs Ponsonby, his rather aged and prim secretary.

Whereupon Masson, now thoroughly steamed up, made his way back into the gym hall, but not before shooting a venomous – not to say, toxic – glance towards Dad and me. Percy turned around and smiled sadly. 'I don't think he's happy.'

They let me phone the practice so that I could give my colleagues, Brian and Jack, the happy news that they would each have a fifty per cent increase in workload that day, and Percy even took pity on Dad and let him contact Ada to know that Texas Homecare was off for the day. Then we just sat there and waited. During the next hour, there was a lot of coming and going past the office, mostly police, although I did see one face that I recognized but couldn't name. 'Who's that?' I asked of Percy.

He was reading a copy of yesterday's *Daily Mirror* and, I suspect, might even have been about to drop off. He just managed to snatch a glance at the man I was pointing at as he went into the gym. 'Dr Bentham. He's our new pathologist.'

Of course. I had been at St George's with Mark Bentham but had lost touch with him. I had known that he had gone into pathology, but not that he had specialized in the forensic area. Time passed, as it generally does, after which Masson came out the gym followed by his new female friend and together they entered the office. He had not noticeably calmed down. He nodded curtly to Percy – who interpreted this as a suggestion that he might like to go forth – and I sought for a suitable adjective that could be used for his expression; I came to the conclusion that 'baleful' just about fitted the bill perfectly.

'Why me?' he asked. Before either Dad or I could suggest an answer, he then added in a somewhat anguished tone, 'And why you?'

I said nothing, although it was hard; I am a doctor and I do not like to see people in pain. All Dad could manage was, 'Ahh . . .' in a sorting sad, dying fall. He offered something of a shrug and his face was a picture of unalloyed commiseration, but Masson just scowled. It began to feel, I thought, quite like old times.

SEVEN

'This is Sergeant Abelson,' Masson said tiredly. 'She's new to Thornton Heath, so treat her gently.' He indicated me. 'This is Dr Lance Elliot, local GP.' Then he gestured at Dad. 'And this is his father, Dr Benjamin Elliot. He is a retired GP.'

We both smiled and nodded at her and she managed to reciprocate with a twitch of her lips that was difficult to read. It could have been shy, but equally it could have been

embarrassed, defensive, even arrogant. Masson went on for
her benefit, 'Welcome to the local slaughterhouse; these two
seem to be the caretakers of it.'

I enquired, 'Is that fair?'

I might then have tried a bit more in the way of conversation had Masson not transgressed the rules of etiquette by
answering my question with one of this own. He asked immediately, 'Do you know how many murders there are every year
in the Greater London area?'

This was one of those questions that I have found through
bitter experience not to answer; if you get it wrong you're
probably going to look a dork by being out by an order of
magnitude and, if you get it right, the questioner hates you
until you die. I therefore remained shtum on the issue and
allowed Masson to say, 'Two hundred and ninety. That means
that in this area, there should be just six.' I looked at Dad
and he shrugged slightly; we both waited for Masson to give
us the punch line. 'In the past fifteen months, there have been
eleven . . . and your faces keep cropping up every time.'

'I *am* a police surgeon,' I pointed out.

To which he said witheringly, 'More like the angel of death.'

Dad tried to appease him. 'It is odd, isn't it? I mean, we
do seem to have a penchant for stumbling across things like
this, don't we? Who'd have thought it?'

'Who indeed?' asked Masson with enough sarcasm to burn
sun-sensitive skin.

'Anyone would think we were somehow cursed,' continued
my pater, in one of those flights of rumination to which he
was prone and which, in turn, were inclined to aggravate even
the most sanguine of listeners. 'But, of course, it's merely
coincidence, random events falling as they will; people think
that randomness means uniformity, but exactly the opposite is
true . . .'

Masson held up his hand, palm forward, a gesture that had
undoubtedly come in useful when, as a young and wet-behind-
the-ears rookie, he had been on traffic duty. 'Enough,' he
commanded angrily. To the comely Sergeant Abelson, he said,
'Take notes.'

For the next half-hour he took us through the events of the

morning; why we were there (Dad still had the replacement alternator in his pocket, which he produced as proof), why we had gone into the gym, what precisely we had seen when we had done so.

'This man, George Cotterill, he was lying on the floor just outside the main hall?'

'That's right.'

'Facing which way?'

'He was on his back. Head towards the body.'

'And was he conscious?'

Dad considered. 'In shock. Almost concussed.'

'A head injury?'

Dad shook his head and I said, 'Not that we could see. The ambulance boys might give you a better idea, though.'

'Was the door to the hall open?'

'Yes.'

'But he wasn't in the hall?'

'No.'

'How long elapsed between the cry that you heard and you finding him in here?'

Dad said, 'No more than five minutes?'

'What does that mean? One minute or four minutes fifty-nine?'

I was proud of Dad, then. He frowned as if concentrating intently and after several seconds said in a completely serious voice, 'Four and a half.'

Masson stared at him and, for the first time that morning, sought refuge in a cigarette. Whilst he was lighting up, I asked, 'Do you know who she is?'

A deep puff and then he asked, 'Do you?'

'She was a PE teacher, I think. I saw her last night.'

He said at once, 'Yes, tell me about last night. It was an open evening for parents, I understand.'

'That's right.'

'And you were both here?'

'Dad helps out running a garden club for the older pupils; Max and I came along to support him.'

'Miss Christy?' he asked in a pained voice. 'She's involved as well?'

I nodded; only a man with a heart of stone would not have felt compassion for him, although when he turned to Sergeant Abelson and said, 'Miss Maxine Christy is an unconvicted housebreaker and serial accomplice to these two, whose various misdemeanours include obstructing the police and interference with a crime scene,' I did have to bite down hard on a witty, withering response. He made us sound like Croydon's three most wanted. 'Take me through your recollections of last night, including the times you arrived and left, what you did, where you went and what, if anything, you noticed that was unusual.'

It didn't take long and after it, he looked no happier, no more informed. He was nearly at the end of his second cigarette and just sat staring at its lighted tip for a while when, abruptly, he said, 'OK, come with me.'

He stood up, and followed by Dad, then me with Sergeant Abelson bringing up the rear, we made our way out of the office, through the foyer and into the gym hall.

EIGHT

We knew, of course, what to expect, but I still felt a palpable nervousness – and from the look on Dad's face, so did he – as we followed Masson across the echoing gym hall and beyond the curtains that had been drawn across.

Things had changed, but not noticeably for the better. The body had been lowered to the floor and was now laid neatly out in a symmetrical pose, the thick rope trailing away from it. Mark Bentham was leaning over it, making notes and directing a photographer. There were three uniformed officers acting as go-betweens and four more in plain clothes who were dusting various surfaces for fingerprints, examining the floor through magnifying glasses and plucking invisible fibres from the clothing of the corpse.

Mark did not look up as we approached and Masson did not try to disturb him. In a low voice, Masson said, 'As you

so astutely observed, the body is that of Marlene Jeffries . . .'
The pause was not hard to read; my easy identification of the
battered body was potentially incriminating in his book; it was
a book that began with the sentence, *Anyone called Lance
Elliot is at best an idiot, at worst a criminal, and always a
source of dyspepsia.* Having left the nasty implication of his
words hanging for a while, he continued, 'As you said, she
was a PE teacher at the school, one of four. She'd been at
the school for five years, according to the headmaster.'

And someone had done something horrible to her face; from
the degree of distortion, it looked as if most of her facial bones
had been smashed, one eye pulped; there was a huge amount
of congealed blood but not enough to hide deep gashes in her
forehead and cheeks, some of which appeared to be slightly
curved. Dad, who was by no means squeamish, winced and
whispered, 'Oh, dear. Oh dear, oh dear, oh dear . . .'

'Someone didn't like her,' remarked Masson in his charac-
teristically sour tone.

Mark looked up, suddenly aware of our presence. When he
saw me, his face was momentarily blank before a small smile of
recognition appeared. 'Lance?'

'Hello, Mark.' We would have shaken hands except that he
wore disposable gloves and on them was rather a lot of Marlene
Jeffries' colourful vital fluids. 'It's been a while.'

Mark had fair hair and faded blue eyes bracketed by laughter
lines; I remember him in the bar at St George's singing rugby
songs about 'dickey-di-do's' with various things attached. It
was a memory that contrasted vividly with our present situation. The smile was the same, though. 'It certainly has.'

'I didn't realize you were working in the area.'

'Just started.' He glanced at Masson, who was clearly in no
mood to stand idly by for a friendly reunion between old
student chums. 'I've heard your name mentioned a few times
already, though.'

'If we could all get on with the task in hand,' Masson said
testily, at which Mark winked at me and said, 'We'll catch up
later.'

'So, what have you got for me, Dr Bentham? The usual
airy waffle that I get from all you pathologists?'

It was clear that, although he might not have been around Masson for long, Mark had clearly already developed a certain degree of immunity to his waspishness. 'Now, now, Inspector. If someone could get you all the information you need without having to have an autopsy done, I'd be out of a job, wouldn't I?'

Masson's face did something that only an eternal, incurable and quite possibly terminally myopic optimist would interpret as a smile. 'Can you tell me anything concrete at all?'

Mark indicated Marlene Jeffries. 'I can't at the moment find any other significant injuries apart from those to her head. I'm not sure what was used, though. Curious, slightly curved shapes to some of the injuries.'

'Some sort of curved blade? Like a scythe?' asked Sergeant Abelson, speaking for the first time. She had a slightly husky, soft voice.

Masson grunted. 'Are you suggesting,' he enquired of his sergeant, 'that Death himself was the killer?' It was asked in a tone that might well have shrivelled a delicate flower.

Dad, helpful as ever, was not backward in coming forward. 'Or it could have been a very old farmhand,' he offered.

This contribution did not help the chief investigating officer cope with his customary incendiary temper, one that he appeared able to control only by several deep breaths and pulling so much air through his cigarette that it was in danger of imploding into his upper respiratory tract.

Mark frowned. 'Hardly anything like that. It wasn't very sharp. These are heavy blunt injuries.'

Abruptly Masson swivelled around to Abelson, a delicate pirouette that I thought he did rather well. 'Any news on her personal circumstances?'

She shook her head but did so almost defiantly and I found myself warming to Sergeant Abelson; she was not about to go readily into that good night. Although Masson was not happy, she did little in the way of flinching, even as he said, 'Well, get some.'

He then turned to us. 'Thanks for your help.' Which, it appeared, was as close as he came to a gentle dismissal. I smiled at Mark and then Dad and I trudged away; we had

almost reached the doors when a cry came from our right,
one that echoed around the vast room. Everyone turned. A
middle-aged, emaciated man in plain clothes was calling from
a side room. 'Sir? We've found something.'

Everyone converged, of course; Dad and I were quite close
so we had a head start, but Masson did a bit of battling and
pulling of rank so that he got to the front. We were crowded
into a side room on the floor of which was a padded mat,
perhaps used for judo or something; there was a trail of red
– clearly blood – across the diagonal,

At the back was an array of body-building equipment –
dumb-bells of all sizes, medicine balls, complicated pieces of
torture equipment – and a man and a woman were standing
to one side at the end of the red trail across the mat. Masson
walked a parallel line to the bloodstains as he crossed the mat;
Dad and I, along with everyone else, walked around the edges.

The exhibit?

It was a small dumb-bell that seemed to have been dropped
in a puddle of blood in the corner of the room. You didn't
have to try too hard to fit the curves of the weights to the
curves in the head and face of Marlene Jeffries.

NINE

That evening I took Max to the cinema – *Annie Hall* –
and was less than impressed. I preferred Woody Allen
when he did funny stuff – *Sleeper* had me almost wetting
my Y-fronts – and this sort of sensitive, caring, witty stuff
seemed a bit tame; I just wanted him to go suddenly into fast-
forward and run around a lot. Max surprised me, though; I
had expected her to love it – what is wrong with women? –
yet, although initially she seemed to fall for the irritating
sentimentality of it all, her mood did not last. She had been
subdued when I picked her up and had only slowly become
her usual self; during the course of the film, she began to fall
back into melancholy. Afterwards, I tried to engage her in

some chat about the film, arguing in a friendly fashion that Woody Allen had become not so much a master of cinema, more a self-obsessed nerd, but it did little good. We had a Wimpy burger (as good as ever) at our usual vendor – St George's Street, Croydon – and it was then that I began to work out what was wrong with her.

Max is a vet and, so I believe, a very good one, but she has yet to learn clinical detachment; if you look after the sick, then you will never be one hundred per cent successful, and you must learn this quickly. Some of them will die; on occasion, it will seem as if every patient you come across has only a fifty per cent chance of survival, as if you dispense death as often as you restore life. You have to accept this, because not to do so leads to a very unhappy life. You are likely to have to become a public-health consultant or, worse, work in occupational health; these are jobs that, like telephone sanitizers and dental hygienists, are completely unfulfilling and unnecessary. It's the same with vets, too; unless they accept that it's a job and not a whole life, they end working for the Ministry of Agriculture, Fisheries and Food.

In this case, she had that day been forced to put down a dog – a beautiful Alsatian. It had been badly injured two weeks before in a road accident, and although Max had initially hoped to save it, this happy outcome was not to be. She had been giving me daily updates on its progress and up until forty-eight hours before she had still been hopeful; that she had failed had hit her hard. Two weeks is a long time to be with a sick person, and if you're not careful, you bond and that way lies disaster; a bond with an animal can be just as strong as a bond with a human.

'Poor Mr Stewart, he was so upset.'

'These things happen,' I pointed out.

'But Major was his whole life. He doesn't have anyone else.' Which summed Max up; she wasn't just trying to treat the animal, she was trying to cure the owner as well.

'Can't he buy another?'

I suppose, in retrospect, this did sound rather heartless and certainly Max's fleeting frown suggested that she had taken it rather badly, although all she said was, 'I don't think he can afford to do that. He's on benefits.'

'Ah . . .'

There was silence for much of the rest of the journey; in fact until we arrived back at her house. I had to park the car about twenty yards down the road, just around the bend to the left of her house, and we continued in silence as we walked to her gate, then up the garden path. 'What's that?' I asked, indicated a dark shape dimly visible against the front door.

'I don't know,' she said in a voice that was partly curious, partly concerned. 'It looks like . . .'

But she didn't have to finish, because the headlights of a car turning the corner swept across us and across the front of her house and we could see precisely what it was.

It was Twinkle, her rabbit, nailed to the front door.

I stayed the night with Max, trying to comfort her, finding her inconsolable and myself a total spare part because of it. She had begun sobbing as soon as she laid eyes on the atrocity and didn't stop until she finally collapsed into exhausted sleep a long time later. My first thought had been to remove poor Twinkle from his undignified resting place but almost at once I knew that I should leave it until the police saw it, so I had to take the key from Max, open the door while she stayed at the garden gate with her back turned, then hurry her past it and into the house with her head buried in my chest. I sat her on the sofa in the back lounge and then phoned the police.

It was Percy Bailey who took the call. 'You what?' he asked in a somehow reassuringly incredulous tone. I wasn't exactly shouting in order to spare Max the verbal descriptions and I suspect he thought he had misheard. After I had repeated myself, he still seemed to doubt his auditory organs. 'Nailed?'

'Yes.'

'A rabbit?'

'Called Twinkle.'

'To her front door?'

'You've got it, Percy.'

I could imagine him scratching his head with the blunt and well-sucked end of his pencil. 'Blimey,' he opined at last, but that was the end of the official police response for a few moments.

'Do you think you could send someone to have a look?' I asked eventually.

'Yes,' he said. 'Yes, of course . . .'

He said it somewhat distantly, though.

Some thirty minutes later and Max had had two cups of sweet tea but was still spontaneously and randomly bursting into bouts of sobbing; I had resorted to red wine before going back outside to make a closer examination of Twinkle. It wasn't enough to inoculate me against reaction to the sight before me, though. Twinkle had been made the subject of mock crucifixion. Spreadeagled and a nail through each paw; two more through each ear, just to add a touch of mockery, I think. I hadn't much liked Twinkle – he, however, had adored me, or at least adored the taste of my flesh since he was constantly trying to bite chunks out of me – but it didn't mean that I wanted such an end for him. Blood had run in irregular trails down the pale-blue gloss paint of the door and Twinkle's eyes were open and clouded. There was an air of cruelty about this that was quite chilling . . .

Because the street lighting didn't reach the house and there was a shallow porch, the sight was fairly well hidden from the pavement, so the two constables who had been despatched to investigate the incident – one male, one female – and who arrived as I was standing in front of this horror did not at once fully appreciate the unpleasantness of the crime scene; accordingly, their demeanour was initially fairly blithesome – I might even have said irreverent – although this soon changed as they hove into sight of poor Twinkle. I had never seen either of them before, but they were fairly young and I suspect that this was most probably their first case of lepicide. The WPC – a fairly sturdy girl with black hair and square features – closed her eyes and dropped her gaze almost at once, and her compatriot (who looked so young he might just only have received his Cycling Proficiency Badge) coughed slightly and frowned, but succeeded only in looking a little sick.

Initial reactions over, though, they did what police people do, which is to ask a lot of questions, most of which seemed (to my mind, anyway) to be either silly or bleeding obvious. We all sat around in the lounge, Max and I together on the

334441234442

sofa, the two of them facing us in the armchairs, both with notebooks and pencils out, like a synchronized police display team. Max was clutching my hand so tightly it hurt and the whole proceeding was punctuated by her sobs.

Is this your rabbit, sir? No, it's Miss Christy's.

When did you last see it alive, miss? I fed it this evening before we went out, at about six thirty.

And you were where, exactly? At the cinema.

You returned when, exactly? Just before we phoned the police. About ten o'clock.

Do you have any idea why this might have been done? (Sobbing.)

Do you get on with your neighbours? I thought so.

And neither of you has any idea who might have done this? To which I lied, because Max said, 'No,' and I agreed.

An hour later, Sergeant Abelson turned up. The Dynamic Duo had reported back and presumably said report had included a lot of puzzlement and little enlightenment, so it had been decided that someone with more experience should attend; killing a rabbit might not be up there with the Ripper murders but it wasn't exactly like a bit of cosy burgling or indecent exposure. After she had taken some photographs, and then examined poor Twinkle (minutely and with great concentration, as if she had seen any number of rabbit-killings and might be able to deduce the identity of the murderer from the modus operandi), she turned to me with a deep frown and pursed lips. She had deep brown eyes and a fringe and pursing her lips made a slight dimple on her chin. 'This is quite extraordinary.'

I smiled weakly. Max had gone to bed, still weeping. 'Just a tad.'

'It's almost like a sign, or warning, or something.'

I said nothing.

'And you really have no idea who could be responsible? Miss Christy has no enemies?'

I shook my head. 'No . . .'

She was quick, because she picked up my tone, spotted that it wasn't a totally unqualified negative. 'No . . . but what?'

'I have an enemy.'

'Who?'

I glanced up the stairs, not wanting Max to overhear. 'Do you think I could take Twinkle down first? It's not very dignified for him and when it gets light, he might upset the milkman, and I know for a fact that the postman has a weak heart.'

'Of course.'

So I put on some Marigolds and detached Twinkle from the woodwork, putting him in an old shoebox (it was a bit of a squeeze since he had fed well on Elliot flesh over the months), then wiping down the door. Once I had done that, I took the Sergeant into the kitchen and across to the small table where I told her all about Tristan.

TEN

'Tristan Charlton is . . . was . . . my brother-in-law.'

'You're married?'

'Was. A few years ago now. Celia. She died, though . . . took her own life.'

She lowered her gaze, made the appropriate response but managed to make it appear that she genuinely meant it. 'I'm sorry.' It occurred to me that her initial somewhat frosty demeanour was going the way of many chilly mornings and turning into quite a warm day.

'She had a history of depression.' I didn't need to tell her any more but it was automatic, a defence against having people think that I might have driven her to it – after all, Tristan seemed to think so. 'She hated being married to me, yet she found that she couldn't live without me . . .' I might have stopped then, but found that I couldn't. 'She'd tried to kill herself before . . .'

Did she look at me slightly askance, perhaps thinking that I was protesting too much? I couldn't tell and her voice seemed to possess the right amount of understanding as she murmured, 'I understand.'

There followed the briefest of pauses before I said, 'Tristan's never been able to accept the loss of his sister. They were close and Tristan is . . .'

I was having trouble finding the right words but she finished for me. 'Not normal?'

I flashed her a smile. 'You could say that. He's always had serious psychiatric problems. He attacked me not long after Celia died; did a pretty good job, too; basically left me for dead. He was convicted for that, but he was released last year.'

'Last year? Where's he been since then?'

And so I went on to explain about Sophie and Leo, her dog, and about what had happened whilst members of the Thornton Heath Horticultural and Allotment Society were dying in their ancient droves. About how Tristan felt that I shouldn't be happy any more, that anyone I fell in love with was a legitimate target.

'He went away, but I knew he'd be back. Tristan has many faults, but weakness of will isn't one of them. He's decided that I'm to suffer no matter what.'

Sergeant Abelson's expression was interesting; I thought I saw several measures of disbelief, perhaps one of sorrow, and a dash – although only a dash – of interest. 'And you think that this –' she waved vaguely over her back towards the front door – 'was done by this by Tristan?'

'Don't you, after what I've just told you?'

But she said, 'Well . . .'

'Look, you have to admit, whoever killed Max's rabbit wasn't normal, don't you?'

Her head bobbed from side to side in cautious agreement, while her faint frown made a faint but pleasing dimple for itself. 'Maybe . . .'

'If not him, then who else?'

'I don't know at the moment.' It was a typical police response. 'There are a lot of strange people around, you know.'

Given what seemed to keep happening in Thornton Heath at the time, I couldn't muster much of an argument against this. 'At least make some enquiries, Sergeant. Don't just dismiss what I'm saying.'

She said at once, 'No, of course I won't.'

And I believed her. 'Thank you.'

'I need to look at the hutch.'

So I took her out through the back door where Twinkle's empty hutch stood on an old kitchen cupboard, its door hanging open, a home without a heart. Not even the rather strong stench of rabbit urine carefully blended with that of rabbit droppings and sweet hay could make it less poignant. Never again would my fingers be at risk as I reached in to take the little swine out so that Max could clean its home out and make everything fresh again. Never again would I wish the little sod would stop wriggling so much. The good Sergeant began to examine the hutch carefully by the light of a torch.

'I expect this is the last thing you could do with, what with the happenings at the school.'

'Things are a bit busy at the station,' she murmured distractedly.

'Any breaking news?'

She looked up at me. 'Now you know I can't tell you anything, Dr Elliot.'

'No, of course.'

She turned again to the hutch; I wondered idly what she expected to find but didn't voice my puzzlement. It was still quite warm and the rumble of traffic along the London Road was starting to lessen. She said almost to herself, 'We've already got a few potential leads.'

I suddenly paid attention. 'Really?'

She nodded, although she was inspecting the hinges. 'The first trawl through criminal records has already netted us a few interesting fish.'

I wondered why she was telling me this if she was breaking confidences and putting herself at risk of disciplinary action, but I asked anyway, 'Can you tell me any more?'

I didn't understand her reaction, though. She smirked over her shoulder. 'I really shouldn't, you know.'

What was wrong with her? Either she was going to tell me or she wasn't. Why was she teasing me? I said uncertainly, 'No, I don't suppose you should.'

Her expression as she said, 'Exactly,' was unreadable. She returned to the hinges and I was left completely perplexed.

ELEVEN

When I went to join Max, she was fast asleep and I tried not to wake her but, not having a double set of X chromosomes, I failed miserably.

'Lance?' she asked sleepily.

'It's all right,' I said softly, because that's what I'm supposed to say. 'Go back to sleep.'

But she was awake. 'What's happening?' she asked.

'Nothing. The police have just left.'

'What about Twinkle?'

'I've . . . taken care of things.'

She began to cry again. 'What a horrible thing. Who could have done that to a small, defenceless creature?'

I thought about telling her there and then, but it was late and she was upset and she needed to sleep. *Tomorrow*, I thought, as I said, 'It can only be somebody who isn't in their right mind, Max. Get some sleep, now.'

And so to tomorrow; more specifically, the next morning, as I ate some Sugar Puffs and Max had a mixture of sawdust and rodent droppings going about its business under the unlikely name of 'muesli'; her reassurance that it was good for me failed to do its job. I didn't point out that I was a doctor and knew exactly what was good for me. Max already knew about Celia and my previous girlfriend, Sophie, but I had left out the details about Tristan until now. It wasn't easy telling her how he had killed Sophie's dog, vandalized her car and then set a fire in her flat; even then, I didn't mention how or why my relationship with Sophie had come to an end.

'He did that?' Inevitably, it was the death of Leo, Sophie's dog, that affected Max the most. I sometimes wondered if she would have loved me ten times more if I had four paws and panted a lot in hot weather. I nodded, watching her, wondering what would come after the initial shock of this news had passed. Would she be angry that I had kept her in ignorance of all this? 'And he got away with it?'

'Yes. I was hoping that he'd had enough and that he was bored with tormenting me, but apparently not.'

She looked scared, and I couldn't blame her, but it passed almost at once. She said firmly, 'He's not going to intimidate me, Lance.'

Much as I admired her certitude, she didn't know Tristan. 'That's good to hear, Max, but—'

She didn't let me finish. 'He killed Twinkle. I want revenge.'

The morning surgery was enlivened only by a small boy who had swallowed a rubber band; his mother was convinced that this was as deadly as ingesting bamboo splinters, the only difference being that her beloved son would die by having his insides tied in a knot, as opposed to haemorrhaging to death from tiny cuts. I was able to reassure her with some confidence that death by rubber band had yet to be reported as a cause of death by the Central Statistical Office. Mr Albert Stewart was last in and (whisper it not lest you be overheard) did not perhaps receive the best of my attention; I like to consider myself a caring and dedicated doctor, but after fifteen patients, even the newest recruit to general practice tends to wilt rather. There are only so many earaches, anal itchings, cases of rheumatism and gouty toes that a sane man can cope with. To make it worse, what Mr Stewart came in with was insomnia.

Insomnia is one of those symptoms that are neither here nor there. It is a matter of opinion: one man's insomnia is another's good night's sleep. You may *want* to sleep for the full eight hours, but maybe your body doesn't; maybe it only wants seven, or even six, in which case you march off to your local friendly GP and tell them that you've got insomnia, while the next patient in will complain because they sleep too much. What is a poor GP to do?

He was new to the practice, in fact this was his first time in. 'How long have you been in Thornton Heath, Mr Stewart?'

He was forty-two years old and tall with athletic muscu-lature. His face was somewhat square-jawed, although not outrageously so, his eyes were widely but not over-widely

spaced and his nose was Roman; in short, the bugger was a
bit handsome. 'About seven months.'

I looked at his medical records, the soft brown cardboard
envelope that accompanies everyone – usually at a distance
of several months – when they move around the country. He
had been born in the area, but had more recently been living
in a foreign land – Highgate, North London, to be exact – and
had spent his early adult years in the army: actually had spent
quite a few of them there. He had been discharged following
a severe head injury that had left him prone to epileptic fits
and mood swings. He was taking not only anti-epileptics but
also lithium. Either could have caused insomnia – most drugs
can cause most ill-defined symptoms – but he had been on
them for several years and it struck me as unlikely that he
would suddenly be having such problems. He was unmarried
and had, as a child, suffered asthma and a burst appendix from
which he had then developed peritonitis; three months' hospitalization resulted. He had then contracted meningitis – another
seven months of hospitalization – and consequent behavioural
problems, including truanting and aggressive tendencies. In
what seemed to me to be akin to using a hammer to cure a
headache, he had been advised to go into the army to help
him 'get over' his problems. The result of all this was that he
might have appeared to be a strong, fit and handsome man,
but he was functionally useless to society.

'What brought you south of the river again?'

He shrugged. 'A change of scenery.' His accent was London
standard, giving no real clues as to his future, his education
or his attitude; he could have been thinking about decking me
or hugging me and I wouldn't have known from that voice.

'Most cases of insomnia are because of stress. Has something
stressed you recently, Mr Stewart?'

He said it at once. 'My dog died.'

Pennies – tuppences, thruppences, five pences and more –
fell. 'What breed was he?'

'He was an Alsatian; a brilliant mate to have.'

The death of Mr Stewart's dog had stressed more than him;
it had upset Max as well. I knew more, though, than to let him in
on that particular morsel. 'Was the dog important to you?'

He showed nothing on his face as he said flatly, 'Major was everything.' It was all the more compelling because of the lack of emotion.

'I can understand that.' He had dropped his head and I saw only very short but very greasy hair as he nodded. I looked again at his records. He lived in Keston Road; not too bad an address but I guessed he wasn't a homeowner. 'He was your life partner,' I suggested.

His head jerked up to show a face full of emotion, but his voice was still curiously unemotional. 'Yes,' he agreed. 'Exactly that . . .'

He had put an ellipsis at the end, so I waited, like all good doctors should.

'Or like a comrade in arms.'

It wasn't the first case of severe depression I had seen following the death of a pet, although the sufferers were usually twice his age and of a different gender. 'You've had similar problems before, haven't you?'

'Once or twice.'

'How does it affect you? Do you have trouble getting to sleep, or do you wake early?'

'I don't sleep.' He said this as if I was being stupid. What else would insomnia be?

'What about your concentration? Has that been affected?'

With unconscious irony he concentrated for a moment. 'I don't think so.'

I went through the usual list of questions one is supposed to ask someone who has depression – about sex drive, about anxiety symptoms, about trembling, about loss of appetite – and all the answers he gave seemed to confirm that he was quite seriously depressed. Having established that, the usual procedure was to move on to the potential consequences. 'Have you had any thoughts about self-harm?'

He had sunk into a deep well and it was a few moments before he became aware of my question. 'Self-harm?' he asked and then frowned.

'Thoughts of death . . . of dying.' More moments were born and then faded and I wondered if he hadn't heard. 'Mr Stewart?' I asked. He had dropped his head, but now it came back up

slowly and he looked at me – actually, he *stared* at me – but
there were tears in his eyes, making them glitter like windows
upon a tumbling stream.

'Oh, yes,' he said in a low, level voice. 'I've had thoughts
of dying.'

I thought, *Oh, Lord.* 'Are you having them at the moment?'

'They come and go. Not now, I'm not, though I did when
Major died.'

'Have you ever actually physically done anything to
yourself?'

He was surprisingly definite as he said, 'No. Never.' This,
at least, gave me hope. I'm not sure what his next remark gave
me, but it certainly wasn't assurance. 'I've hurt and killed too
many people to do that. I know everything there is to know
about pain.'

Looking on the bright side – dim as it was – I began to
surmise that he was not at immediate risk and I wouldn't have
to go through the rigmarole of sectioning him under the Mental
Health Act for his own protection. I considered my options. 'I
think the immediate thing to do is help you get some sleep.
Then, when you're feeling a little less tired, perhaps things will
seem a little brighter and we can perhaps think about some
sort of psychotherapy.' He didn't react, seemed to have sunk
again into despond. I went on, 'I see you're on Phenobarbital
for your epilepsy.'

'For all the good it does.'

I felt compelled to defend the drug, as if I had invented it.
'No anticonvulsant can stop seizures completely.'

'So I've been told.'

I gave up. Some patients need to be cynical and there was
no reason for it; you have to take it on the chin or else become
a vet. 'I'm going to prescribe you some Mogadon.'

Slowly, he asked, 'What's that?'

'It's a shortcoming relaxant. It takes away anxiety and calms
you down. Also, it's completely non-addictive too, unlike a
lot of similar drugs.' I wrote out the prescription and handed
it to him. 'Take one at night, about half an hour before you
intend to go to sleep. There's a month's supply there, but I
want to see you for a check-up in two weeks; if you start to

experience thoughts of self-harm, come back straight away
– don't hesitate.'

He took the script and read it slowly and I wondered if he
had literacy problems. Then he crumpled it up and thrust it
into his pocket; for a moment I feared that he was going to
ignore my advice, but then he nodded and said, 'OK.'

As the door closed behind him, it struck me that there was
suddenly an awful lot of doom, gloom and dying around the
place.

TWELVE

Dad was incandescent. He had rung early and, as was
his wont when worked up over something (which was
not an infrequent occurrence), he had dispensed with
the formalities. 'Are you awake?' he demanded . . . no, shouted
. . . no, demanded *and* shouted. His voice was naturally hoarse
but emotion made it almost rasping; that the phone line wasn't
too good – in those days before digital communications and
optical cables, telecommunications relied on copper wires and
paper insulation, so a drop of rain anywhere in the country
was liable to result in a veritable sea of background white
noise – didn't help either.

'No,' I said tiredly. It was Saturday and I had only just
got up, had only just managed to make a cup of overly
strong tea; somehow I had known that the telephone had
been ringing at the behest of my progenitor and no one else;
it seemed to reflect his character, to be exigent, unreasonable
and taxing.

'Do you know what they've done?'

I repeated the negative with a sigh. He might have been
referring to the latest slightly bizarre choice of the England
cricket-team selectors in their increasingly hysterical efforts
to avoid a complete five-test whitewash by the touring West
Indies. He might, just as easily, have been referring to the gas
board, the water board or the pixies that he used to tell me

lived at the bottom of the garden; I was, in truth, never sure
whether that last was just a joke or whether he really believed
in them himself.

'I'm coming round,' he said by way of inadequate explanation. The phone went down before I could suggest that I might
have something better to do.

Thirty minutes later and he was striding past my opened front
door, launching straight into the topic of the day by asking
again, 'Do you know what they've done?'

Once upon a time I might have tried a dose of sarcasm on
him – 'I know it's amazing, Dad, but I'm half an hour older
and I *still* don't know' – but I knew from bitter experience
that it would be like wasting a thing of beauty on the sweet
desert air. 'Tell me.'

'They've arrested George Cotterill.'

I did not follow. 'George,' he repeated impatiently. It was
one of the many fascinating things about my father that he
said things that in his head were part of a connected thread
of dialogue, but that to the outsider seemed completely disso-
ciated with reality; as, indeed, they often were. It made talking
to him an interesting intellectual exercise in Holmesian
deduction. There followed a pause as I stared into space help-
lessly. 'Who?' I asked eventually, at which he tutted and sighed
with annoyance and explained as if to a particularly simple
simpleton, 'George, the caretaker at the school.'

'Oh . . . Why?'

'*I* don't know, do I? Ada told me this morning. She woke
me.'

'You mean she rang you?' I asked, before I could help
myself.

He stared at me. 'Of course,' he said and I could not tell
whether he said this with outrage or sadness, or possibly a
mix of the two. He explained, 'She lives opposite him in
Kingswood Avenue and saw it all. Masson and two others in
plain clothes, plus a car full of uniformed bobbies. She said
it was as though they were arresting one of the Great Train
Robbers, not a sixty-seven-year-old man.'

'But presumably they think he's a sixty-seven-year-old man

who might have murdered someone, Dad. That would make him potentially quite dangerous.'

'Pshaw!' he said. Or at least I think that was what he said. It had a single syllable and involved both his lips and the back of his throat, but was basically an unspellable sound. 'George had nothing to do with it.'

I wasn't about to argue; great experience told me that along with trying to lick your own eyebrows and learning to love Stockhausen, it was an impossible task. 'In that case, I'm sure they'll release him fairly soon.'

This time the sound was different but equally beyond my powers of literacy; it approximated to, 'Kkeukk!' and came from a heavily camouflaged face that, I imagined, radiated disgust beneath the beard. 'With Masson in charge, anything could happen. Look at the mess-up he made of the Lightoller case.'

Well, I suppose I have to admit that the good Inspector Masson had not covered himself in glory on that one, but then no one had really. It had only been good fortune that had allowed Max and me to discover the truth. 'He's not a bad copper, Dad. We all make mistakes.'

His eyebrows were hoisted up his frowning forehead like two over-hairy greying caterpillars on puppet strings as he stared at me. He said nothing but his entire demeanour suggested that for the life of him he couldn't recall the details of any mistakes that he had personally made. After a pause and an all but inaudible grunt he took a sip of tea and recoiled at once, as if it had bitten him. 'My God, Lance. What is this?'

'Tea.'

He stood up from his chair at the kitchen table, strode over the sink and poured it in, then peered at the liquid as it drained away. 'Well,' he said thoughtfully, 'it doesn't seem to dissolve metal, so it can't be *too* acidic.'

'Dad . . .'

'No, Lance. This has to be said. I appreciate that you have the domestic habits of a warthog, that you can't cook, can't keep the pit you inhabit in any state approaching tidiness and that you dress like the last, blind customer at a jumble sale, but you really must draw the line at the poisoning of innocent parties. In future I shall be bringing all my own food and drink into this abode; I may even resort to bringing my own crockery and cutlery if the standard of washing up doesn't improve.'

'Now, really . . .'

He held up his hand; it was a gesture I remember from my earliest days. It meant 'be quiet' and when I was in short trousers I learned that it was not to be disobeyed; this Pavlovian learning reflex remained unshaken even now. In my silence, he said, 'What I want to know is what you're going to do about this.'

'Do? Do about what?'

'About poor George's arrest.'

Only years of training enabled me to keep both breathing and talking at this point; someone less used to the idiosyncratic unreasonableness of my papa would have been rendered all but comatose by the implications of this question. 'What am I supposed to do?'

'Masson's your friend. Find out what's going on.'

Which was such a ludicrous description of the relationship between the Inspector and me – akin to asserting that Hitler and Churchill were pen pals who cooked up the Second World War for a lark – that, used as I was to his incorrigible habit of voicing outrageous assertions, I reacted badly. 'You what?' I squeaked.

'You seem to get on. I've noticed it.' He looked up at the polystyrene tiles on the ceiling, two of which were coming away. 'Oh, I know he makes out he's angry with you all the time, but take my word for it, he's got great respect for you, both as a doctor and as an amateur detective.'

'He keeps all this deep inside, then.'

He stood up. 'That's your problem, Lance. You just see what's on the surface. I would have thought you'd have learned by now that a good doctor looks past the superficial; it's inside people that you find reality.' I wondered what I'd find if I looked inside him; somebody sane, perhaps? I sincerely doubted it. He continued on his way out of the kitchen, 'Anyway, see what you can do, will you? Tell him that I can vouch as a character witness for George. If that man's a murderer, then I'm a madman.'

I said nothing; I didn't even smile.

On his way down the garden, he turned and said, 'And for goodness' sake have some mercy on these shrubs and give them some water. It looks like the Kalahari out here.'

As it happened, I didn't need to talk to Masson. Having washed and dressed, I then phoned Max to see how she was. She had taken the day before off from work and had spent most of it bursting into tears; Sergeant Abelson had taken Twinkle away, presumably for a post-mortem (I had wondered if there was such a thing as forensic veterinary pathology, but hadn't liked to ask), and I had cleaned up as best I could in the morning before surgery; removing all the physical evidence didn't help erase her memories, though. In the evening, I had taken her out for a curry, but even a lamb vindaloo and mushroom bhaji hadn't cheered her up; she had insisted on going back home and refused the offer of company.

Her voice sounded a little brighter now though, which gave me some cause for hope; she was just about to leave to spend the day at her parents' in Hampstead and we agreed to meet at the Norbury Hotel at seven that evening for a drink. I had thought about visiting a pet shop and perhaps buying her a baby rabbit, but decided against it, suspecting that it was too soon after the tragedy; accordingly it looked as if it was going to be a day spent with Frank Bough and *Grandstand*, alternating (when the racing was on) with thinking about watering the garden; the hosepipe ban meant that to achieve this was going to require a lot of watering-can action and the prospect did not appeal as the heat of the last few weeks had not lessened in the slightest.

'Maybe I *want* to live in the Kalahari,' I murmured.

The doorbell sounded and when I opened the door I found the culprit to be Sergeant Abelson. She had a nervous smile on her face. 'Sorry to bother you, Dr Elliot.'

I ushered her in. 'You're not bothering me,' I said politely. 'What can I do for you?' I asked as I showed her into the front room and hastily cleared a space on the sofa so that she could sit on the loose cover rather than several days' worth of newspapers, a simultaneously impressive and impressively

untidy back catalogue of the *British Medical Journal* and a
pair of dirty socks. She smiled as I was doing this but didn't
comment. Having seated herself, she explained, 'I thought
you'd like to know what I've found out about Tristan Charlton.'

'Of course I do,' I said. 'Can I get you something to drink,
perhaps? Tea, coffee, a cold drink?'

'Orange squash would be nice.'

I returned in about five minutes to find her examining a
photograph of Max that I had in a frame on a low table by
the sofa. Max was photogenic and this one, taken on her
birthday a couple of months before, had found her especially
so; her eyes (always large and luminous) seemed to glow, even
shine, and her slightly lopsided mouth always became somehow
perfectly asymmetrical as she laughed delightedly. The
Sergeant put it back down and said to me with a smile, 'She's
very pretty.'

It gave me a strange sort of shivery feeling of pleasure as
I said, 'I think so.' I handed her the squash. 'Sorry, run out
of ice.'

'It'll be fine.' She put it down next to the photograph without
sampling it then, as I sat down opposite her, said, 'Tristan
Charlton has been an in-patient at Springfield Hospital,
Tooting, since April. He was a voluntary patient and has been
treated for paranoid schizophrenia.'

'And he's still there?'

'Yes.'

'Can he come and go at will?'

She nodded. 'He's not regarded as dangerous either to
himself or anyone else.'

I barked a bitter laugh as my opinion of psychiatrists was
confirmed; they would have diagnosed Ted Bundy as merely
neurotic. 'Really? They haven't sought my views on the
subject, I notice. Nor those of Sophie: nor indeed Twinkle.'

She made a face of sympathy. 'I appreciate what you say,
but the reality is that he has paid his dues for what he did to
you; in fact officially he's kept out of trouble since he was
released from prison last year. To all intents and purposes,
he's done the right thing by seeking psychiatric help.'

'Does he have an alibi for Thursday night?'

'No, but that's hardly surprising. The voluntary patients are free to come and go between ten in the morning and ten at night.'

'Have you spoken to him?'

'No.'

'Are you going to?'

She hesitated. 'When I get the chance to. We're rather busy at the moment, what with the school killing.'

And I saw at once that fate, for once, had been my friend and given me an opportunity to keep my father happy without having to beard Inspector Masson in all his terrifying glory. 'How is that going?' I asked in a cunningly disinterested way.

'Well, I shouldn't really say.'

'No, of course,' I hastened to say. 'It was wrong of me to ask, Sergeant.'

She hesitated, then said with a faint, modest smile, 'My name's Jean.'

I was slightly taken aback and it was after a short hesitation that I allowed, 'Jean it is, then.'

I had assumed that that was that, but she continued in a low voice, perhaps fearful that Masson really did have the supernatural abilities he seemed to threaten, 'We made an arrest this morning.'

'Really?' I think I did quite well with the feigned surprise.

'The caretaker.'

'George Cotterill? You think he did it?'

She nodded. 'His story concerning his movements contains certain inconsistencies. There is at least sixty minutes unaccounted for between the time he claims to have locked up and left the school and the time he arrived home.'

'Is that all?' It didn't sound much.

'And he has a record.'

'Oh? What did he do?'

Her smile was that of someone with a very, very big secret. 'Something bad. Something very bad indeed.'

THIRTEEN

The weather had been having its effects on my patients and, in turn, this was having its effects on me. With increasing numbers of cases of heatstroke, especially amongst the elderly and those under two, surgeries were always busy and we were making huge numbers of house calls; something that in itself was becoming a problem. Every day now, by about one in the afternoon, the tarmac of the roads and pavements felt soft as I walked on it; I felt completely drained of energy and my skin greasy and dirty. As I passed women in light summer dresses, men in T-shirts and children in swimming costumes, I (in my suit because I am a doctor) felt even hotter than I actually was. And everyone, it seemed, was upending fizzy drinks bottles, licking mountainous ice-cream cones or, if they were children, slurping Jubbly-Wubblys, the melted bright-red ice water running down their chins and over their hands; I had to make a conscious effort not to stare in naked envy.

The fact that I had arranged to meet Max in the Norbury Hotel for a drink kept me going that afternoon through five house-calls, three of them heat-related. I wasn't finished until half-four, and then I had an evening clinic which was completely booked and didn't finish until six-fifty, giving me no chance at all to shower or change before it was time to meet Max. I could only hope that I wasn't exuding too many unpleasant odours. I reckoned, though, that my news about George Cotterill would drive all olfactory unpleasantness from her mind.

I was not wrong.

'Oh, my God!' She was shocked in a way that only she could be; Max was in many ways an innocent, in many others the most knowing person I have ever met. I suspect that she enjoyed – perhaps even revelled in – shock, excitement and incredulity. She delighted in her constant surprise at the variance between the world as she thought it should be and the world as it was, obstinately refusing to behave. 'Really?'

I nodded glumly. 'Apparently so. A young couple.'

'He battered them to death?'

'With a hammer.'

She winced. 'Why?'

'Apparently he saw himself as some sort of moral guardian. He had a strict Christian upbringing mixed with a healthy dose of schizoid paranoia; they lived in the same block of flats as him and weren't married. He was constantly remonstrating with them – the usual stuff about saving their souls, turning to God, and suchlike. They laughed at him, apparently; laughed once too often, though. He went completely bonkers, ranting about how he was going to save their souls, no matter what they did. He was convicted of their manslaughter on grounds of diminished responsibility and sentenced to twelve years' imprisonment.'

'He should have been put in a secure mental hospital, surely . . .'

I shrugged. 'At least fifty per cent of the prison population should be in mental hospitals. There just isn't the room for them.'

'How long ago was all this?'

'Twenty-three years ago.'

'Where's he been since then?'

We were enjoying the faded, not to say sepulchral ambience of the lounge bar of the Norbury Hotel; as usual it was only sparsely patronized but the amount of cigarette, pipe and cigar smoke in the atmosphere was enough suggest there was a large conflagration in a not too distant location; there was a definite resemblance to Victorian London as I looked around while sipping a pint of Watney's Red Barrel bitter, and I half expected Jack the Ripper to jump out from one of the alcoves, perhaps waving a human pancreas, spattering the cream and gold flock wallpaper with gobbets of clotting blood. 'No one knows,' I said. Max was sipping Dubonnet and lemonade, a drink I found curiously repellent and sweet, not at all helped by the Day-Glo pink that seemed, in that ghastly smoke-filled atmosphere, to shine with unearthly power. She liked it, though.

'It's Dad's reaction that's worrying me.'

'He'll be upset, you mean?'

'Upset? He'll go ballistic. I can see him now, ranting and raving about the incompetence of Masson and the local plod in general. His opinion of the Inspector hasn't been particularly high, given Masson's predilection for arresting him at every available opportunity, so this is just going to be pouring petrol on the bonfire.'

'But they do seem to have reasonable cause for at least suspecting him.'

I drained my pint; there was always something about Watney's Red that seemed acidic; it left a peculiar fuzzy feel to my teeth as if, like rhubarb, it was dissolving them. 'That won't matter,' I assured her. 'Dad spent forty years practising medicine as an art, not a science. He worked by premonition and he thought he had a consummate talent, no matter what the laboratory findings told him. He applies the same principles to life; if he thinks George is innocent, no amount of evidence to the contrary is going to persuade him otherwise. George could have been found covered from head to foot in human blood, and with entrails draped over his shoulders whilst gibbering about his lust for pagan murder, and my good pater would suspect a frame-up. You mark my words.'

I got up from the table and made ready to trudge through the Stygian atmosphere to the bar for refills, trying to keep at bay the nagging fear that, given the gloom, I would not be able to find Max on my return journey.

It was as I predicted, except that maybe Dad's reaction was even more violent than I expected.

'That man is a disgrace to his uniform,' he declared.

'He doesn't wear a uniform, Dad . . .'

'Don't be an imbecile, Lance. You know exactly what I mean. For God's sake, I don't expect members of Her Majesty's Constabulary to be endowed with the intellectual capacity of a genius, but I do at least hope that they aren't all gibbering idiots and buffoons.'

It was the middle of a Friday and I had dropped in to see him during the course of my midday home visits. 'Dad . . .'

'Why on earth would someone as harmless as George Cotterill do something like that?' I hadn't yet told him what I knew about George's previous misdemeanours, but I wasn't allowed a chance to do it. 'And how strong must the killer have been? George is in his sixties, for goodness' sake.'

'He's quite fit and strong for his age.'

'Pshaw!' This strange syllable – perhaps a relic of a lost, ancient tongue, or perhaps an imitation of a steam engine with the collywobbles – served to let me know that my progenitor had little truck with my arguments. He carried on what he was doing, which was searching through his large, unwieldy and over-ornate wardrobe. He had deposited various items of clothing – socks (all grey), casual shirts in various strikingly offensive colours, slacks (including a pair that were pale blue and, if I am totally honest, painful on the optic nerve) and woollen pullovers.

'What are you doing? Is there a jumble sale?'

He stopped what he was doing – folding a vaguely grey pair of underpants that looked as though they had seen service on the Eastern Front during the Great War – and stared at me. 'I'm packing,' he replied coldly.

'What for?' For some reason I immediately leapt to the conclusion that he was off to hospital for an operation.

'Ada and I are going to Brighton for the weekend,' he said. He was continuing to stare at me but I detected a degree of defensiveness in his words, as if he anticipated an adverse reaction to this announcement. In fact I was too stunned to say anything immediately, other than a slightly dazed, 'Oh.'

He resumed his packing, searching under the bed for a few moments, in the end almost having to disappear completely under it. When he wriggled back out, he began to cough and was covered in dust, duck feathers and a small but extremely active spider. He produced an ancient brown suitcase that, with no little effort, he lifted on to the bed. When opened, I saw that it contained women's clothing, all carefully and reverentially folded. I knew at once what they were and in that instant, he saw me looking, saw that I knew, and quickly shut it again. There was an unmistakeable sense of embarrassment in the air of that room then, one that was reflected in the way that he kept his head low and muttered, 'I'll finish this later.'

'Dad . . .'

It was far from cold in his bedroom, but the ghost of my mother – my mother whom for some reason we rarely mentioned, perhaps because we had both loved her too much – was there with us, and even the most loved and loving of ghosts brings with it a chill. He asked so quickly that he interrupted me, 'What is it, Lance?'

I hesitated, thought about saying nothing, then said as gently as I could, 'There's no problem, you know, Dad.'

I was seeking to reassure him, but I think I not only failed, I made things worse; certainly for me, if not for him; being my dad, though, he merely frowned, then said a touch too loudly, 'What on earth are you talking about, Lance? You're lapsing into feeble-mindedness again.'

I smiled. 'You're right. I know.'

He nodded assertively. 'I really don't understand it. Most of the time you seem to be quite bright, and then suddenly you stumble into meaningless lunacy. It's clearly not inherited; I blame the television.'

I loved him so much then that I felt tears hot in my eyes. He was thinking exactly what I was thinking – that Mum wouldn't mind him having a bit of female company in his life now that she was so long gone, that she had loved him too much to begrudge him that and that I should have kept my mouth shut. 'You're probably right, Dad.' I had four more visits to make before evening surgery and used the excuse of these now to make my exit. 'Where are you staying in Brighton?' I asked.

'At the Grand,' was the reply, his tone suggesting that the notion of staying anywhere else was clearly yet another sign of my loopiness. 'We're due there at seven.'

'And you're back . . .?'

'Sunday afternoon. We might stop off for lunch on the way, perhaps in Hurstpierpoint, or somewhere.'

'Well, have a nice time.'

He smiled. 'Thank you, Lance. I think I will.'

With which slightly gnomic remark, we parted.

FOURTEEN

I've never been entirely sure why I decided to become a police surgeon; I hate being on call – it had always been the worst aspect of medicine for me – yet this entirely voluntarily (albeit paid) duty involved a lot of the bloody stuff. I suppose part of it was because my father had been one in his day and I rather love him; when I announced my decision to him, I was unaccountably moved almost to tears that he was so delighted. If I'm honest (which I try not to be and, as a doctor, tend not to be out of habit) part of it too was the money, and part of it was stupidity because we had just amalgamated with the London Road practice, so that the on-call rota had gone from one in three to one in seven; as a consequence of all this I had thought, *Why not?*

Anyway, whatever the reason, the phone rang that Saturday night and I knew immediately that it wasn't Dad telling me how bracing the weather was down in Brighton. 'Dr Elliot?'

It was Sergeant Abelson; she sounded bored. I, however, could have done without being called out; not that I was doing much, what with Max having disappeared two hours before because of a Great Dane with a brain tumour. 'I was last time I checked.'

'I'm afraid we need your help, Dr Elliot.'

'Where?'

'At the central nick in Croydon.'

'What's the problem?' Usually it was drunk drivers.

'One of our customers is complaining of chest pains.'

Which could mean anything, from complete fakery (far from unknown) to injuries unavoidably obtained when 'resisting arrest' (also, lamentably, far from unknown). I looked at my watch. 'Give me half an hour.'

'No hurry,' she assured me.

Bruce Forsyth was doing what only he could do – making an imbecilic game show interesting *and* not making the contestants look undignified – but duty called. I was halfway through eating with some delight something I had recently discovered – 'Toast Toppers' (strangely, Dad had looked at me with some despair when I had informed him of my epiphany) – but in no time at all I had polished these off, and then I was on my way. The traffic was light and the tarmac at least beginning to harden up as I drove into the centre of Croydon, along Wellesley Road and into Park Lane; I had special dispensation and parked in the police station's ample car park beside a heavily armoured police van. There was still plenty of light, although there was all about the late evening's crepuscular remnant of a hot day's dust, the kind that seems to hide more than it reveals, that seems to suffocate. The central police station had never been a particularly beautiful building – red-brick, rectangular, old before it was born, and possessing only the character of characterlessness. The entrance hall smelled of disinfectant; it might have been my imagination but I had the impression that it masked a faint tang of vomitus; at which, I suddenly wondered if it was poo. It wasn't that many years since the foundation stone of the imposing headquarters of the Croydon stretch of the thin blue line had first been laid but, internally at least, the constant battering and physical abuse from the less than enthusiastic customers had left their marks; there were holes in the wall caused either by fists or toecaps, while the once pristine magnolia emulsion was badly scuffed and covered in what I can only describe as an 'interesting and thought-provoking' variety of graffiti (much of which was most appallingly spelt and gave me scant optimism in the Labour government's faith in comprehensive education).

Having presented my credentials, I was forced to wait for fifteen minutes in the company of a drunken gentleman of the road who possessed the reddest face, the longest beard and the most pungent body stench I have ever encountered (and believe me, I have worked in NHS casualty departments where I have experienced a fairly broad range of bad breath, body odour, gangrene and smelly feet). He mumbled a lot too, looking towards me but not at me; I moved to sit diagonally opposite him but it seemed to make no discernible difference in the intensity of his perfume, as if no matter how far I travelled, I was doomed to share the same atmosphere with this harbinger of pong for ever. During this time, there was a string of visitors, all in the company of police officers, all professing very little enthusiasm for their environment and all doing so in ripe language.

Eventually I was dragged away from the entertainment by a tall, saturnine constable who seemed not to notice that life's rich pageant was being displayed before him for his entertainment. Having asked of me briefly, 'Dr Elliot?' and received an affirmative, he punched a five-digit code into a lock on a door, carefully shielding his actions with his other hand and thereby demonstrating a highly commendable attitude towards security, despite the fact that it was only the drunk and I who were in the room at the time, and he was a good twenty feet away. He led me down a short corridor, then down two flights of stairs, then along another, longer corridor; the atmosphere improved for a short while, then deteriorated again, although now the overwhelming note was one of perspiration and cabbage stewed for a week or two, so that it had been turned back into primeval pond life. My guide saying nothing, I decided to make a venture at conversation as we walked along the drab corridor.

'Busy night so far?' I asked, by way of a start on this resolve. My escort looked at me, his expression suggesting that he had heard there was an imbecile in the vicinity and nothing else that he could see would fit the bill so perfectly. He said after a short pause and in a voice that was both sepulchral and vexed, 'It's not yet nine o'clock and the cells are already almost full.'

'Oh, dear,' was all I could find to say. I could understand how the working environment might predispose to a distinctly pessimistic view of life.

At the end of the corridor was a T-junction at which seated at a desk was another uniformed police officer, this one no sunnier than his colleague. Along the sides of the perpendicular corridor were arrayed the cells, sixteen in all. The smell here was a heady mix of odours that did not so much assault the olfactory organs as decimate them, while there was an equally disagreeable attack on the auscultatory apparatus from the cells' inhabitants as they sang, groaned, shouted and profaned with gay abandon. This custody sergeant – for thus it was – looked up after writing with intense concentration something in a ledger. He was a tall, well-built man of middle age, running to fat and beginning to lose his hair. Fearful that he should consider me a felon and instantly incarcerate me, I said quickly, 'I'm Dr Elliot, the police surgeon,'

This evoked no enthusiasm, even when my escort nodded assent at the questioning look from this stout guardian of the cells. Returning his attention to me, he said without noticeable gusto, 'He's in number three. Making a terrible fuss, he was.' How he had determined this given the unholy cacophony that seemed part of normal life down there was beyond me. My escort, keys clanking on his thigh, moved forward and I followed. We turned left and walked perhaps twenty yards along the corridor, passing through a bedlam of sound that changed with every three steps. We stopped before a door that was like all the rest; it was made of heavy steel, painted in a sort of green-grey paint that was curiously reminiscent of the contents of a boil. There was a small semicircular indentation in the door at eye level at the base of which was a small window of thick glass; the constable grasped his key ring but looked into the cell through this before selecting a key.

He said suddenly, 'Oh, Christ!' and began fumbling in earnest for the correct key.

'What is it?' I asked.

He didn't reply and I was in the metaphysical dark until I followed him as we hurriedly entered the cell. There was a body, face down on the floor by the side of the bunk; the feet were near the slop bucket but thankfully they hadn't made contact with it. There was vomitus on the floor under the head. 'Get out of the way,' I ordered, feeling some enjoyment at being able to boss him around. He obliged at once and I was able to lean down beside the body, although there was precious little room. I felt around the side of the neck for a pulse and, albeit with some difficulty, found one. I said, 'Help me turn him.'

The constable took a moment to react, but then squeezed in beside me. Together and with some difficulty in the cramped space, we turned the man over. It was George Cotterill.

FIFTEEN

'He died shortly after we got him to Casualty.'

I was cooking. For my A-levels I had done chemistry, biology and physics, and got A grades in all of them, much to the delight of my father. It had always seemed to me that cooking was just the practical application of these three academic subjects and, moreover, most cooks, no matter how bright, were not particularly academic. The logical corollary of this was that I should have been a brilliant cook, since I was both bright and knew the theory.

How wrong I was.

My father had had occasion in the past to pass adverse comment on some of the products of my culinary experiments that had passed the frontier of his false upper-plate gnashers. The first time that this had occurred, I had laughed it off as mere envy, but the years had gone by and he had been joined in adverse commentary by most of the people who had summoned the courage to partake of my cuisine. One of my early girlfriends had once left the table while I was dishing up the dessert only to be heard throwing up in the toilet.

Max's problem, though, was that she was completely incapable of any kind of cooking at all. Until she met me, I think she was quite cheerful about it, not seeing it as a particularly major problem; she had a career as a vet and, presumably, she thought she would either meet a man who could cook any matter of delicious repast at her whim, or she would soon be earning enough to live her entire gustatory life in restaurants. Unfortunately, she ended up with me. She had yet to regurgitate my attempts (at least within my earshot or eye line), but there had been times when even I, a man with the social sensibilities of a rhinoceros, could see that things were proving a strain.

On this particular Sunday, I was preparing roast beef. I would say 'with all the trimmings' but all I had been able to manage was roast potatoes, carrots and cabbage. I had just opened the oven door to discover that the cookery book had lied yet again and what should have been a nicely browned rolled silverside looked more like an incinerated dinosaur turd; thankfully, all I could smell was charcoal. Add to that the fact that I had previously over-boiled the spuds and now they were rapidly becoming over-roasted potato sludge, the carrots had been on for nearly an hour and were still slightly less hard than my grandmother's wooden leg and the cabbage had turned to soup as soon as it had hit the water, and all in all I could sense that I was building to a repast of climactic awesomeness.

Max was sitting in the garden, unaware of what delights were heading her way, enjoying the arid, waterless delights of my own personal slice of desert, whilst drinking deeply of a glass of Black Tower. She said, 'That poor man. What a horrible place to spend his last hours on earth.'

She could have been talking about the casualty department of Mayday Hospital, but I guessed she was referring to Croydon Central nick. 'It certainly isn't my favourite place to spend Saturday evening,' I agreed.

'Why do you think he died?'

'I would say his heart.'

'So it was natural?'

'I think so, but there'll still have to be a post-mortem.'

'Why?'

I poured myself some Riesling. 'Because he died in police custody.'

'What difference does that make?'

'People get skittish when suspects die in the cells. It's just to reassure the public.'

She was astonished. 'Why would the public need to be reassured?'

This innocence was part of Max's attractiveness (and it was the same part that made her the most irritating person I have ever met); she lived in a world parallel to the one that housed the rest of the human race, one in which the police were incapable of wrongdoing for no better reason than they were the police and in which, unbelievably, my father was a sane and rational human being (and not one of the most irksome entities that has ever bothered the universe).

'Because it has been known for the police to treat people in their cells without due care.'

'Really?'

In reply to this I said only, 'Sometimes, yes.'

I got up and went back into the kitchen, having become aware of a strange odour emanating thence: it was the carrots that were the perpetrators of this; having silently suffered total dehydration, they were beginning to turn into carrot caramel on the bottom of the saucepan. 'Is everything all right?' called Max through the kitchen doorway.

'No problems,' was my response, with quite breathtaking mendacity as I furiously scraped sweet brown toffee off the bottom of a copper-bottomed saucepan that had once been a wedding gift for a marriage that had lasted only one tenth of the period of the pan's guarantee.

Max's expressions told the story, although she said not a word of criticism. I have to admit that it was a curious culinary experience; the vegetables had the texture of partially digested seaweed and the smell of inspissated mucus, while the meat (I always like to create different textures in my cooking efforts) defied any attempt at mastication; nor did it have much flavour, although I did on rare occasions detect the tang of sweat-soaked lederhosen. The only way it could be ingested was by cutting extremely small pieces, and even that took a great deal of effort. This was a cow that had clearly decided that, dead though it might be, it was not going to go gentle into that good night; conversation died as we struggled to overcome this curiously obstinate foodstuff. Eventually I gave up, and although I was only halfway through the meal, put my knife and fork down; my right arm was tired and the exertion combined with the heat was making me sweat rather uncomfortably. Max took my surrender as a cue that she could do likewise; there was, I think, an air of relief as she did this.

The doorbell rang and a few moments later I opened the door to Inspector Masson. He had his jacket over his shoulder and his tie was at half-mast. 'May I come in?'

I stood aside and showed him through to the back patio where we had been eating. He nodded at Max. 'Miss Christy.'

'Hello, Inspector.'

'Something to drink?' I asked him.

'Iced water,' he said, without appending the usual niceties. He sounded even more exasperated and tired than usual. When I returned with his libation, he was seated at the garden table eyeing the remains of our recent repast with something that I can only describe as a jaundiced eye, while Max attempted the impossible and tried to make small talk with him; I could see from her expression that he was proving as sociable as ever. He grunted something – possibly thanks, possibly not – and took a deep draught. Then he put an empty glass down and, gesturing with his chin at the half-eaten meal, said acidly, 'What the hell is that muck?'

'Roast beef,' I responded, and I think I did so in a voice that told him he had overstepped the mark.

'It was very nice,' added Max loyally.

Masson curled his lip. 'It looks it,' was his only comment. His fingers were fidgeting with each other, with the edge of the table, with everything and nothing; anyone who didn't know him might have assumed that he was nervous, but I knew that the reason for this unconscious finger-jiving was indicated by patchy yellow-brown stains on this fore and middle fingers, and by the ever-present odour of stale tobacco smoke that he moved around in, as if he were an alien creature who required his own atmosphere. Since we were (in theory at least) still eating, I reckoned he could wait a while longer to knock another seven minutes off his life.

'Aside from your part-time role as visiting food critic for the *Croydon Advertiser*, what brings you to my house, Inspector?'

'I need a statement from you.' He actually sounded as if he needed nothing less.

'What about?'

'Your part in the death of George Cotterill.'

Well, there we were. I'd played a part in his death,

apparently; and there I had been thinking that I'd played a part in trying to save his life. Presumably the good Inspector suspected me of slipping him a capsule full of potassium cyanide during the twenty minutes I had been in the cell giving him mouth to mouth (I could still remember the taste of that particular experience); I had, after all, been on my own for most of that time. 'I beg your pardon?'

He was preoccupied, staring at the green plastic surface of the table, whilst Max did a bit of her own staring at me, hers with some shock, clearly seeing me with new eyes. 'Inspector?' I prompted.

He came to. 'You were there in the cell and thereafter accompanied him to hospital where he died. All deaths in custody have to be investigated; all the witnesses have to be interviewed and statements taken.'

Did Max look disappointed that I was not suspected of manslaughter? I fancy she did.

Whilst Masson consumed a second glass of iced water, and Max and I had some Riesling, I recounted what had happened; he did not take notes. Eventually, I ran out of things to say and he ran out of questions to ask, and everyone ran out of things to drink. I asked, 'Do you know what George died of yet?'

'The post-mortem examination was done this morning by Dr Bentham. Pending further investigations, he's fairly certain it was heart disease.'

Max asked, 'What about the murder?'

'What about it?'

'Are you satisfied that George Cotterill did it?'

He laughed, as ever, sourly. 'Oh, I am. Trouble is, I doubt I'll be given the time and money to prove it now. Even if I was, I doubt whether I could, he was too clever.'

'Was he really?' Max had a knack of asking such questions; the words said one thing, the tone of voice another entirely. She sounded even to my ears to be entirely genuine; for all I knew, she was.

Masson's face told me that he was unsure of whether she was being authentic. Momentarily bereft of speech, he soon came back with, 'Yes.' I thought that, as a witticism, it probably wouldn't even have made Oscar Wilde's discard pile.

Before she could say any more, I intervened. 'You can chalk up another successful case, though.' I don't know what it was, but whenever I was around Inspector Masson, I felt this irresistible desire to try to cheer him up. I think it was the medical training; the Hippocratic oath probably had a word or two to say on the subject of bringing cheer to misanthropic members of the police force.

'Can I?' he enquired, demonstrating that my bedside manner could have been improved.

'Well, nobody can prove he *didn't* do it.'

'The point, Dr Elliot,' he said tiredly, 'is that I can't prove he did. That's the important thing. There'll always be a doubt now.'

I wondered why that mattered to him but didn't dare ask. There was then a pause, the like of which I can only recall when I was a small child and barged in on my Auntie Barbara when she was doing number twos in the downstairs cloakroom; inevitably it was Max who broke it. 'Maybe he didn't do it,' she suggested. 'Maybe he was innocent.'

And, thankfully, the phone rang inside the house; it stopped what I feared would be a fit of apoplexy that would see the end of my good friend Inspector Masson. I said, 'Max, could you answer that whilst I fetch another glass of water for our guest?'

She opened her mouth but shut it again when I looked at her warningly. Masson, meanwhile, was doing an ace impression of a boiled lobster being inflated by an air pump, although he said nothing. I deliberately took my time finding the ice tray in the freezer, not wanting to go back out to our guest alone; Max came into the kitchen and said, 'It's your father. He wants to talk to you.'

Part of me was asking silently, *What now?* Another part was highly delighted that I could delay returning to Masson and thus give him a little time to calm down a bit. The heavy Bakelite of the handset was, for a moment at least, a small pool of coolness in an otherwise sweltering world. 'Dad?'

'Is that you, Lance?'

It was my father's habit to ask questions such as this, questions that invited acidic sarcasm, that required the forbearance of a saint not to answer through painfully gritted teeth. Through long practice, I enquired of him, 'Is everything all right?'

'Slight hitch in the plans, that's all.'

Which could have meant anything, everything or nothing. 'What's happened?'

'The car's broken down, just outside Crawley.'

'What's the problem?'

'Have you ever been to Crawley? Dreadful place. Absolutely horrid. I remember visiting it just after the war with your mother and it was delightful little village. Now they've turned it into a giant concrete necropolis; it's got about as much soul as a prefabricated garage.'

'Dad, what's wrong with the car?'

'I think the water pump's gone west.'

'Have you phoned the AA?'

'They said they might be some time; a lot of calls because of overheating.'

'Are you and Ada all right?'

'Oh, yes. Don't worry about us. We've found a very agreeable pub, but that's not the point . . .' And here, I knew, was coming the crux of the issue; I knew also that, as it was my father talking, I was probably in for at the least perplexity, quite possibly embarrassment, conceivably some pain. 'I was wondering if you were going to be in tonight.'

'What time?' I asked this not because I was going out, but because my father would have been quite capable of turning up at one in the morning, completely oblivious of the fact that he was waking not only me but also, because of his car, most of the neighbourhood.

'Well, that rather depends on the AA. Do you know, I'm paying them fifteen pounds a year, and for what? They don't even salute any more . . .'

'Why don't you let us know when you're on the road again? Then you'll be able to give us a better idea of when you're likely to get here.'

'Will Max be there?' He asked this in a tone that was difficult for me to read; Dad had mixed feelings about my girlfriend, sometimes succumbing to her charms, at other times . . .

'Probably.'

'Good,' he said at once, and put the phone down.

It was not unusual for me to emerge from a conversation with my father feeling slightly winded, as if I had been exposed to a weakly hallucinogenic gas, but I had a guest to take care of and could not bother about such things. Accordingly, I strove to overcome the slight dyspnoea that was sometimes an inevitable consequence of contact with my father; conversations with him could on occasion prove to be similar to being punched in the stomach.

Masson had abandoned his rather pained survey of my cooking and, now upright, was looking intently at the wilting hydrangea bush, wreathed in the grey, sinuous tendrils of cigarette smoke. The airless, still heat not only allowed them existence but seemed almost to animate them. His back was to the house and behind him Max had cleared the table. She looked at me and raised her eyebrows, to which I shrugged. I went back into the kitchen and brought out from the oven the dessert. Putting it on the table, I called to him, 'Would you care for some pudding, Inspector?'

He turned, then spotted my creation. 'What is that?' he asked, and sounded partly genuinely puzzled, partly wary and partly horrified.

'It's rice pudding,' was Max's stout and rather touching defence. I could see his point, though; I had put all the ingredients in that the recipe promised would turn into rice pudding but, somehow, somewhere along the line, it had become something that looked as though it had been born in the slime pits of the Jurassic period and survived undisturbed in my oven until the present day. There was a dark brown, focally burned skin on the top that strange ripples and bubbles from the depths occasionally disturbed. It hinted at things from beyond the great abyss, as Lovecraft might have put it.

Masson continued to stare at the pudding. 'No, thanks. I have to get going.'

He stepped on his cigarette and started forward, then paused. He resumed progress after a moment but appeared to want to keep as far away from the table as possible as he moved back into the house. As I showed him out, he said, 'Sergeant Abelson will be in contact to take a formal statement.'

When I returned to the garden, Max had dished up the rice pudding. Even before I started to eat it, I could see that it possessed interesting properties, possibly ones previously unknown to science. It flowed slowly, but for all its torpor, it seemed to possess a curious animus, as if it were slowly disassembling itself and exploring its environment. I hesitated before plunging my spoon in, half expecting it to react badly to such an indignity. As I put it slowly in my mouth my eyes met Max's; she was watching me, her own spoonful poised at about chin level, her eyes filled with curiosity. The taste was *interesting*, being almost like rice pudding, which was good. What wasn't so good was that it had the adhesive properties of wallpaper paste, which made speech impossible for some little time, and made swallowing an exercise in suppression of the gag reflex.

By mutual agreement we soon abandoned any attempt at mastication and ingurgitation, and finished the wine instead. 'What did your father want?'

'The Red Hornet's broken down in Crawley.'

'Are they all right?'

'They're fine. All he wanted to tell me was that he doesn't like Crawley New Town. Apparently they've taken a delightful village and turned it into a blot on England's green and pleasant face.'

She smiled. 'He's on good form, then.'

'He's calling in when they finally get back.'

'That's nice.'

I had to wonder about that; if I knew my father, he was up to something.

SIXTEEN

Mourning takes many forms, and if it is not dealt with (much as if dry rot is not dealt with) it spreads without obvious movement, certainly without purpose and without outward sign. Yet this thing that does not move, does not bother, does not raise its head and does not appear to be in any way menacing, this thing will destroy as surely as acid and as completely as a fusion blast, without any of the fuss, any of the bother, just all of the devastation. Yet all of us have to deal with it; sometimes when we are young, sometimes when we are old; sometimes many times, sometimes on just one, completely overwhelming occasion. And for each of us, there is a different way of dealing with it. Nowadays there are advice lines (many different kinds), counsellors (many different kinds) and therapists (even more different kinds). In the nineteen sixties, there were only the now alien concepts of friends and family, and nothing else; if you didn't have those (and Dad and I didn't), society provided only one other resource.

Yourself.

Don't get me wrong. Dad and I loved each other, but each of us found our grief for the loss of my mother, his wife, too personal and intense to be shared by anyone. We both knew her so well, yet we knew her in entirely different ways; his memories could not be mine, nor mine his. We both had intimate remembrances, but they would always be completely personal to each of us; and we both understood that, even without saying anything about it. Perhaps it was because nothing was said – and that was because nothing needed to be said – that we drew so close without any wailing, or gnashing of teeth, or tears when we were in each other's company. We had lived through the experience, perhaps even grown through it, because learning to live with a disability (and the scar that bereavement leaves is, believe me, a disability) empowers you.

Yet it also tethers you.

Without saying a word, without ever acknowledging our bond, we had become conjoined as completely as any pair of stage Siamese twins, as irrevocably within each other's orbit as binary stars. We had a common centre of gravity around which we spun, trying to live our present lives; it was one that was an absence, as dark and as powerful as a black hole, and just as inescapable.

That night, something happened to disturb the harmony of our system, though.

Dad and Ada arrived at about eight thirty that evening, tired either from the weekend or the journey home, or both; they wasted no time in announcing their engagement.

The following morning Jane, our practice nurse, seemed oddly compassionate when I told her my news. She said, 'Never mind,' and said it in a tone full of sympathy, which struck me as odd as I didn't think I was in need of sympathy.

'Never mind what?'

She looked nonplussed, as if it was all obvious; it was not an unfamiliar situation to be in when Jane and I talked things over. She saw things in a different way from me; I hesitate to say that she saw them with greater clarity, or greater depth, but she certainly always brought a refreshingly insightful and novel view with her. Then she took a deep breath in and, with a slow nod of her head, sighed, 'Oh, I see.'

'See what?'

'You're not bothered, then?'

'Why should I be bothered? If the silly old fool wants to plunge into the deep end of the matrimonial pool for a second time, why is it anything to me?'

The body language of my father and Ada had been instructive and told me at once that something had changed. They sat in my living room on the sofa, perhaps a little bit closer than they ever had previously, whilst on my father's face was a slight but noticeable smirk, one that I always associated with him when he had achieved some success in one of his lunatic schemes. Little did I know how lunatic this particular scheme was, although there was the usual kerfuffle that is associated with my dad and his doings before Max and I were released from our state of naive ignorance.

'We got a lift with the AA man. Very nice, he was,' he said, sipping some red wine. Ada nodded; she was on sherry, and I have to admit that she looked every inch a sherry woman. 'He said how much he admired the lines of a Hillman Avenger.'

'Beats a Maserati any day,' I agreed, although Dad didn't seem to hear the sarcasm that dripped from every syllable.

'We had a nice time, waiting for him, didn't we, Ada?'

She nodded and finished her sherry; well, I reasoned as I

refilled it, it was only a small schooner. 'What's wrong with it? Was it the water pump as you said?'

'Eric – that's the man from the AA – was fairly sure it was the starter motor.' He spoke as if he suspected Eric was a charlatan, clearly not up to the job. 'Maybe it is,' he added generously. 'Whatever it is, she's certainly fairly poorly at the moment.' He said these words sadly, as if he were talking about the family pooch that kept getting a variety of minor and annoying ailments but was really loved by all.

'When can you get it fixed?'

'I'll phone the garage tomorrow. Hopefully they'll be able to fit me in this week.'

Max asked, 'How will you get to the school to look after your vegetables?'

I kind of wished she hadn't made that enquiry because it would be just like Dad to assume that I would be able to provide a free, on-demand taxi service, but I need not have fretted. 'I shouldn't need to go over there until the end of the week. I know the children will keep up with the watering, which is the most important thing at this time of year.'

The conversation waned, a lull into which Dad jumped with both heavily shod feet. 'Ada has kindly consented to be my lady wife,' he announced pompously, while she stared at the side of his face as an enigmatic smile played around her thin lips and I was uncomfortably reminded of the Mona Lisa, or perhaps of the way a cat will stare at a small, unknowing mouse that is trapped in a corner.

I opened my mouth, aware that I was expected to pronounce something and that it had to be something politic and at least vaguely enthusiastic. All I could find in the locker, though, was, 'Wow.'

Max, so often my cavalry in social situations, said quickly, 'Congratulations to you both. We had been wondering, hadn't we, Lance?'

Had we? But everyone was looking at me and I agreed effusively.

'Have we got any champagne?' asked Max.

Well, of course we didn't, so we had to make do with a bottle of hock that I had been saving for a special occasion.

We toasted the happy couple whilst I felt immersed in a sense of surreal disconnection. Max did the talking. 'When's the happy day?'

'We haven't decided, have we, Ada?'

Ada said, no, they hadn't. 'We haven't yet told my son.' Her voice was thin and slightly nasal.

'But we're not going to hang about,' he assured us.

'Well, no,' I said without thinking. 'You wouldn't want to . . .' There was an uncomfortable silence whilst the unintended meaning of my response hung about the room. '. . . I didn't mean . . .'

'Any more wine?' asked Max.

It hadn't been the best of evenings.

And now Jane wasn't quite smiling, but then she wasn't quite *not* smiling either. I felt as I used to do when sitting in medical viva-voce examinations and I was trying to convince the learned professors that I knew what I was talking about; I nearly always failed and they nearly always had that smile on their faces when I did so. We were standing in the receptionists' area, Sheila and Jean pulling notes in preparation for evening surgery, not listening to what we were saying, honest. Jane nodded in faux agreement. 'Absolutely. It'll be nothing to you at all.'

'What does that mean?'

'He was very happily married, Lance,' she pointed out. 'Maybe he can swim.'

I found that remark curiously unsettling, but didn't know why. 'Maybe there are sharks in the pool now,' was all I could find to say. She nodded and didn't reply, which I thought slightly unfair because it forced me to say something more. 'Are you implying I'm worried about my inheritance?' I hissed. Our two ever-busy clerical staff worked even harder as they began to listen even harder.

Jane laughed. When Jane laughed it was because she was amused, not because she wanted to make someone feel small. 'No, Lance. I know you better than that.'

'Then what?'

Jane had been nursing for nearly twenty years. During that time she had been forced to cope with every possible situation, whether it involved physical injury, lunacy, tragedy, farce, complete anarchy or total idiocy. She had come through it all but, more than that, she had come through it all with her humanity intact, and that was a miracle. She had never married; when I had asked her why that should be, she had replied simply, 'I found I only had enough emotion for my patients.' In that simple statement, I found both joy and sorrow in such amazing quantities, it left me almost breathless, and certainly in awe of her.

'I think you're worried about your mother . . .'

'What?' My voice was unexpectedly loud.

'And I also think . . .'

'Rubbish!' I was astonished. Aware that Sheila and Jean were ever ready to be the best and most attentive of audiences, I lowered my voice even more. 'I'm not twelve years old, you know, Jane. I think I'm adult enough not to be still fixated on my mother.'

'And I also think,' she went on, her own tone considerably more confidential now, 'you're afraid of losing your father.' Which was patently absurd as my spluttering, wordless response told her. She added, 'And I think that's wonderful.'

'Rubbish,' was all I could find to say.

The phone rang and for a moment neither Jean nor Sheila moved, as if they were transfixed. I turned to Sheila, raised my eyebrows at her and nodded at the phone. She came to and picked it up. 'Brigstock Road Surgery.'

She listened for a moment, then held the receiver out to me. 'It's for you.'

It was Sergeant Abelson. My immediate assumption was that she wanted to arrange a time to take a formal statement from me concerning George Cotterill's death, but I was wrong. 'Can you come to 121 Keston Road immediately?'

It was half-past eleven and I didn't have any house calls until one. 'I'll be there in twenty minutes. What's the problem?'

'We have a suspicious death.' Her tone was odd, although I couldn't identify why.

SEVENTEEN

Have you noticed how the police like to play things down? They don't interrogate people; people 'help them with their enquiries'. When there is a demonstration, police estimates of the numbers are always half the demonstrators'. When they tell you that a death is suspicious, it's bound to be blindingly obvious that it's a murder.

Keston Road was long and almost completely straight, only dog-legging slightly to the right; it ran from Thornton Road almost to the London Road. It was not a particularly prestigious address – even less so, now – with its small front gardens and general lack of recent painting. Number 121 was just beyond the dog-leg, distinguished only by the attention it had now acquired – three police cars, an ambulance, sundry police officers, a lot of plastic yellow tape and a crowd of onlookers. This last was composed of the usual motley assortment – those who whispered to each other, those who pointed whilst whispering to each other, those who gawped and then whispered to each other, and those who just gawped.

The object of their attention was not your average terraced house. Although architecturally I suspect it was nothing for Christopher Wren to get too excited about – upstairs were three bedrooms (although one was little more than a cupboard) and a single family bathroom, and downstairs were two living rooms and a reasonably sized kitchen – it proved yet again what an interesting creature is *Homo sapiens*.

Not that, on first sight, it seemed to be anything too much out of the ordinary. The exterior was drab and somewhat in need of redecoration, the hall ornamentation lacklustre and, although not dirty, somehow utilitarian and without inspiration; indeed, my first impression was that these were students' digs and not a family home and I wondered who lived there. I had trouble making any progress once past the front door because of the number of sweaty male police officers there were in

the hall, as if they were attempting to break the world record
for cramming constabulary into domestic premises. I even
began to feel slightly dislocated; perhaps it was the heat of
the day made so much worse by the concentration of foetid
male pheromones. At the end of the hallway, Masson was
standing in the doorway of what was presumably the back
living room; despite this being a crime scene, he was smoking
and staring through the doorway, a look of concentration on
his face. When I came up to him he said nothing but stood
back to let me see what it contained.

At one time, this room would probably have looked just like
most people's idea of suburban normality. There was a two-
seater sofa in loose covers with a floral pattern, a single armchair
that was similarly attired, a fake stone fireplace in which there
was a three-bar electric fire, a wooden trolley on which was a
bottle of British sherry with three glasses, an oval wooden
dining table with two fold-down flaps and an elderly television
set that looked as if it had heard there was a third television
channel, but was going to have nothing to do with it. On the
floor was an ornately patterned square carpet that was slightly
worn in the middle and surrounded by a border of bare linoleum. The windows looked as if someone had been cleaning
them and then got bored halfway through – which was odd
– but, all in all, it reminded me slightly of my grandmother's
sitting room, although she had been dead some twenty years.

I say 'slightly', because there were one or two alterations to
this room that I'm fairly sure Granny would never have had in
her house. Firstly the room had been wrecked – all of the cushions ripped and thrown on the floor, all of the drawers rifled,
even the television set destroyed. Secondly, there was a body of
a woman, and this woman was lying on her front and covered
in blood. Indeed, she almost seemed to rise out of the stuff, so
much of it was there on the carpet. Even from the doorway I
could see several long, deep gashes in her arms and on her back.

Masson said, 'I can't get hold of a pathologist at the moment
– the bugger's in court.' He made it sound as if Mark was
skiving. 'We've got Scenes of Crime on the way to take the
photographs; I just need you to confirm death and give me
your opinion on the likely cause.'

It was a peculiarity of English law that even a decapitated corpse required a doctor to confirm death; plainly ludicrous and I knew it, so I could understand Masson's frustration and anger. Biting back the urge to be facetious that always seemed to rise to my lips whenever I was in Masson's company – 'I can't be absolutely certain, Inspector, but I have the strangest feeling she may have been stabbed' – I put my bag down in the hallway and gingerly entered the room. From what I could see of her (which wasn't much) she was about fifty years old, with blonde, permed hair, and sharp, pinched features giving her a suspicious face, even in such a death. She was short and quite stocky. I fished out some disposable gloves from my jacket pocket and put them on before crouching down beside her, aware that I would be lucky to come away without at least some of the blood transferred somewhere on to me. What I saw then made me freeze with shock. I hadn't noticed it before – probably no one had – because of the considerable quantity of blood and because the head was in the far corner and in some shadow, but up close you couldn't miss it.

She had the point of a compass sticking out of her right eye.

Deep breaths, Lance, I told myself.

I gently touched the neck, feeling for a pulse, and finding myself actually hoping that I wouldn't find one. The blood was markedly congealed and she had obviously been there for some time, so it was no surprise when I was unsuccessful. In doing this, my fingers found one of the cuts, found how deep it was. Then, still being as gentle as I could, I tested as best I could for body warmth and for rigor.

I stood up, stepped away backwards.

'Well?'

'You won't be surprised to hear that she's dead.'

'How long?'

I had known he would ask that and my insistence that precise timing of death was as much a thing of crime fiction as Sherlock Holmes with his calabash, Inverness cape and deerstalker cap would be as but a whisper in a whirlwind. 'This is only approximate,' I replied.

'I know that. It's what you lot always say.'

'*Very* approximate . . .'

His colour was forever somewhat unhealthy – sometime sallow, sometimes grey – but the rising deep puce did little to enhance the impression of rude health; indeed, he looked as though it would not be long before he came dangerously close to apoplexy. I said hurriedly, 'Less than six hours, since she's still slightly warm and there's little sign of rigor. I'd say maybe as little as three hours.'

'And did she die of the stab wounds?'

'I would say so. Obviously I can't say if there was a decisive one or it was just blood loss, but she's got quite a deep one that could have reached her right internal jugular . . .'

But he wasn't listening. 'A frenzied attack,' he said.

'You could say that. She's got a compass stuck in her eyeball.'

Even he winced at that one.

'Who was she?' I asked.

He didn't reply directly, instead moving back along the hallway (magically finding a clear path opening before him) to the foot of the stairs. He called up them, 'Sergeant?'

Abelson's voice came from the first floor. 'Sir?'

'Would you show Dr Elliot what we've got upstairs?'

His face was unreadable as he gestured up the stairs to me.

The back bedroom, at the top of the staircase, might have been a back bedroom in any one of a million homes in the UK, except that it had also been ransacked. There was a double bed with an identical bedside cabinet to right and left, made out of white laminated wood or wood substitute; a mechanical alarm clock was on one, on the other was a Teasmade. Beside the clock was a hardback copy of *Humboldt's Gift*; beside that most decadent of household appliances was a paperback copy of *Salem's Lot*. The bed had a pink quilted cover pulled over it and there were fluffy white cushions on the pillows. In the window was an ornate dressing table in a similar laminate, before which was a stool and above which was a round tilting mirror; the table was crowded with cosmetic products. Fitted wardrobes – same laminate – ran across the wall behind the door. A shag-pile carpet covered most of the floor area.

All had been thrown about and disordered in what seemed to me to have been a furious search.

It would have been a good place to sleep, I thought, but I soon discovered that this was not something that could be said of the front bedroom. Sergeant Abelson was standing in the open doorway, but she stood aside as I approached and looked around it. There must have been a look of some awe on my face, for Sergeant Abelson said, 'Impressive, isn't it?'

Looking back, I'm fairly sure that impressive was one of the adjectives running through my wonder-filled brain, but it was only one among many, jostling for attention with *surprising*, *shocking*, *amusing*, *titillating*, *staggering* and *puzzling* and many others. I could find only one thing to sum it all up.

'Wow.'

The room was a sexual torture chamber.

The walls were painted a deep red, as if to hide the blood stains, and the woodwork matt black. There was no bed, merely a flat wooden tabletop, although one that had been erected on some sort of tilting mechanism, and that had manacles at the top end. At the bottom end were poles at either corner, on each of which was a stirrup; it brought to mind the slightly less than pleasant memories of hot and embarrassed days spent in the gynaecology outpatients' clinic when, as a callow medical student, not yet amnesiac of puberty, I had been introduced to the emotionally draining world of bimanual pelvic examination. On the wall to the left of the window was hung an assortment of leather goods, by which I most definitely do not mean high heels and purses, but this was less unnerving than the wall opposite, which was the home of a shelving unit that had been emptied of its contents, again apparently in some sort of search. On the floor beneath it were various 'toys' but, try as I might, I could see no Lego, no Stickle Bricks and definitely no Barbie dolls.

The good Sergeant said, 'I've been doing this job for ten years and I'm still amazed by what our citizens choose to do in their private time.'

'And to their private parts. My eyes are watering.'

She said at once, 'They would if you were trapped in this place.'

'Who lives here?'

Masson had joined us and Abelson deferred to him. 'The

house is in the name of Yvette Mangon. We're assuming at the moment that it is Yvette Mangon downstairs.'

My head was overflowing with questions about Yvette Mangon's domestic arrangements, chief amongst which was, 'Was she married?' If so, her husband could hardly have been in ignorance of what had presumably been going in the front bedroom. Either he had been her manager – by which, of course, I meant 'pimp' – or she had been unmarried.

'Did she live here alone?'

Masson's voice was dry, but that wasn't unusual; when he really wanted to convey sarcasm, he tended to desiccate everything within a ten-foot radius. 'Of late, she had been.'

I didn't know what he meant, although that he had meant something was plain from his tone. He walked out of the room and led me into the box room. It, too, was a bit chintzy for my taste – all pink and satin and frilly bits – and it had also been the object of someone's search. He turned to me and said, 'Yvette Mangon's lodger supposedly slept here.'

His voice was heavy with sarcasm.

'Where is he now?'

'*She* is at Mayday mortuary. Her name is Marlene Jeffries.'

EIGHTEEN

I arrived back at the practice just before it was time for evening surgery. I was standing in the small staff room by the reception area looking at the list of my patients who were going to seek my help and advice, sifting them into those who were relatively infrequent visitors and those who were regular attendees (and subdividing these into the ones with problems that were more medical, and the ones with problems that were more social), when Sheila came in. 'Your father phoned.' Her voice held amusement and her cheeks contained a smirk, although they were clearly struggling to keep it confined. 'He says he's going to be working at home tonight. He wants you to go and see him there.'

'He said it like that?'

She nodded. 'Oh, yes, Dr Elliot. He sounded a little bit terse.'

I arrived at my father's house at just after seven thirty to find him in his garden, watering assorted vegetables and fruits. The air still held the heat of the day, a wet warm embrace that didn't seem to have much time for clear thinking or cool temperament. Certainly my father seemed a little on the steamy side. 'Lance,' he greeted me. Before I could do the decent thing and respond, as one is supposed to do, he continued, 'George Cotterill is dead.'

His announced this as if it would be news to me and I was about to assure him that I already knew when I realized my faux pas; I had completely forgotten to tell him. 'Dad, I'm sorry . . .'

'Why the hell didn't you tell me, Lance?'

He wasn't just angry, he was hurt; quite rightly, too. 'I completely forgot. What with all the excitement about your announcement last night, it just went from my mind.'

'How could you, Lance? It was such a shock to see an item about it in this morning's paper.'

'Yes, I know I should have told you but . . . it was just that the news of your engagement to Ada was such a surprise . . . such a joyous surprise . . . that I didn't want to spoil it, not last night. I should have phoned you this morning but, as I say, I forgot. I'm sorry.'

Considerably mollified, he nodded, accepting my explanation whilst I struggled with a not inconsiderable amount of guilt at my massaging of the truth of how Max and I had received the news of Elliot Senior's impending nuptials. 'Yes, well, I understand now.'

And we were left with his grief at the loss of a friend. He asked, 'What was it? Do you know?'

'His heart, I think. I don't know what the results of the post-mortem are yet.'

His head bobbed up and down slowly, his face a thing of sad reflection. 'He'd been having angina. I told him to get it looked into, but he wouldn't.' It was an epitaph that could have been written on a million tombstones. He picked up the watering can – rather a fetching red one – and resumed drowning some ants who had innocently been doing ant-like things at his feet.

Intending to show interest and concern, I asked, 'Have you and Ada told her family yet?' He ran out of water just as I asked this and yet he didn't seem to notice, which was odd; he just stood there, looking at something just in front of the onions, as if mesmerized. 'Dad?'

He came to, pulled himself out of a slight slump of his shoulders. 'Yes, well, that didn't go quite according to plan,' he said.

And although his voice was not overtly sad, it held a wistfulness and a tone of puzzlement that were together a paradigm of melancholia. He clearly needed some form of therapy so I asked, 'How about a pint?'

It has to be said that Thornton Heath was not overly endowed with public houses to which could be applied the terms 'friendly', 'cosy' or 'welcoming', but the Horseshoe, on the corner of Thornton Road opposite the pond, came fairly close, thanks in large part to Vernon, the landlord. He was one of my patients, but out of necessity, not habit; Vernon, you see, was dying.

'Hello, Doctors,' he said with a grin that I swear was in danger of meeting on the far side of his head and thus splitting it into two perfect hemispheres; that his head was completely hairless only seemed to add to this illusion. I had noticed before that sometimes – only sometimes, mind – people who were dying were genuinely, deeply cheerful; it was something that, every time I met it, left me feeling inadequate, insignificant and totally worthless. 'What can I get you?'

He had retained at least some vestiges of normal publicanism, though, so he didn't offer to give us the pints on the house and pocketed my pound note, providing only a twopence coin in return. Dad tutted under his breath as we took our seats by the window. 'I remember when you could get change out of a crown when you bought two pints of bitter.'

'And go from here to Trafalgar Square on the trolley bus for sixpence?' I asked.

'Thruppence,' he corrected and, following a sip, asked of

the world in general and no one in particular, 'Why did they have to get rid of the thruppenny bit just because we went decimal?'

'Because three doesn't divide into ten with any elegance?' I suggested.

He snorted, then sighed. 'Ten's a rubbish number,' he declared, undermining with a single sentence of four words and six syllables some thousands of years of civilization.

'I've always thought it fairly reasonable.'

'It's only got two divisors,' he said incredulously, as if this were the arithmetic equivalent of halitosis.

'At least it's not prime.'

He brightened at that. 'Yes, you're right,' he agreed, then lapsed into reflection before admitting, 'As I said, the announcement didn't *quite* go as I'd expected.'

'No?' I'd already guessed as much.

He was frowning deeply, perhaps even wincing as he went on, 'Mike had only just got home – he works nights, you know – and perhaps he was still feeling tired.' He spoke as one trying to explain matters to himself, and not for the first time, either.

'He wasn't pleased?' I guessed.

'Um . . . no, he wasn't.' He considered. '"Not pleased".' A nod, then, 'I think that would be a fair way of describing his reaction. Yes, that about sums it up.'

As uneasy as I was at the prospect of having Ada as my mother-in-law, the last thing I wanted was to see Dad unhappy, and I felt for him; I said nothing, feeling it better to let him talk as and when he wanted to. It didn't take long. 'I must admit that we don't really know each other.'

'It was a shock, obviously,' I sympathized. 'I own to having been a tad surprised myself.'

'Yes . . .' His tone told me that there was something he had yet to tell me. I didn't remain in ignorance for long. 'And, of course, you'd known about Ada for a long time, even if you hadn't actually met . . .'

It took a moment for me to catch on and, when I did, I was stunned. 'Ada's son didn't know about you?'

'He knew about me, obviously,' he corrected. 'But he didn't appreciate, I think, the *nature* of the relationship.' He shook his head sorrowfully, took a sip of bitter, then explained, 'Ada didn't seem to think there'd be a problem and it's not been easy arranging to meet, what with his job and everything.'

This all sounded distinctly odd to me, but I didn't say as much. 'But there's a problem?'

'He doesn't like the idea. Said so in no uncertain terms. He even went so far as to call me a "toe-rag"'. I've never been called one of those before.'

'What's the problem? Does he think you're after his inheritance?'

'He wasn't particularly specific about his objections. He just said she was a stupid old woman; after that he became slightly incoherent . . . Ada assured me it was just because he was tired because he'd been working hard, but I wonder if he was also drunk. I'm told the pubs around Fleet Street have opening times to suit the journalists and printers.'

'He struck me as rather a testy individual when I met him.'

'He's not always like that.'

I frowned. 'How would you know?' I asked before I could stop myself; I think I might have struck a little close because he looked momentarily disconcerted.

'That's what Ada's told me, anyway,' he mumbled after thinking about it.

We had nearly finished our drinks and so I rose to fetch two more. When I sat back down, I asked, 'What are you going to do?'

'Ada said she'd work on him. She's certain that he'll come round.'

'And what about her grandchildren, David and Joanna?'

He pursed his lips. 'Difficult to say, really. Ada says that Joanna's been pretty subdued recently – probably puberty or something, I suppose. David's his usual self; he seemed to think his father's reaction was quite funny, actually.'

I could imagine that; David had struck me as someone who would think that tying a firework to a donkey would make great family entertainment. 'And Ada's daughter-in-law?'

He sighed. 'Well . . .' He looked uncomfortable. 'It may come as a surprise to you, but I don't think Ada and Tricia get on very well.'

I thought back to the parents' evening at the school but didn't say that Max and I had the impression that the relationship between Ada and her daughter-in-law had been akin to that of Stalin and Hitler around the time of the siege of Leningrad. 'It's a common problem,' I said in a voice that was as anodyne as I could make it.

He agreed glumly and then there was silence while he presumably rued his misfortune and I pondered what Dad was potentially getting into; the more I heard of the Clarke clan, the more they seemed to me to be a right load of herberts. Ada might have been a God-fearing Christian (and was there any other kind?), but her descendants and her daughter-in-law seemed to inhabit a very different world and I wasn't entirely convinced I could see Dad fitting into it; I was as sure as sugar I couldn't see myself feeling entirely at home on planet Clarke, and was desperately trying not to think of Christmases to come when we might all have to congregate around a roaring log fire and play Scrabble together.

Suddenly he seemed to brighten, drawing in a long breath through his nose, and doing it with so much force he actually seemed to disturb some of the taller foliage around him. 'Still, I'm sure Ada will sort it all out.'

I managed to place a smile on my face although, I confess, there wasn't one in my heart.

NINETEEN

'We have a visitor.'

In all the time I'd known Max, I'd never heard her speak like that; she hissed this at me, sibilance lurking just behind her teeth, where it held hands with anger. I had just come in, and was feeling the effects of the heat, a day's work and a couple of pints of bitter and, perhaps because of this, wasn't feeling totally up to pace. 'Do we?'

Looking back on it, this might not have stood up well amongst the great ripostes of history and, in retrospect, it was a fair way inferior to, 'You will, Oscar, you will' or 'My dear, I don't give a damn' (with, as is *de rigueur*, emphasis on the wrong word). Certainly, Max was unimpressed. 'Yes.'

'Who?'

'Your Sergeant Abelson.'

I was unaware that I had come into possession of a police person, so this came as something of a surprise. 'What does she want?' I enquired, making my way into the kitchen to pour a beer.

'She said it was to take a statement from you.'

I couldn't see why Max seemed to be so worked up about things; after all, Masson had said that I would have to give a formal statement regarding George Cotterill's death, yet Max's implication was that the comely Sergeant was here with an ulterior motive. 'Fair enough,' I said, in what I thought was a placatory tone; oddly, Max snorted, glared at me and then snarled, 'Well, I'm going for a bath,' as if this were the ulti-mate weapon to deploy.

In the sitting room, Sergeant Abelson was standing in the bay window, looking out at the comings and goings. 'Something to drink?' I asked her, realizing that Max had inexplicably failed in her duties as a hostess.

She turned and smiled. 'Some water would be nice.'

I fetched it for her, then we sat down and got to the busi-ness at hand. It only took fifteen minutes, at the end of which I asked, 'What are the results of the post-mortem?'

She nodded. 'It was his heart, as you suspected.'

It was quite nice to be proved right by an autopsy for once; it didn't always happen, which could sometimes be a blow to the professional ego. 'A natural death, then.'

'Whatever the cause, it doesn't look good when people die in custody. People tend to talk.'

I couldn't resist pointing out, 'And he wasn't even guilty, was he?'

It was quite interesting to see how she went into standard constabulary defensive mode. 'We have yet to determine that.'

I did a bit of gaping at this brazen bit of stonewalling, before asking, 'Do you know something I don't?' Looking back on it, this was a question that was not one of the most perceptive that has ever been asked; it was highly likely that she knew something about the case that was at that moment hidden from my not-quite-all-seeing gaze.

'Probably,' was her quite reasonable reply and which left me slightly bereft of where to go next.

I decided not to argue. 'Just who was Yvette Mangon?'

Without any hint of irony, she answered. 'She was a maths teacher at Bensham Manor.'

I must admit that I lapsed into a little bit more gaping. 'You are kidding, aren't you? First Marlene Jeffries, then Yvette Mangon? Two women who worked together, lived together and . . .'

She smiled despite herself. 'Played together?'

'You could put it like that.'

'And their deaths aren't connected?' My question had gone into a slightly higher register than normal.

For a moment, I think she was going to argue, but all she said was, 'Officially, George Cotterill is still a suspect in the murder of Marlene Jeffries.'

'Two murderers? Is that likely?'

'No,' she admitted. 'But then, statistically speaking, murder is a very unlikely occurrence, anyway.'

I knew enough statistical theory not to try arguing, even though it sounded slightly on the side of sophistry to me. 'Is that the theory that Masson's working on?'

Her smile said it all; her only vocal response wasn't one at all. 'I don't think Inspector Masson would appreciate me discussing the lines of enquiry concerning the murders. I just came here to take your statement regarding the death of George Cotterill.'

'Has she gone?' Max, no less frosty than before, came down from her bath, dressed only a towelling bath robe.

'She has.' I was laying the table for our supper, which was to be a cheese salad; I hoped this would not overtax my culinary abilities, but was prepared to be disappointed. She might have snorted, might not have done; it was difficult for me to tell. 'What's wrong?'

'Nothing.' She said this too quickly, too flatly.

'Yes, there is.'

'No, there isn't.'

I was about to repeat my insistence, but I had been in this situation before and decided to be discretionary rather than valorous. 'Do you want beetroot?' She made a face which I took as a negative. 'You're going to have to admit soon to my father that you don't like it. Judging from the amount he's been growing at the school, in his garden and on his allotment, I expect we'll soon be receiving at least ten a week to boil and pickle.'

Max thought that she was equal to this. 'We'll just throw them out when he's gone.'

Such naivety. I felt slightly sad for her. Shaking my head slowly I explained, 'He'll want to see what we've done with them. He'll be looking forward to tasting them. He'll keep on about them; the strain of lying will eventually prove too much and you'll find yourself crumbling.'

The implications made her pause, think, pause, then think again. Her expression told me that she had got the message. 'Oh . . .'

'Exactly,' I said grimly. At least I had transformed her mood from one of inexplicable irritability to one of entirely explicable gloom. I cast around for something to distract her and the only thing I could find was the news about the latest poor soul to find that living in Thornton Heath was not always good for the health. It worked, though, as was obvious from her widening eyes as my tale unfolded.

'A compass?'

I nodded. 'No pencil, though.'

The table laid, we were by now sitting down and eating, the jar of beetroot sitting between us untouched, an air of reproachful isolation seeping from it. I may have to say so myself but, all in all, it was a pretty decent salad, with or without roots of the beet variety. 'And she shared a house with the dead PE teacher?'

'She did.'

She snorted triumphantly, which is a pretty impressive feat, especially since she remained just as pretty whilst doing it. 'I *told* you.'

'Did you?' I own to a degree of nonplussedness at this assertion.

'Yes. At the open evening. I said that all PE teachers are lesbians.'

I found something in the lettuce that didn't taste entirely lettuce-like, in that it was soft and slimy and possibly slugoid. I tried my best not to show any emotion. 'Just because they shared a house doesn't mean they were . . . like that.'

She snorted again, this time giving it a veneer of incredulity; incredulity, I surmised, at my ingenuousness. She replied in a tone that one might use to a small boy who had just asked why girls didn't have willies. 'Oh, come on, Lance. With a dungeon where the front bedroom should be?' was her not unreasonable enquiry. 'And a nice cosy double bedroom at the back?'

She had a point, I conceded. 'So you think they were killed because of their proclivities?' I asked.

'Maybe.' She sounded as if she didn't think so.

'Have you got another theory?'

'They were both teachers.'

'And?'

'Marlene Jeffries, a PE teacher, was battered to death with some lifting weights, and Yvette Mangon, who taught maths, had a compass stuck in her eye. They've both been killed with things that they use in their jobs.'

Well, it was a theory, I had to admit. 'We don't know that Yvette Mangon was killed with the compass,' I pointed out, rather hoping that she hadn't been. 'In fact it's more likely that she was killed by the stab wounds.'

'It's symbolic, Lance,' she insisted.

'So who's the killer? Some deranged pupil? One who hated cross-country running and failed mathematics O-level?'

'Possibly,' she said, somewhat defensively.

It was my turn to snort, although I did it quietly and a long, long way under my breath. 'That would apply to ninety-seven per cent of people in the country.'

'It doesn't mean that it couldn't be true.'

'No,' I agreed, but only because I didn't want to upset her.

At that moment she did the female thing of completely contradicting herself; Dad once explained to me that it's evolved over the millennia to disorientate men and make them feel stupid and, my God, it works. 'Or, of course, it could be someone who doesn't like lesbians.'

'I've always known that maths teachers were weird, but not like that,' I said thoughtfully.

She agreed thoughtfully; the concept that Yvette Mangon might be archetypal of all maths teachers was mesmerizing. The idea that instead of going home of an evening with a worn leather briefcase to eat a tea of sardines on toast, then watch the nine o'clock news followed by the Open University, they routinely retired to an epicurean feast of swan stuffed with goose stuffed with duck, followed by a couple of hours with the anal beads and the stirrups filled my head to bursting. Indeed, I think it filled Max's. There was a look on her face that spoke of strange visions.

She suddenly stopped chewing, then made a face. 'Did you wash this lettuce?'

TWENTY

The journey from Thornton Heath to Tooting Graveney can be made only by bus, bicycle or car for the Underground does not extend to the London Borough of Croydon, in which Thornton Heath sits like a resplendent jewel in a particularly impressive and ornate crown. Because my trusty BMW was sick with a disease it was beyond my capabilities to cure (it had refused to start), I was forced to choose between two self-powered wheels and a London omnibus; neither prospect was entirely of the pleasing variety, but that of cycling in the afternoon heat was infinitely worse. The upside of all this was that I had a grand view of the verdant pleasure that is Mitcham Common as I sat atop the number sixty-four bus (although that adjective was at the present time perhaps not entirely appropriate in view of the drought, since it temporarily resembled more the Arizona dustbowl than a tropical oasis). It was still, though, a welcome break in what even I have to admit can be the slightly claustrophobic environs of South London, in that one can see for more than twenty yards in any direction; I am certain it was my imagination but I even felt the first vague stirrings of agoraphobia as I sat there, feeling slightly sick from the jerky swaying, the heat of the day and the fumes of the bus's throbbing diesel engine. This was not helped by the presence of large numbers of loud, excitable and rumbustious schoolchildren, just out of lessons, who accompanied me. Once past Mitcham Common, one comes through the delightfully but somewhat oddly named Amen Corner (I know of no strong ties between that area and evangelicalism), thence on to Tooting; all the while one is on this journey (perhaps 'pilgrimage'?), one is aware that one is heading for the central parts of London, and perhaps one is even afraid that one is nearing a heart of darkness.

In those days, Tooting was noticeably more cosmopolitan than Thornton Heath, although that may not be true in this age. It held an air of much greater mysticism, almost exoticism, and I always found myself excited by this. I knew that there were well-advanced plans for St George's Medical School – my alumnus – to relocate here from the somewhat more rarefied and refined landscape of Hyde Park Corner, and I looked forward to this with somewhat mixed feelings. The old St George's building, Lanesborough House, was a magnificent early eighteenth-century edifice, and I found student life in the centre of London to be an intoxicating experience (pun intended); from what I had seen of its replacement, it looked as though architects with all the soul of malfunctioning, right-angle-fixated automatons had been let loose. However, given the ethnic mix of Tooting, the medicine was likely to prove far more exciting (if not entirely baffling) to the medical students than it had been in Knightsbridge.

My goal that afternoon was not the Fountain Hospital, where construction work on the medical school was nearing completion, but a place I had always found rather pleasant, although my reason for going there was less so. I alighted from the bus, being jostled by huge numbers of shouting, cackling children, then turned to take my bearings. I was standing near the statue of Edward the Seventh, who was looking rather forlorn, covered as he was in verdigris and pigeon poo; it reminded me rather of the fate of Ozymandias, albeit with somewhat less dignity. A large flower stall was behind it, the blooms trying to suck whatever coolness they could out of the shade of the Tooting Broadway tube station canopy. People streamed in and out of this latter, looking severely hot and stressed, blending right in with the rest of us. Try as I might, I could not see much resemblance with the area's namesake in New York. I crossed the road when the green man said I could and began to make my way up the High Street towards Tooting Bec, which was (whisper it quietly lest ye be overheard) perhaps slightly posher.

It was not long before I turned up Selkirk Road on the left, then right into Fishponds Road. This is a long road and there is neither a fish or pond in sight. It also rises inexorably with a slight but, in that heat, killing gradient; by the time I reached its end to turn left again into Beechcroft Road, I was not so much exuding as pouring perspiration, and there was yet more ascent ahead of me, although the worst was now over. By the time I reached Glenburnie Road I was feeling none too good; at least, though, I was at journey's end.

Springfield Hospital was built in early Victorian times when they really knew how to build a loony bin, when no expense was spared to make sure that, just because you're one sandwich short of a picnic, it doesn't mean you shouldn't have a nice view. There were large immaculate grounds, an ornamental pond (perhaps *that* was where the fish were), some nicely tended formal gardens and, like poor relatives, quite a few barrack-like buildings It had everything a modern hospital needs and it exuded an air of calm tranquillity, which I am sure was wonderful for the more disturbed patients. What was perhaps slightly more troubling was that some of the outbuildings had obvious high-security measures such as chain-link fencing topped by barbed wire; I suspected that these were not there to keep people out . . . I knew also that there was somewhere in the main house (although I had never seen it) an operating theatre, a piece of information that made my flesh creep some-what. It was bad enough that I remember witnessing as a medical student the application of electroconvulsive therapy here, a sight once seen never to be forgotten. Thus does medical science make its slow, ponderous progress, leaving in its wake crushed innocents, unremarked and rewarded only by death, who have lain down their lives and well-being in a fashion just as valorous as those who die or are wounded on the battlefield; those given radium for tuberculosis, or arsenic for warts, those bled within a pint of their lives because of fever, or those with dog bites who were treated by the topical application of aqua fortis (guaranteed to make your eyes water a bit).

So all in all, Springfield Hospital presented me with a curious, perturbing amalgam of memories and association.

Not least because of one of its present patients.

The district health authority could have made a pretty penny had it been opened to the public, even without the added entertainment value of the patients. The scents of the flowers as I walked up to the main entrance were almost intoxicating, given the heat and my dehydrated exhaustion; I wondered how they managed to keep the gardens so neat, weed-free and, above all, moist. The fountain tinkled merrily, adding to the sense of oasis in this driest of summers; the black-faced rhomboid clock at the top of the building said that it was three thirty but had said so when I had been there as a student, so I guessed it had stopped. Inside the impressively tall light brown doors, the picture of opulence was tarnished slightly by the interior furnishing in the entrance hall. It was difficult to put my finger on precisely why – it could have been the chairs of moulded orange plastic that were arranged around the walls, or perhaps the scuffed black-and-white flooring that had, over the years, become seriously pock-marked, but I think it was mainly the magnificent marble fire surround that had been boarded up with plywood on which were pinned an assortment of health posters. Not that the rickety looking reception desk in the corner helped, covered as it was in light blue Formica and a bored-looking girl of twenty years and twenty stones. Elton John and Kiki Dee pretended to love each other for perhaps the thousandth time in my hearing and the receptionist looked as convinced as I did. She barely looked at me as I approached and only reacted when I said, 'My name's Dr Elliot.'

You see, in those days – the good old days as I call them now – although I knew that to Dad the 'good old days' had happened twenty-five years before then (and so on, ad infinitum) – people looked up to other people who called themselves 'Doctor'. There was none of this 'whatever' attitude, and a better world it was, too. Accordingly, she reacted. She jumped, straightened up what I had seriously thought might be a congenitally deformed posture, and said, 'Oh. I'm sorry.'

'I'm here to see a patient. Tristan Charlton.'

Without complaint, without question, without even appearing to think, she turned her back on me and went to a desk against the far wall, whence she picked up a clipboard; she didn't ask for identification and I didn't expect her to. She ran her finger down the clipboard, then flipped over a sheet of paper, repeating the process until she reached about three-quarters of the way down. 'Here he is,' she said. 'Jupiter Ward.'

'Where's that?'

She came back to the front desk and pulled out from underneath it a Xeroxed sheet that was a map of the hospital. She pointed at it with a stubby finger; her nail polish was bright red and badly chipped; the colour did not go well with her nicotine stains but I kept my mouth shut. Jupiter Ward was on the far side of the grounds, and they were extensive grounds; it would mean another long, hot trudge. When I murmured, 'Oh,' she grimaced, I think in sympathy, but didn't actually speak. I asked, 'Do you know if he's there at the moment?'

A shrug. 'I really couldn't say.'

I sighed and repeated my exclamation of woe. She was unmoved, apparently having run dry of the social lubricant that is sympathy. She enquired, 'Is there anything else?'

'No. No, thanks.'

I left her to the unlikely and revoltingly platitudinous love waffle of Elton and Kiki, and went back out into the weather.

Jupiter Ward was in a single-storey block at the south-west corner of the hospital grounds. There was a sense of that kind of annoying yin-yang thing in the way that it contrasted sharply with the main hospital block. It was probably about forty years old and was built of prefabricated sheets; there had clearly been a considerable shortfall in the maintenance budget at Springfield Hospital for several years, given the amount of entropy that seemed to hang about the place. I had uncomfortable flashbacks to my days of National Service for the barracks had looked just like this. During those twenty-two months it had never once ceased to rain and I seem to remember having to run seven miles a day through the north Devon countryside for no very good reason; and, impossibly, it seemed to be wetter and draughtier inside them than out.

A middle-aged man came out of the front entrance, the latter being plain double doors painted in shiny dark red that was peeling badly at the bottom. He looked at me and I looked at him. We were each caught in that age-old mutual dilemma that is the inevitable consequence of finding yourself in a loony bin; he was wondering if I were a patient, or visitor, a doctor or a nurse, and I was doing exactly the same. It would be so much easy if each category wore a different uniform, but I could see why they hadn't opted for that one. He dropped his gaze and hurried past, and neither of us will ever know the truth about each other.

I went in.

There was a small foyer in which were four more of the orange plastic chairs and, by the door, a rubber plant; when I brushed against it, I realized it was plastic, which seemed to say something significant about psychiatry. The carpet had once been blue but it was now merely looking sad and depressed; it was covered in many rather disgusting-looking stains. Three doors led off this room; above the left-hand one was the sign 'Jupiter Ward', above the right-hand one was the sign 'Ellis Ward'; above the one straight ahead was the sign 'Private'. The only other thing in the room was a small table on which was an opened book like a ledger, and a pencil on the end of a string. I looked at it curiously and discovered that it was a register in which the patients could sign in and out. I began to scan it for Tristan's name but the door to Jupiter Ward opened and a rather large Afro-Caribbean man came out. He stopped when he saw me. 'Can I help you?'

'Um . . .'

The assumption had to be that here was a member of the

psychiatric establishment (as opposed to a guest of it), but, as I have already said, you can never be sure; I'd heard a story when I was a medical student about a girl in the year above mine who had been taken advantage of by 'Professor Welsby', an elderly gentleman in pince-nez and bow-tie who, it transpired, had been a long-term patient with a fetish for courgettes. 'I'm here to visit Tristan Charlton.' I added then, just to establish my credentials (whatever his were), 'My name's Dr Elliot.'

He looked less than overly impressed. It was with a deep frown that he said suspiciously, 'Dr Martindale didn't say anyone was coming to see Tristan today. May I ask what it's in connection with?' From his reaction, I strongly suspected he wasn't a patient.

'It's a personal visit.'

His face lightened. 'Oh, I see.' He was clearly relieved that no professional toes were going to be trampled on. There was a clock on the wall to his right and this he glanced at. 'He's due for group psychotherapy at five, but you've got some time. He's towards the end on the left of the ward.'

With that he went out of the main front door and I went into Jupiter Ward.

It wasn't perfectly reminiscent of the barracks in which I had spent many 'character-building' months of my late adolescence, but it wasn't a bad attempt. It was a lot wider and taller, and the atmosphere was permeated not just by a mix of foot odour and sweat, but also by the scents of over-boiled cabbage and disinfectant; the finest parfumiers in the land could not have done a better job. Also, there was a lot more lying down than I recall, much of it being done whilst pyjama'd. It was quiet, too, save for the sound of gentle snoring, which was sort of disappointing; no screeching, no maniacal laughing and no sobbing. There were doubtless numerous insects about the place, but not a one was being consumed by any of the patients. All in all, it was a peaceful scene and I heard my footsteps on the linoleum as I made my slow way down the centre of the aisle. About half of the patients, I estimate, were present. Most of these were just lying on their beds, either asleep, or staring at the ceiling. Some were sitting on the side of the bed or up against the pillows, of which five were reading – either magazines or books – and one was talking to himself, an archetype of concentration as he discoursed in a mumble that I could barely hear and certainly not interpret; I am afraid to admit that he rocked slightly. Each of them – they were all men, of course – had just a bed, a cheaply made combined wooden cupboard and drawer unit, and another of those ubiquitous orange plastic chairs; the beds, though, were not crowded together, giving at least a nod towards privacy.

Tristan was where I had been told I would find him, towards the end of the ward. Just beyond his bed were open double doors that I could see opened on to a day room. I could hear a television and peeked around the door jamb to discover that it was like every other NHS hospital day room, in that it was depressing and soulless; as was the rule, the furniture was upholstered in brightly coloured artificial leather and specifically designed to be totally uncomfortable. There were five people in there, and presumably at least one (and possibly every one) was a nurse.

Tristan was lying on his back on his bed, dressed in day clothes, but asleep. I didn't know whether to wake him or wait. In truth, now that I had arrived, I was unsure of why I had come at all. Perhaps somewhere inside me there had been the idea that I would march in here and let him have a piece of my mind, that he might be able to fool the psychiatrists, but he hadn't taken me in; I think, too, I was going to assure him that he might have beaten me to a pulp on a previous occasion, but that was then and this is now . . . et cetera, et cetera; and I would say all this in a calm but commanding tone. Now I was there, though, it didn't seem quite so simple. I wouldn't go so far as to say that I was timorous or anything but, for the first time, I came to appreciate that I had a position in society to consider, that it wouldn't look seemly to brawl in public, especially not with a patient of the NHS.

He suddenly opened his eyes but he was not immediately aware of me, I think. He just stared up the ceiling, not blinking; it was as though the on-switch had been thrown but the current had yet to increase to a level at which any other muscular movement was possible. In accord with this hypothesis, after a few seconds he turned his head so that he was looking at me; it was a smooth action but accompanied by no other, not even a change in his blank expression. I was still standing by the side of the bed but, feeling slightly oppressed by this passive scrutiny, I sat down on his chair.

Nothing more happened. We regarded each other, but he did not appear to recognize me. He had aged, I decided, but then so had I; I had aged considerably following his determined assault on my person. He was tall – a few inches over six feet – with ginger hair that was long and untidy, and mild blue eyes that belied his facility with violence. His hair was shoulder length – longer than I remember it, but not unusually so for that time – and he was unshaven. He wore jeans and a T-shirt with Pink Floyd's prism and refracted light on it.

Had I not spoken we might still be there to this day for all I know, because he seemed disinclined to do anything more than peruse me without obvious emotion. 'Tristan?' I essayed, and I heard my voice to be slightly husky and, a surprise to me, edged with a tremor.

He frowned. It was a reaction, although not a particularly animated one, in both senses of that word. I repeated my salutation. Still nothing, so I felt it incumbent upon me to go a bit further. 'It's Lance. Lance Elliot. Do you remember me?'

It took a couple of seconds, but this did eventually induce him to lift his head and frown; not brilliant, I'll grant, but I was desperate by then for anything. A slow, lazy grin spread over his face, enticing his lips to part slightly so that I could see a sliver of teeth; he hadn't been keeping up on his dental cleanliness and these nameless, dateless dental dead appeared somewhat squalid. 'Lancey. You came to visit.'

He had always called me that because, despite my best efforts, I had been unable to portray my disgust at the nick-name. He wasn't too good though, that was clear. He struggled to raise himself on his elbows but seemed uncoordinated; it took quite a while and was accompanied by small, delicate grunts. I waited, my thoughts of a manly confrontation evaporating in the presence of this performance. At last he raised his shoulders, whereupon he yawned mightily. 'What time is it?' he enquired through this.

'Just after four thirty.'

'It's fucking hot.'

'Rather.'

He nodded groggily. 'It's good of you to come.'

'Well . . .' I began, not sure where I was going to end, but it didn't matter because he interrupted me.

'Fucking load of loonies in here.' He began to laugh softly, looking around at those around us. Suddenly he pointed at the man sitting on the side of his bed quietly jabbering to himself. 'Look at that old cock! Talk about bonkers!' I was programmed not to take the Mickey out of patients and had to fight hard not to tell him off. He continued, 'He spends his time reciting the seventeen times table; every time he gets it wrong, he swears enough to make the paint peel, then he just goes back to the beginning. Not sure what his record his, but I bet it's pretty impressive.' A soft laugh, one that might have been a cover for tears held back, then, 'I've seen some scenes over the past few weeks, Lancey. Some unbelievable sights.' He laughed again, but this time it was as if to himself, as if to a private, unheard joke.

I couldn't see the funny side myself, but Tristan could; after a while he could hardly control his merriment, in fact, so that he collapsed back on the bed, continuing to chortle, more of his rather unpleasant teeth making an unwelcome appearance in my ken. What could I say? I actually began to feel sorry for this man who had terrified me and broken up an important relationship in my life. He was clearly addled by an example of the latest addition to the psychiatrists' arsenal against severe psychiatric problems – 'the liquid cosh' or, as it was known in the trade, a 'major tranquillizer'. These were extremely effective in suppressing the symptoms and signs associated with psychotic depression and schizophrenia but, perhaps inevitably, they were also extremely effective at suppressing any signs of sentient life.

But then suddenly he stopped and, as if taken over by something, got back up on his elbows without apparent effort and turned once again to look directly at me. 'We've got unfinished business, Lancey-boy.' There was no amusement in his voice now. It was all rather spooky, horribly reminiscent of *The*

Exorcist, which Max and I had been to see a few months before and was still prone to pop up in my dreams now and again. 'I might have consented to come in here, but that doesn't mean that I've forgotten what you did.'

I hadn't done anything, but we had agreed to differ on that point a long time ago, although it had never been an easy accord, especially for me. I took a deep breath, relying on the fact that although I couldn't actually see any nursing staff, they couldn't be too far away. 'What you did to the rabbit is unforgivable.'

He stared at me, his expression unreadable, for just a second, then he neatly flopped back down, eyes on the ceiling once again. He said contentedly, 'The rabbit sure won't forgive me.'

And that was all he said, whilst I discovered that insouciance was the perfect defence against anger and thus was I rendered without appropriate words. I heard the evocative tones of 'Barnacle Bill' coming from the day room and I subconsciously lamented the loss of Christopher Trace from the lives of the nation's children. Without taking his eyes from the ceiling (which, as far as I could discern, was just a normal ceiling covered in painted polystyrene tiles), he asked, 'Was she upset?'

'Of course she bloody was!' I had tried not to lose my temper, honest.

He considered. 'But she's still alive, isn't she?' he asked slyly.

He was referring obliquely to his sister, of course, and I was thinking that I had to remain calm, and only by doing that could I remain in command of the situation. 'It was unnecessarily cruel, Tristan.'

He made play of considering this, tilting his head, distorting his lips, frowning in what was supposed to convey considered contemplation, every inch of him portraying a man who was intellectual and refined and, above all, sane. His answer, though, gave the lie to that. 'I have yet to be convinced by anything that has happened to me, or anything anyone has said to me, that there is any such thing as *unnecessary* cruelty.'

'For God's sake, Tristan.'

'In fact, I would tend to adopt the opposing rhetorical position; I think that, given the indifferent, Godless universe in which we have crawled from the primordial ooze, given the

fact that there are no moral absolutes other than the compulsion to survive – a compulsion that is mine yet for which I
cannot be made responsible (and therefore, by the simplest of
logical deductions, I cannot be made responsible for its consequences) – I would say that cruelty is a necessity. I must
survive and therefore must adopt whichever strategies are most
likely to achieve that end.'

His voice was thoughtful, as if he were reading from his
doctoral thesis – 'An Explanation of Sociopathy' – and he
didn't once look directly at me, although it was clear that every
word was aimed at me, and my loved ones, and the wrongs he
imagined had been perpetrated by me. The gentleman of
the mathematical bent suddenly uttered a word of eye-
watering profanity; it was beyond the abilities of my imagination
to conjure up the images of group-therapy sessions in which he
and Tristan participated.

Suddenly, Tristan yawned; it was an impressive thing, something so deep and so long, that paused at its peak for so long,
that I wondered if he was suddenly going to plunge into uncon-
sciousness at the end of it, but he didn't. In a quiet voice he
said, 'Fucking pills. Screw your head right up, you know, Lancey.'

What was I supposed to say that? I didn't have to fret too
long, though, for he went on, 'Anyway, I bet she didn't cry too
long. Bet you went right out and brought her another bunny,
and she dried her eyes and was a happy little girly again.'

I had thought about doing just that, but hadn't got around
to it; it was characteristic of Tristan that he should be so
unerring in his assessments. 'Max is a vet, Tristan,' I admon-
ished him. 'She's not like that.'

No reaction. From his position on the bed, his eyes looking
straight up, his sole response was to say, 'If you say so.'

There was some commotion from the day room; someone
began screaming and this brought with it sounds of someone
– actually two people, I think – trying to comfort whoever it
was. Tristan didn't react other than to comment, 'Happens all
the time with that one. He thinks General Zod is after him for
medical experiments. Fuck knows why he thinks that; probably
quite fancies the idea of a good anal probing.'

The noise eventually abated but only temporarily for then

a bell rang, which started the kerfuffle anew. Still Tristan didn't react, other than in speech. 'Time for you to go, Lancey, That's the end of visiting and I have an appointment.'

It was five but it appeared I was the only visitor. I thought about exercising my prerogative as a doctor and staying for a while longer – it didn't look as if anyone cared anyway – but couldn't see the point. I had never been sure what I had been expecting to achieve in coming and certainly hadn't thought to convince Tristan to leave me and my loved ones alone. I supposed it had been just to reassure myself that he really was seeking help and, perhaps also, to see my bogey man again, to fix him once more in my mind.

I got up, not bidding him any sort of farewell, although he did call after me languidly, 'Ta ta, Lancey. Thanks for coming.'

The journey home was no less hot and uncomfortable than its predecessor. In fact, it was considerably more unpleasant because, just as the bus sailed past Mitcham Common Golf Club, I realized what I had potentially done. Perhaps I had been wrong in assuming that Tristan had nailed Twinkle in mock crucifixion to Max's front door; in which case I had told him her first name and her profession. Not much for sure but, in Tristan's hands, quite probably enough.

TWENTY-ONE

Pathologists and general practitioners don't get to meet very much, except if they're married to one another, and not many are. Actually, pathologists and any normal kinds of doctors don't get to meet much either, which partly explains why most doctors think pathologists are odd; the other reason why your average doctor thinks they're odd is because they're pathologists, and they do what they do, which is exactly what any normal person would not want to do. Simple, really.

Mark had been one of my closest friends at medical school and had originally shown no signs that he was anything other than a normal medical student; he worked extremely hard (albeit for three weeks every year just before the exams), drank extremely hard and didn't give a proverbial. (I know that this is a stereotypical image of medical students, but it's stereotypical for a very good reason.) We were wild but, I hope, good-hearted and harmless. We feared no one, except possibly dental students (the dental students scared us, because they did what medical students do, only did it with even more depravity), and we felt good about ourselves because we were learning how to treat diseases and save lives, and all that sort of tommyrot which these days is widespread.

Anyway at the time, as far as the rest of us knew, Mark was going to turn into a proper doctor; instead he became the curious hybrid that is the pathologist – interacting not with patients but with body fluids or corpses, in fact usually so disordered of personality that they do not want to meet living patients. They spend their lives sequestered in laboratories, seeing the grist of the medical mill only when it is too late to be of immediate practical benefit to anyone.

I apologize. I rant. It comes of a bad experience as a fourth-year medical student when the professor of histopathology made me slice a fixed brain as if I was preparing cuts of steak, and then humiliated me in front of my peers because it looked, as he so cruelly said, as if it had been done by 'a luetic gorilla with the shaking palsy'.

Mark had, however, seemed to remain a surprisingly decent chap, although the only contact I had had with him was at the medical school reunions where he had behaved perfectly normally; certainly he had drunk prodigiously so, to all intents and purposes, he had appeared not at all brain-damaged. Until I had met him over the rather badly used body of Marlene Jeffries, I had assumed that he was still in Sheffield, investigating cases in which death was due to poisoned Bakewell tart or suffocation by Eccles cake. I was delighted that he was now in my vicinity, even more pleased when I bumped into him again in the car park of Mayday Hospital, which is the local Croydon infirmary, and not nearly as bad as people insisted. I had just been paying a courtesy call on Sylvie, one of my oldest patients, who was unfortunately celebrating her one hundred and second birthday (statistically, she had just reached the age at which she was more likely to wake up dead than alive) in the hospital because she had overdone the Tio Pepe and fallen over, thereby breaking her humerus).

'Hello, Lance,' he called across to me.

He was a tall man, surprisingly self-confident for a pathologist, with pale eyes and ash-blond hair. We approached each other just as a number 109 bus rumbled past on its way to Croydon, each of us pleased. He said, 'Sorry we haven't had a chance to catch up, Lance,' he said as we vigorously shook hands. 'A murder scene isn't exactly the ideal place for back-slapping reunions.'

'How are you?' I asked.

'Well, thank you. And you?'

I assured him I was. 'Is this where you're based now? I thought you were in Yorkshire.'

He winked, then rubbed the first two fingers and thumb of his right hand together. 'More spondulicks in the metropolis, Lance. A *lot* of coroner's work.' Which summed up pathologists as far as I was concerned; not interested in anything except corpses and cash. He continued, 'But I'm not based *here.*'

Now, I have a lot of time for Mark, but that last comment rather wounded me. He made it dismissively, and did so whilst looking back at the fine part-Victorian, part-ramshackle conglomeration that was Croydon's finest (albeit only) acute hospital. Before I could defend the reputation of this wonderful, not to say unique, sanatorium, he added, 'I have NHS sessions at King's.'

'Nice,' I remarked.

'The folk of South Yorkshire are fine people, but you can only take so much coal-miner's lung.' He spoke in a jovial manner.

'So what do people die of around here?'

He grinned. 'Murder, apparently.'

Once again, I felt the reputation of my homeland had been impugned. 'It's not always like that.'

'No? Inspector Masson told me that this place was some sort of murder magnet, and you were the centre of it. He was of the opinion that people coming into contact with you were more likely to die than to get better.'

I suspected that this was technically slander, but made a rapid once-and-for-all decision not to pursue Masson through every court in the land about it. Changing the subject I enquired, 'I do hope Yvette Mangon was dead when the drawing compass went in her eye.'

A normal human being would have winced at this, but Mark did autopsies for a living. 'I think so. She had seventy-seven incisions, all told, and some of them were very deep. The photographs showed a huge amount of blood at the scene – as you'll be aware – and several of the neck wounds severed major blood vessels.'

There was a certain degree of cheeriness about his demeanour that mere words cannot render. The more blood the better seemed to be the Bentham family motto. 'Yes, I remember,' I said weakly.

'Quite frenzied,' he said with relish.

'Quite.'

'I think I'm going to enjoy working around here.'

It did appear at that moment that a man whose spiritual home was an abattoir might well see Thornton Heath as a desirable place to pursue his career choice. We parted, he presumably to his blood-spattered dungeon, me to my brightly lit, clean surgery and I own to being in a thoughtful mood as I did so. That the two murders were linked seemed impossible to deny, the nature of that connection was obscure to me, hidden as it was amidst a bewildering number of possibilities. Was this the work of someone who hated teachers, as the facts that Marlene Jeffries had been killed with the tools of her profession and Yvette Mangon had been stabbed in the eye with a compass suggested? Was it perhaps connected with that most peculiar of front bedrooms? Perhaps it was someone who, like Max, was convinced that all female PE teachers were (how can I put this tactfully?) of a different persuasion, and didn't like it?

There were deep, muddy, but fatally swirling waters here.

TWENTY-TWO

I was not looking forward to that night because I was on call. Merging practices had meant that the on-call rota was now considerably better, in that I was only on call once in every seven days; it was therefore also, of course, now considerably worse when it did come round, because that one night in a week was one hell of a humdinger. Not only did we not get to sleep, we barely got to sit down; these days, after a night's on-call we had to take a day off, whereas before we would have made do with a half-day. There was, of course, variety. We got to see all ages, all sexes, all predicaments, all moods and all reactions. We saw the trivial and the serious, we saw the extreme and the exasperating, the hilarious and the appalling; unfortunately, by the time it got to four in the morning with barely time for a fluid break (either in or out), I didn't care. By that time, I could have been called to the scene of a bug-eyed, two-headed, slime monster from Venus giving birth and I wouldn't have been capable of reacting in any way other than as I had been taught by experience and learning to do; this was fine, as long as my subconscious was fully functioning but, as every pilot knows, once the autopilot goes tits up, you very quickly find yourself in unpleasantly odiferous waters without a means of propulsion.

On that night it went pretty much as expected – the highlight being the drunken man with a ferret bite and a tear in his trousers – until I was called to attend to Albert Stewart, a forty-two-year-old man who had collapsed. I thought nothing of it – was incapable by then of thinking anything of anything, as it was three in the morning – and duly attended the drab upper-floor maisonette not far from the junction of Keston Road with Thornton Road. It was starting to drizzle but, despite the heat, it was still so hot that this gift of moisture was almost a joke, as if it were merely the gods applying a bit more sweat to my brow. I was shown in by the woman who lived on the ground floor and who, it transpired, was the landlady. She was a short woman, broad about the beam and, it must be said, slightly shabby; I tried to make allowances, given the hour and given the fact that I probably looked as if my suit was a charity shop reject, but I think there was little excuse for the smell of urine that seemed to envelope her. I say 'envelope her', but what I mean was the stench hit me with eye-watering intensity as soon as she opened the door. Her quilted pink dressing gown of the finest pseudo-silk had seen better days, largely in the way that a corpse has.

'I'm looking for Mr Stewart,' I said. 'I'm the on-call doctor.'

She bore a look of wide-eyed excitement. 'He's upstairs. I found him.' She spoke triumphantly, as if she had won a treasure hunt. 'I heard a crash and I went out to see what was going on, and I called up the stairs but he didn't answer . . .'

Like Rolf Harris, she appeared to have mastered the art of breathing in and out and vocalizing all at the same time; certainly I didn't notice any pauses in her monologue. We were standing in a small hallway, off which two doors led; the one through which she had come showed a living room that was crowded and untidy, the wallpaper sporting a garish orange pattern that fought ferociously with the deep red of the carpet; only the eye of the beholder was the loser. She continued, 'So I fetched me key . . . I wouldn't normally go in, of course . . . I mean, I may be the landlady and he may be only a tenant, but he's entitled to some privacy . . . anyway, I went up and found him on the floor . . . he was twitching . . .' At last she paused but, before I could speak, she carried on in a stage whisper, 'I think he *wet* hisself . . .'

The irony of this remark did not strike her, although I had to try mightily not to point it out to her. Indicating the other door, I asked, 'Is he upstairs?'

'Oh, yes,' she said and delved deeply in her pocket for the key. Whilst she did so, she said over her shoulder in a wounded tone, 'He was very rude, you know. He told me to go away, only he didn't use those words, if you know what I mean . . .'

'Does he know you've called me?'

'No.'

Which meant that he might well tell me to take a walk, in

which case, I would have to wish him 'sayonara' and be about
my overly fatigued business. Oh well . . .

I began to trudge wearily up the stairway that the opened
door had revealed, but was a bit disconcerted to discover I
was still not alone. I paused and turned, smiled and suggested
firmly, but I hope not impolitely, that she should stay downstairs. Her look of disgruntlement might have been hard to
take had I not been so tired and had the thought of fresh air
not been so enticing, but she complied. At the top of the stairs
was another door, upon which I knocked.

'What is it?'

'It's the doctor, Mr Stewart.' Saying the name out loud made
me realize that it was familiar, although I could not place it.

'Go away.'

'Your landlady called me, Mr Stewart. She's worried about
you.'

'Sod off.'

'She said you collapsed. Perhaps I should check you over.'

There was a pause, then the door was suddenly wrenched
open, something that made me jump so that I almost took a
tumble backwards down the stairs. The man in front was
dishevelled, clearly very distressed, angry and probably drunk;
I finally recognized the name as that of the man who had so
recently been in my surgery. He had his mouth open, presumably to exhort me once more to depart the scene in rich and
ringing Anglo-Saxon, but on seeing me, he paused. A look
came over his face, one of recognition true, but one in which
there was something more; it was something I couldn't place.
'Oh, it's you.'

'May I come in?' I asked, eager to do my Hippocratic duty.

A pause, then he stood aside, but said nothing.

It was tidy. That was the first and overwhelming impression.
It was basic, much of it looked second-hand, and some of it
looked broken, but there was a dignity about that room. This
was a man who had little but, most importantly, amongst it
was order. A bed, a small bedside table, two chairs and a
bookcase; I could see a bedroom through a doorway, a kitchen
in another; the carpet was thin and focally worn, but clean.
The only thing in that room that wasn't neat was the bed; he

went and sat on the edge of it, gesturing that I should sit in one of the chairs. 'I told you. I'm epileptic. I had a fit. Nothing serious.'

Saying that having an epileptic fit wasn't serious was a bit like saying that it was only an amputation. I said, 'Maybe not this time . . .'

He considered this. 'I did a couple of stints in Ulster.'

That was all he said, but it was all he had to say, especially using the tone that he did. To him, an epileptic fit was nothing and I was a naive fool if I thought otherwise. I looked around for something to say, found nothing. Then my eye caught the empty dog's bed in the corner. 'Are you going to get another dog?'

He stared at me with an intensity that was quite striking, if not frightening. Slowly and in a voice that was calm, and yet all the more chilling for that, he replied, 'I haven't decided yet.'

'It was probably the stress of his death that precipitated the fit,' I suggested.

'I expect.'

There was then a silence between us. It wasn't a comfortable silence and inevitably one of us felt compelled to say something; just for once, this time it wasn't me. He suddenly said, 'I've done some terrible things in my life, Doctor.'

It was a long way into a day that was rapidly becoming everlasting, at least in my mind, and the last thing I wanted was an in-depth therapy session with a man who had clearly seen and done things that would probably give me sweat-drenched nightmares for a year; a man, moreover, who was undoubtedly trained in various ingenious methods of separating people from their lives, and who had a physique that was ten times better than anything *I'd* ever seen in a mirror. However, he was also a man who was clearly in some sort of torment and, for better or worse, I had once made the colossal, stupid mistake of applying to medical school.

'You were a soldier, Mr Stewart; it goes with the job. We – the rest of us – expect you to do it, because if you didn't, there wouldn't be anyone else to.'

I know he heard because he replied, but there was no change

in his lost, distracted expression, no flicker of the eyes away from the grimy carpet. 'I know that. It doesn't make it any easier for me, though.'

I suddenly discovered that my counselling skills were a tad limited; all I could find to say was, 'No, I don't suppose it does.'

He suddenly breathed out as if he had been holding it in for hours in some sort of personal dare; I thought for a second that he had relaxed, and that I was a natural counsellor all along, but his next words disabused me. 'So that's my tough shit, then.'

'There are types of therapy you could try . . .'

His face told me what he thought of that, but just to make sure I got the message, he said, 'I don't think so.'

Somewhat awkwardly, I countered with, 'Yes, well, if you haven't seen a neurologist recently, it might be an idea to get checked up. Have you ever tried Tegretol?'

'It gave me the shits.'

'Ah, well, it can do that. But there are new things coming along all the time . . .'

'No, thanks.'

It was a polite refusal but a most definite one. 'Fair enough. Has the Mogadon helped you sleep?'

'No.'

'Oh . . . OK . . . Perhaps we could try something else?'

Until then he had been hunched, head down, but now he suddenly jerked his head up to stare at me, and his whole body became tense. 'Perhaps there are some things that drugs can't fix.'

I found myself nodding enthusiastically purely out of instinctual self-defence. 'Absolutely.'

It was obvious that I wasn't going to do any more good here and I had a man in Fairlands Avenue with breathing difficulties to see. I stood up. 'I'll be on my way, then.'

His head was back down and his posture was once again one of despair. He was mourning. Perhaps it was for his dog, perhaps it was for a life lost but still too-well remembered. He did not respond. I made my way to the door. On the bookcase to the left was a single black-and-white photograph of a group of schoolchildren, perhaps in their mid-teens. It was some sort of end-of-term class photo; they were all dressed, more or less smartly, in white shirts or blouses, dark skirts or trousers and striped ties. They were standing outside what was clearly the main building of Bensham Manor School. I wondered what connection it had with this strange, sad, angry man, but didn't dare ask.

TWENTY-THREE

And so, dear reader, to bed. I am unaware to this day of the exact time, but would suppose it to be around eight forty-five or so in the morning. My last patient had spent most of the night being sick; it was associated with central abdominal pain that had moved to the right lower quadrant, and she had been febrile with a coated tongue. Thus it was that I confidently diagnosed acute appendicitis and had waited with her – she was only twenty and had newly moved into the area, knowing no one – until the ambulance had arrived. During that time we had chatted and she had told me that her mother had just been diagnosed with pre-senile dementia and she had moved to be close to her. She had struck me as a nice girl, and I treasure meeting nice people because there are so few about.

It was the kind of sleep that only the truly, wretchedly, incontestably exhausted can ever know; it doesn't so much knit the ravelled sleeve of care as darn it badly, so that you awake not refreshed, just ordinarily tired. Only problem was that halfway through – so that the darning this time was even more than usually threadbare and not destined to last long – a knocking came upon the front door. 'Knocking' is a euphemism; it would be described more accurately as 'thumping', or perhaps 'battering'; maybe even 'hammering'. More door abuse was committed before I made my bleary, semi-comatose way out of my bed, into the bathroom (by mistake), down the stairs and thence to my poor front door. This I opened.

My gaze fell upon a man who was the epitome of disgruntlement. Such was my state that I failed immediately to recognize him, an omission that this man – six feet or so in height, broad across the shoulders, getting broad about the beam – seemed to take amiss. I say 'seemed' because at that moment, the whole of reality 'seemed', if you get what I mean.

'I think we should talk,' was his opening sally in lieu of the usual niceties.

'Do you?'

Now, you read those two words and maybe you will appreciate that I was extremely dozy, but they could be conceivably be misinterpreted; should you be so inclined, you might think that the tone was facetious, perhaps even in gladiatorial. Whatever *you* think, my visitor certainly formed his own opinion, and did so quickly. He grabbed the lapels of my light cotton dressing gown and brought us face to face; his breath smelled of beer but God only knows what mine smelt of. 'You what?'

It took a couple of seconds for my lenses to contract to the right spherical diameter but, when they did, cogs meshed, synapses were triggered, bio-electric relays did their things . . .

Mr Michael Clarke occupied approximately eighty per cent of my visual field. To judge by the amount of perspiration he was excreting, he was hot, but then the morning was already warm. 'Don't be funny,' he advised.

'Mr Clarke,' I said. For want of anything else to add and, given that I was somewhat befuddled, I continued, 'Come in.'

And in he came.

To cut a long story off at the knees, he had a problem with the forthcoming matrimonials 'twixt my pater and his mater. This he made clear immediately, having pushed past me and sort of planted himself in my kitchen. 'What the bloody hell is going on?' he enquired; he had a richly South London twang.

Given that he had barged into my house and was acting in an unmistakeably hostile manner, I thought this a bit rich, but forbore to point this out and thus had to extemporize. 'Well . . .'

Not brilliant, I admit, but I felt somewhat inhibited, what

with being in my jim-jams and all. I was spared yet more embarrassment by his desire to do the talking. 'Your father's well out of order.'

I've been of the opinion that Dad was well out of order for a long time, but the men in white coats had yet to cotton on. The clouds of ambiguation were clearing, though, which was perhaps good for my well being, since I was getting the impression he was short on patience. I ventured, 'Mr Clarke . . .' dimly aware that I was in danger of becoming rather repetitive.

He brought his finger into action, using it with vigour to underline his points. 'One, my mother is not available.' He poked me hard about halfway between the sternal notch and the xiphisternum. 'Two, even if she was, I wouldn't want her having anything to do with some chancer like your father.' Another poke. 'Three, I'm holding you personally responsible for this situation.' I tried again; if there's one thing that being a doctor teaches you, it's patience, although his choice of designation for my father was distinctly trying. In addition, you must bear in mind that I was tired and, in my opinion, Mr Clarke was a bit of a wanker (although I didn't use that phraseology out loud). Therefore, instead of being anodyne, I reacted and did so loudly. 'What situation?' I was rewarded with a frown and a pause in the ranting, so I did what Wellington would have done and pressed home this small advantage. 'In the first place, I am not responsible for my father and what he does. In the second, even if I were, I would applaud what he's doing. In the third, you should be delighted to have him as a stepfather.'

I was quite pleased with this riposte, right up until the moment he produced a blow to my epigastrium followed by a well-aimed upper cut to my jaw, and I discovered that the art of debate (at least in South London) had died with the ancient Greeks.

What's supposed to happen is that darkness gradually gives way to blurred light, shapes and colours emerge from blackness, while sounds come to you from a long way off, approaching slowly, and becoming less reverberant, more meaningful. Ideally, the shape of a face should fill your vision, a loved one talking in concerned tones as consciousness returns and you slowly recall what has happened to you.

That's what is supposed to happen. What actually happened was I came to all alone, starring up at a cobweb in the corner of the ceiling; the only other entity in the vicinity was the spider – one of those incredibly long-legged ones that must have trouble when the soles of its feet get itchy – in the midst of the aforementioned web. My jaw hurt but then so did my whole head, and my stomach wasn't going to be easily outdone in the pain stakes, either. I rolled over and got slowly and agonizingly to my hands and knees. I felt sick, but I feared that if I did start vomiting it would hurt big time; luckily a few deep breaths seemed to help. After five minutes I was able to get to one of the kitchen chairs and sat on it heavily. The ring of the doorbell was not well timed. Was it Michael Clarke back for a bit more sparring? I was in two minds whether to answer it but decided it was unlikely to be my nemesis again and made my giddy way up the hall. It was my father.

'You all right?' he asked, his face assuming a frown.

I considered giving him a brief résumé of my recent past, decided that there was no point. 'Just tired.'

He grunted and there was a moment where I sort of stood aside and he sort of came in without being overtly asked, which is the way that close friends and relatives do things. 'Been on call?' he asked as we arrived in the kitchen.

'Yep.'

'Shall I make the tea?'

'Yes, please,' I sighed, sitting down heavily at the table. There was no point in saying anything more.

As he stirred the pot, he said conversationally, 'I think things are going to be all right with Michael.'

'Do you?'

'Ada and he have had a heart-to-heart. She tells me there isn't a problem. It was all just a bit of a shock for him. Give him a couple of days, she says.'

I nodded understandingly. 'The news must have been like a blow in the midriff.'

He was putting my mug down in front of me as I said this; it had a picture of Einstein on it. 'What?' he asked, and I couldn't really blame him. Thankfully, he didn't want an answer; I had long ago noticed that my father often asked me questions without wanting a reply. We sat at the table for a few silent moments of familial companionship, after which he suddenly ventured, 'I never had a problem with relativity.'

'No?'

He shook his head gravely. 'It was quantum mechanics that gave me trouble.'

'Really?'

He had both hands around his mug, which bore a line print of Newton. 'There's logic about relativity, so you can accept the consequences, no matter how odd. You can see that, can't you?'

'If you say so.'

'There's no logic about quantum mechanics, though. It's just odd.'

'Like life, then.'

He brightened, as if I had said something witty. 'Yes!' he exclaimed. 'I suppose it is.' Then, his face suddenly perplexed, 'Is your jaw all right?'

I don't know what it looked like, but it felt huge and it throbbed. 'I've got toothache.'

'Oh.'

More silence. I wanted to ask him why he was there – because there was obviously another reason for his visit, although its nature was as yet unknown to me – but I knew that I couldn't, that if I did, all the uncertainties would collapse around us (an ironically quantum mechanical situation). We both imbibed more tea; Dad always made a good mug of tea. Eventually he took in a lot of air and said, 'I know you think I'm a stupid old fool.'

'No, I don't . . .'

'Yes, you do, and yes, I am.'

'No . . .'

'Lance, please. I am not completely demented. Not yet, anyway.'

I smiled, although I was suddenly, unaccountably sad. 'I know that, Dad.'

He nodded seriously. Opened his mouth, was about to speak, didn't, breathed in, breathed out, shut his mouth, then drank the last of his tea. Only at this point did he speak. 'They're not the most attractive family, are they?' I had a thousand things to say and could say none of them for a moment. He laughed but it was a melancholic thing, one that might come from someone who has just seen the back half of a maggot poking out of the apple he has just bitten into. 'I've been trying to tell myself that I'm being judgemental, but it's tough. It's odd, because they all seem completely different from Ada.'

Being a family doctor means having to react instinctively and caringly whatever you are shown or whatever is said to you, no matter who is in front of you; you must never leave a pause, never allow the patient to begin to feel embarrassed and, above all, never suggest to them that you have opinions about what they say or what they show you. Being a professional means presenting yourself as a perfect replica of a human being, one who appears caring and knowing everything, yet at the same time one completely without emotion. You can get a long way as a doctor if you perfect that art.

I like to think I'm pretty good at my job.

I knew at once what he was talking about, and knew at once what to say.

'Dad, you're marrying Ada, not her family.'

'They come as a package. She's very close to them. She lives with them in the loft of their house; Michael converted it for her.'

From what I'd seen she was very close to her son and grandchildren, but I reckoned you could drive a supertanker through the space between Ada and her daughter-in-law. Not that that mattered; at that particular moment, I was more inclined to the distaff side of the Clarke family, given the fact that my mandible was groaning with silent, throbbing agony. 'I'm sure things will grow easier as they get to know you, and you get to know them.'

He looked less than convinced. 'I hope so.'

'And you and she will be living together in your own house.'

'Obviously.'

'You can choose your wife, but you can't choose her relatives,' I pointed out.

'Mmm,' he said thoughtfully and, to my ears, there was a distinct lack of chuffedness about him as he did so. 'You're not bothered, are you, Lance?'

'What about?' I asked, although I knew exactly what he meant.

'About me and Ada.' I tried to respond but it still wasn't my turn and he went on, 'I know we're close, but . . .'

He had run out of steam, which was maybe just as well. I rushed into the vacuum. Before either of us knew quite what was going on, I had moved towards him and we were hugging in a decidedly un-English way. 'Dad, there's no problem. Really.'

It had been a while since we had had more than five per cent of our body surfaces in contact, so he was a bit taken aback. There was a feeling of release and I felt the brush of his beard on my shoulder; I tried not to shudder or look at my epaulette. 'Yes, well . . .' he muttered, breathing quite deeply, as if I had just showed him a picture of me in women's underwear and nothing else. We stared at each other for what seemed like an hour, was almost certainly only a couple of seconds. Then normal Dad was back and he remarked in the tone I have heard him use an uncountable number of times before, 'It's just that I can't say that Michael and Tricia would have been my first choice from the catalogue.'

I cast around for positives, which took a while. 'David's a fine lad,' I said after what I hope wasn't too long a pause. 'You and he get on really well.'

This produced a nod and a smile. 'Yes, we do, don't we?' A pause. 'He hasn't been at school for the past couple of days.'

'Is he ill?' I asked out of politeness rather than professional or emotional concern.

'Ada says he's a bit below par.' Which is one the commonest diseases known to mankind; it is also completely impervious to medication or any sort.

'Probably a virus,' I suggested.

He nodded. 'Probably.'

I put out my hand to rest it on his and suddenly I found

that I couldn't recall the last time I'd touched him so often. He didn't react, which was just the right thing to do, but it wasn't long before he asked, 'More tea?' and stood up.

He was English, after all.

'Why not?'

He looked at me more closely. 'That's one hell of a tooth-ache, Lance,' he observed. 'The side of your jaw looks as though it's been clobbered.'

Clobbered. I thought, *What a wonderful word.* It was the type of word only my father would use. I said without answering, 'There are some paracetamol in the cupboard above the kettle. Would you get them for me?'

TWENTY-FOUR

That night Max and I went to see *One Flew Over the Cuckoo's Nest* at the Fairfield Halls, which is the ventricle of Croydon's cultural heart; the atrium is the Ashcroft Theatre in which, I am ashamed to admit, I have never set either of my feet. The date was the price that Max was paying for making me go to see *Tommy* earlier in the year; I am not a fan of pop music, and have a positive dislike of Ken Russell's work (I will not say 'of Ken Russell', since I have never met the man); in truth, the music wasn't too bad, but it was set in his usual lurid, polychromatic and psychedelic style, one that distracted rather than attracted. *One Flew Over the Cuckoo's Nest* was altogether different; it was an intelligent, thought-provoking film, well-acted and one that asked as many questions as it answered. In short, apart from the intolerable temperature we had to endure in that foetid darkness, it was a thoroughly enjoyable experience. We had a drink in the bar afterwards, as much to rehydrate as anything.

The Fairfield Hall complex is a fine example of post-war architecture, in that it is a concrete chancre on the landscape. Many years' experience of it has, however, turned an ugly thing into an icon of beauty, the beast into a beauty, at least in my eye. It has the advantage of space, for before it are flat concrete vistas in which there are fountains – these water features are an attempt to provide something fun and joyful, but this fails because after twenty years they have become slightly *grubby*. The traffic rumbles past interminably, waxing and waning with the hours but, as year follows year, on an imperceptible and inevitable crescendo. The Brighton to London railway line is not far away and this brings its own intermittent additions to the sonic background that is an indivisible part of Croydon. There are graffiti but, somehow, these seem normal and perfectly in keeping with this bleak, Orwellian location.

The interior, though, is slightly less harsh on the retinas; it is done out with a lot of varnished wood, although the lighting is a little postmodern and very subdued. There are interesting paintings on the walls, none of which seems anything more than a vivid, slightly coarse, multichromatic regurgitation of paint; try as I can, I have never seen a recognizable object in any of them. The beer is pretty dire too, but any port (or beer) in a storm . . .

'What did you think?' I enquired eagerly.

She frowned. 'Honestly?' she asked diffidently.

'Of course,' was my confident reply. I was enthused by my recent cinematic experience.

She hesitated to assemble her thoughts, then took a detour. 'Do you mind if I'm honest?'

Now there, in case you've missed it, is the red flag; me, I'm colour-blind. 'Of course not.'

More of the same hesitation, this time with a side order of a sip of her drink, before, 'I thought it was all very silly.'

I was stunned. Actually, that is an underestimate on the scale of, 'I see no ships'; actually, I was nearly concussed with shock. I managed four syllables – 'You are joking' – but the effort cost me dear; I had to finish my pint of amber dishwater (that they called 'ale') for sustenance.

'Mental hospitals aren't really like that,' she pronounced confidently.

Springfield Hospital loomed into the rear of my consciousness; asylums in Oregon certainly appeared to be a lot whiter and cleaner than those in Tooting, but McMurphy hadn't been a patient of the NHS, and I had seen a lot of higher truth in that film. 'Not in Britain,' I extemporized, hoping for a slightly firmer argument to pop up.

'And nurses aren't really that beastly, are they?'

I had a fairly solid foundation on which to contest that one; as a medical student, I had quickly learned that experienced nursing staff treated me and my kind as amusing but ultimately irritating simpletons, to be either abused or laughed at. I could see that Nurse Ratched wasn't too far from reality. 'I don't know . . .'

'And that Red Indian man wrenching the water fountain out of the ground and throwing it like that . . .'

'I'm not sure that that was . . .'

'It was all a bit unbelievable, really,' she concluded. With this, she drained her Cinzano and put the emptied glass on the water-ringed table between us. 'Can I have another one?'

My journey to the bar, although short, was a dazed one. Having sat through nearly two hours of appalling acting, strangled singing and disconnected narrative in the name of love when she had dragged me along to see *Tommy*, I thought her criticisms to be at best misjudged, at worst close to hypocritical. She had completely missed the point. How could someone as intelligent as Max not appreciate the subtleties of the film? More importantly, how could she not see how vacuous *Tommy* had been?

Please believe me, I am not pompous. I like mindless entertainment as much as the next sad bugger – I found *Star Trek* quite fascinating, if increasingly ludicrous as the episodes went by – but I have my limits; in any case, the important thing is to appreciate the finer things in life whilst still enjoying those that are slightly coarser. Also I must insist that I like modern music. Max introduced me to Barclay James Harvest at the end of last year and I have not once failed to look back.

I made my way back to the table, still slightly shocked not just at her artistic insensibilities but also at the price of the drinks. I was about to wax lyrical about this but Max cut me vocally short. 'Who's that man?' she asked.

For a moment I didn't comprehend what she was talking about, and looked around the various couples and groups that were dotted around the room. I looked back at Max, my face questioning, and she nodded at the bar, towards the far-left end close to the windows that gave a panoramic view of Croydon's ceaseless activity. There was a long angled mirror at the back of the bar, reflecting everything – the drinks, the glasses, the upper halves of the bar staff, the bar, those sitting at the bar and much of the room.

And Tristan.

He was sitting at the bar, lazily drinking lager of some sort, his eyes looking up at the mirror and directly at us; he didn't have the dazed expression I had seen on his face at Springfield.

'Oh, shit,' I breathed. She looked at me oddly and I had to collect myself before I could smile reassurance that was, I have to admit, not mine to give. 'It's one of my old patients,' I said as calmly as I could. 'Hang on.'

I stood up and went over to him, nice and steady, like. His eyes remained fixed on me all the time that I approached him and, believe me, the seconds seemed to pass so slowly I would have come last in a race with a glacier. Tristan didn't react at all, just kept sipping his lager and looking at me. I came to a slow and steady halt at about east-south-east of him but, before I could assemble some dignity from the wreckage of my nerves, he raised his half-empty glass in salute. 'Hello, Lancey.' He peered at me with a frown. 'Has someone hit you?'

Everyone had asked me that. My colleagues had found it most amusing, nearly wetting themselves about it: my feeble excuses had gone unbelieved. Max had been most solicitous when I had told her what had happened, though. Accordingly, I ignored the amusement in his voice; in fact I ignored the words in it, too. 'What are you doing here?'

He frowned. 'Enjoying the lager. Not the best, but the ambience here is better than my closest local. Do you know the Selkirk? A bit run-down, and really only good for the Guinness, if you get my meaning.'

'You don't intimidate me.' Which was so patently untrue I felt embarrassed when I heard myself saying it.

He gave this due consideration. 'Good,' he said simply. 'Cos you don't intimidate me.'

He drained his pint, then got up. If I had been bound in calico ropes, I could not have more immobile. He smiled and winked at me as he made to go. Leaning in close to me, he whispered, 'Nice bird, Lancey.'

And he was gone before I could recover from my bewildered shock.

TWENTY-FIVE

'Sorry about this,' said my father, although he hid his remorse well.

I said nothing. The *Radio One Breakfast Show* had just started and some annoying nerk or other was trying to persuade me that I should be happy, whilst all I felt was irritation and despair, made worse by his inane imbecility. Dad liked it, although I wasn't sure whether that was a plus or a minus. Dad filled in my silence whilst I negotiated the tricky bit of driving that is represented by the Pond during the morning rush hour. There were thunder clouds in the sky, but I had little confidence that it was going to rain any time soon. 'Bit of an emergency with the carrots.'

'No problem,' I said tersely as a milk float, driven by a man who clearly thought he had eaten invulnerability cereal for breakfast, cut me up from the left.

'I think we might be wide open to carrot-root fly.'

'Really?'

'Something of an epidemic this year. Must be the heat.'

'Probably.'

'Got to nip that in the bud – or, I suppose, the root – or else you can lose the whole crop.'

'Disastrous.'

'Ada said the plants are looking really good, but I doubt she knows what to look for. It can be very subtle in the early stages.'

'Can it?'

'Oh, yes. You need experience in these matters.' A bus pulled out away from the stop without indicating, as buses do. I swore, and Dad said in the knowing manner that I knew so well, 'I thought he'd do that.'

It was half-past seven, the temperature well up to speed already. I had spent the night at Max's in a state of paranoia; it was one that had become intense as I left her that morning. I had tried to sound ultra-nonchalant as I had suggested that she should take care, and I had scanned the street as I went to my car; of course I had seen nothing, and I fervently hoped that it was only because there was nothing to see. We drove along Thornton Road in relative peace and at a relatively good speed, then turned left up Keston Road.

'This was where Yvette Mangon lived, wasn't it?' he asked.

'That's right. Up there, on the left.'

'Ada says the whole school staff is in turmoil.'

'I can imagine.'

'The favoured theory is that it's an old pupil with a grudge.'

'Not many suspects, then.'

He didn't get the joke. 'I wouldn't know. She says that Inspector Masson interviewed her. She said he was the epitome of charm.'

I nearly ran a pedestrian down on the zebra crossing, so shocking was this news. 'You're joking.'

'No. Apparently, he was kind and gentle with her. Very understanding.'

'Is she sure it was Masson? Did she see his ID?'

'I know. Interesting, isn't it?' He thought for a while. 'I wonder if he's got his eye on her.'

I did well; I didn't laugh. My voice was ever so slightly strangled as I replied, though. 'Now there's a thought.' I was thankful that this concept was sufficiently unsettling for my father to be completely immersed in a pool of deep, dark gloom until we reached the school. I parked where I wanted, then waited for him to get out so that I could be on my way but, my father being who he was, suddenly grasped my arm and said, 'There's Mr Silsby.' I could not argue with this ejaculation. The tall, thin and slightly austere figure that was standing outside the arched main entrance to the school, some fifty yards distant, did indeed belong to that beleaguered head-master. It appeared, moreover, that he was for the moment doubly beleaguered because he was being accosted by a short individual in rather florid clothing, even given the year and its prevailing tendency for fashion eyesores; he had a green velveteen jacket, light blue trousers of an indeterminate mate-rial, a grotesque black Stetson and shoes that, although not curled at the toes, were clearly far longer than the gentleman's feet; because he was not only short but somewhat rotund, the name 'Little Tich' kept recurring annoyingly to my mind. So egregious was his attire that even a person of perfect bodily proportions would have looked a bit – even a large bit – of a prat in it.

He was clearly animated, in that he waved his arms around a lot and did his best to get into Mr Silsby's face, an impos-sible feat given the disparity in heights. His face was red, too, although it was conceivable that this was either its natural hue or the heat of the morning. Mr Silsby, to be fair, was giving as good as he was being given; his features were set and he kept shaking his head in what can only be described as a determined manner; occasionally he would make small hand gestures, all of which were clearly dismissive or negative.

'Who's the little chap?' I asked.

'One of the teachers,' said my father, his voice hesitant and slightly high with uncertainty.

'He certainly dresses flamboyantly.'

Dad frowned. 'I'm fairly sure he's an art teacher.'

Which made sense.

The performance lasted a few more minutes whilst we, an unbidden and unexpected audience, looked on; Demis Roussos warbled through the car speakers whilst we did so, a ghostly yet huge metaphysical apparition providing a bizarre sound-track. Eventually, just as Demis's respiratory system gave up gasping its way through 'Ever and Ever', Mr Silsby turned and walked away from his strange gnomic aggressor. He walked in an upright and stiff gait with something of the military about it; he carried with him a sense of offended dignity that was evinced by a slight nodding of his head as he walked. I felt for him but, whilst I was ready to utter private sympathies concerning his plight, I did not expect my father to erupt from the car and call him over. Mr Silsby hesitated but eventually did as he had been bade. As he approached, I judged from his expression that he would rather have retained a little privacy of his own at that moment.

My father said, 'My son, Lance. You'll remember him. He took over in the practice.'

Perhaps Mr Silsby did, and perhaps he didn't; his faintly strained expression suggested that he didn't particularly have the urge to bother trying. He said, 'Yes . . . of course.' The headmaster's handshake was firm but slightly damp; perhaps it was the climate, although perhaps it wasn't. 'Your father is proving of great help to us, Dr Elliot,' he said, but everything about him told me that his heart was elsewhere. Out of the corner of my eye I could see the spheroidal figure of his erstwhile combatant stalking off to his car.

'That's good to hear.'

There was a pause, one of the type that concerns a gorilla in the corner of the room. It demonstrated the inescapable truth of Einstein's revelation that there is no universal time, for whilst the world at large went on as usual, our little trio seemed embedded in a reality that oozed rather than flowed. My father broke first. 'How are things?'

I knew that this came from his training and years of practice; some patients walk into the surgery and never get around to telling you stuff without a bit of prompting. Mr Silsby, though, looked as if one of his pupils had just passed wind in his assembly. 'What?' he asked, showing some shock at my father's lack of etiquette in not avoiding the subject that we were all thinking about. 'What?' he then repeated in exactly the same tone, timbre and volume; it was just emphasis, I supposed, although I held a diagnosis of deafness in reserve.

Dad did his ingenuous act; it was the way that he said the most outrageous things or asked the most gauche questions, and then got away with it. 'It must be difficult to cope at the moment?'

Mr Silsby goggled at him for a moment, clearly containing

a raging internal debate as to whether or not my father was taking the proverbial, then replied weakly, 'Yes . . . yes, it is.' I saw his eyes twitching towards the retreating figure.

Mr Silsby smelled of tobacco and he had about him an air of dehydration, the weather notwithstanding; when he spoke he did so through his nose whilst smacking his lips and tongue. I began to appreciate that the more stressed he got, the more he did this smacking. Dad sailed on. 'A colleague of yours, was he?'

'Eh?'

'That gentleman.' He indicated the distant corpulence.

'Yes. What of it?' Mr Silsby replied, a tad defensively.

'Seemed worked up. He should avoid undue exertion in this weather. Even at this early hour, it's starting to get warm, and there is a definitive increase in the incidence of cerebrovascular accident when the temperature is high. Ask Lance.'

Mr Silsby failed to do as he was bid, however. 'Why are you here, Dr Elliot?' he enquired of my father tiredly; I had heard a similar tone used before when my father got into his stride.

Dad reacted with astonishment, perhaps because he was surprised that Mr Silsby evinced little interest in his titbit, perhaps because his schemes and stratagems were not working. 'To tend to the allotment. I fear we may be prone to an infestation of carrot-root fly and that, as I was only just explaining to Lance, can be . . .'

'Well, I suggest it would prudent of you to attend to it as soon as possible. The sooner you tackle it, the less damage will be done, presumably.'

Dad was surprised. 'Oh, yes. You're right. There are several pesticides we could turn to, but I was hoping . . .'

'Good. Now, if you will excuse me, gentlemen, I have work to perform.'

He turned on his heel in what was really quite a balletic manoeuvre and marched off in his military gait, into the shade of the school's entrance hall.

TWENTY-SIX

'That, if I haven't lost all my clinical acumen, is a man under stress.'

I could only agree, all the while reflecting that, being the man he was, my father must have been constantly surrounded by people under stress. Abruptly he cast the good headmaster into the wastepaper bin of oblivion, grasped my arm and insisted, 'Come and look at the allotment.'

I risked a peek at my watch. 'I really ought to get to the surgery.'

'Come on. It won't take long.'

'I really haven't got time . . .'

'Rubbish. Patients expect the doctor to be running late; Hippocrates said it did them good.'

I sincerely doubted the accuracy of this assertion but I was distracted and did not reply. My eye had been caught by another little scenario that was being played out just beyond the school gateway. It involved the man who had just been giving it large to Mr Silsby; now he was being given it large by someone else, because yang inevitably follows yin. That in itself was interesting enough, but it was with whom he was once again in dispute that interested me.

It was Albert Stewart. This time, however, the dyspeptic globular teacher seemed to be on the receiving end, because to judge from the body language, Albert Stewart was an angry man, and making sure that his interlocutor knew it.

'Come on,' urged Dad, tugging at my arm, 'I thought you said you were in a hurry.'

I looked away as he pulled me and protested, 'Hang on a second.' When I looked back, events had progressed. The teacher was sitting on the ground and Albert Stewart was striding away, clearly very angry about something. As I watched, with Dad making noises of consternation and impatience, the little man slowly stood up, apparently none the worse for his encounter. That wasn't all, though. As I hurried to follow Dad, I caught sight of Mr Silsby through a window in the main school building. He, too, was staring at what had gone on between Albert Stewart and the angry little man; his face was fixed and, although I could be mistaken, it was very, very scared.

'Lance,' called my father. I was a hundred yards away and he, as is his wont, was impatient.

And so we went to see the vegetable garden.

It held a shock in store for us, for it had suffered grievously from dehydration, even though my father had only been absent for a few days. 'Oh,' he sighed, disappointment writ in large script all over his heavily bearded face.

If I had been given the use of only a single word to describe the vegetable garden, it would have to have been *wilted*. Nothing stood tall, with the exception of the weeds – 'the devil's houseplants' as my father called them – and in one or two species, there seemed to be even more deterioration, so that a further word – *dying* – needed to be added. I looked at Dad. His eyes held more moisture than they should have done, although no tears had yet escaped. He sniffed and set his lips so that his cheeks puffed out. 'They said they'd water it for me . . .' he murmured.

I put my arm around his shoulders. 'I'm sure they're very busy, what with preparing for the start of a new school year and everything.' He neither did nor said anything, just continued to stare. I went on, 'And you said that David hasn't been at school. That must have had an effect. I expect things just drifted, without anyone being around all the time.'

At last he reacted, taking a deep breath and nodding. 'Yes, you're right. This wouldn't have happened if David had been around . . .' His voice subsided then, 'I wonder why Ada didn't tell me.'

'She presumably didn't get over here to look at it. Too busy, I expect.'

'But she said she had.'

Which was a tricky one to counter. 'Maybe only from a distance?'

He looked at me for a brief moment before agreeing. 'Yes, I expect that's it.' There was something in his voice that suggested to me that he was still puzzled.

About fifty per cent of the lettuces had gone to seed and their leaves were bordered in brown. The tomatoes, too, looked distinctly thirsty; Dad commented, 'They'll be thick-skinned now,' and was clearly completely oblivious of the irony. The radishes – once such a prize exhibit – were severely affected, with not many destined to survive; the potatoes formed a flat, flaccid mat of foliage. Dad announced manfully, 'I reckon we'll be able to salvage a lot of things.' His voice was that of a Napoleon following his Waterloo.

I had a sudden panic that by his use of the plural pronoun he had been referring not to the pupils, but to his one and only son.

'Dad, I haven't got the time.'

'What?' He was contemplating the distressing state of his spring onions and didn't take in what I had said immediately. 'Don't be an imbecile, Lance. I know that. I'll have a word with Mr Silsby and get some of the children to help out, the lazy little beggars.' This, I noted, seemed to denote a subtle change in his attitude to the pupils of Bensham Manor School.

I made my goodbyes and left him. As I walked around to front entrance of the school, I noted with some relief that the way was clear for me to escape. I hurried to my car past the main front doors, got in and was making my way out when I caught sight of Mr Silsby; he was visible through one of the windows, presumably sitting at his desk in his office. He had his head in his hands, a picture of despair.

'I'm really sorry, Dr Elliot, but there's nothing I can do.' As we were conversing by phone I couldn't judge by anything more than the sound of her voice but Sergeant Abelson sounded genuinely sorry.

'You know what he's doing, don't you?'

She hesitated. 'As a policewoman, all I know is that Tristan Charlton had a drink in a public bar; as it was within licensing hours, he wasn't drunk, he paid for his drink and he didn't breach the peace, there's nothing of interest to me. As a civilian and, I hope you won't mind me saying your friend, yes, I know exactly what he's doing.'

'Well, then . . .'

'Dr Elliot – Lance – I can't do anything. Until he commits a crime, we can't touch him.'

'Don't you have a commitment to prevent crime? Haven't I heard something along those lines somewhere?'

'And how much of its time does the medical profession spend preventing illness? Doesn't it usually just attempt to treat it . . . especially if the patient goes private?'

Ouch. I thought it would be unproductive to enter into a political argument about means of medical provision. 'But surely there's something you can do,' I pleaded. 'You do believe me about Tristan, don't you?'

'Of course I do. I've looked at his file. I read the medical report on your injuries.' She sounded genuinely shocked. 'He's clearly done horrible things.'

'Well, then . . .?'

'Do I really have to give you a lecture on jurisprudence?' she enquired, her tone leavened. She was right. Justice was blind; in the past Tristan could have slaughtered and tortured a million and it would have made no difference. The police needed evidence of what he was up to *now*.

'No,' I admitted.

'The Inspector's already made it plain that he thinks your allegations about Tristan Charlton are irrelevant and, to quote him, "hysterical"; he wants me to concentrate on the murders of the teachers.'

'He's wrong. He's underestimating what Tristan is capable of.'

'According to his doctors, he's no longer a threat.'

'They're wrong, too.'

There was a pause before she said in no more than a soft whisper, as if she was afraid of being overheard, 'I'll do what I can.'

TWENTY-SEVEN

That night, things were not easy. We stayed in and Max cooked a lasagne and did her best, I have no doubt. I was still tired from my night on call and I was also intensely anxious about Tristan, and the threat he represented to Max; yet I felt that I could not tell her about it. I was irritable and Max, understandably, did not really appreciate why. We didn't row but, in a way, things were the worse for that. I have made many mistakes in my professional life, many of which have endangered patients yet none, as far as I know, has ever resulted in a death. I could only now hope that I would be able to say the same of my personal life . . .

That next day I was the on-call police surgeon; were this not sufficient to make the day wondrous beyond comprehension, it was also the monthly urology clinic. This was an innovation for the practice, and one I could have done without; it was the result of yet another campaign that had just about reached our suburban ears (albeit gasping and about to expire) from the disturbing, unknowable edifice that is the Department of Health and Social Security, and I had clearly not been at the meeting when we had decided who should be responsible. The rationale was that we were taking part in a blitz on venereal disease, but I found that anyone with a todger-related problem turned up; there seemed, moreover, to be a distressingly large number of male patients on our lists who felt the need (and who had the time) to come into my surgery, drop their kecks and cup their genitalia proudly in their (usually right) hand. Often it was just poor hygiene, sometimes it was warts, occasionally it was phimosis or a similar anatomical problem. There was a regular trickle of gonorrhoea and syphilis (if you'll excuse the image); once an extremely shy member of the clergy had come in (inhabiting mufti), explaining that he was slightly worried about something. It had taken twenty minutes to persuade him finally to allow me to examine his problem; he had a cancer on the end of his not inconsiderable member, and one that was well advanced. He had been separated from his Percy within the week and I think even a man of God found that a hard thing to bear.

All in all, it was never for me an afternoon of fun.

Luckily, there was little to do during the evening and I was able to go to bed at just after midnight. I was allowed by the fates to sleep until the call came through at about seven in the morning, which is never a particularly good time for me. As I made my way down to the hall to answer the metallic, robotic ringing, I debated not for the first time whether it was better when on call to fall asleep and then get woken, or to stay awake the whole night. I continually swung between these opinions on the subject. On this occasion, it wasn't helped by the dull ache in my mandible and the impression that my lower lip was little more than a fat juicy blood-bag.

'Hello?' I said.

'Dr Elliot?' I knew at once who it was and the realization brought no comfort.

'Inspector.' I didn't bother responding to his question since I knew he wasn't interested in any answer I might have given. 'Is this a social call?'

He laughed, much as Prometheus probably had a good chuckle every morning when he saw what the day held for him, bird of prey-wise. 'Not this time. I wonder if you could oblige me with your presence on the Thornton Heath allotments. I have need of your expertise.'

His pronunciation of the last word was laden with quotation marks. 'A body?' I asked.

He sighed and I could see the disgust in it. 'It's not because I want you to judge the biggest parsnip in show, Doctor.' The telephone line, although never actually alive, went dead, and did so suddenly.

I have had occasion to talk before of Thornton Heath Allotments, where my father spends much of his time and not a little of his energy. It is a rural oasis in what is otherwise a somewhat 'over-urbanized' town, one where the sounds, if not the smells, of the traffic are not prominent, and where nature retains a delicate, ever-threatened foothold. During daylight hours it is rare, even in the coldest part of drear winter, for the allotments to be completely deserted but, even allowing for that, when I arrived about half an hour later there was an unusually large number of people and vehicles. The centre of attention was on the north side, not far from the fences that marked the ends of the rear gardens of the houses in Mayfield Road. Several police cars and about a dozen police were clustered around what at first I thought was a shed. The inevitable lay audience was there; in the front stalls were a motley assembly of adults standing at the ends of their gardens, peering over the fences, while in the upper circle were their children, faces framed by the opened back bedroom windows.

Sergeant Abelson greeted me wearing a very nice light brown trouser suit. 'Thanks for coming.' Since I was being paid for attending, it struck me that this was nice but unnecessary. Her expression turned to one of concern. Before she could ask any questions, I explained, 'Toothache.' She winced and it was at once plain to see that she did a very good sympathetic wince. I moved on briskly. 'What have we got?'

'It looks as though someone's drowned.'

Her face was serious, but there was an unmistakeable tone of irony in her voice; when I stopped short, she turned and looked back at me, her eyebrows raised, her lips framed by laughter lines. Despite the early time, she was turned out, as far as I could see, immaculately. 'Are you joking?' I enquired. She didn't reply but just turned away from me and began walking into the melee of police officers; one on the periphery was trying, rather unsuccessfully I thought, to control a small brown-and-white Jack Russell. It was on the end of a choke collar but that wasn't particularly useful to the ginger-haired constable who had to keep dancing in the high-stepping Irish manner to avoid the dog's ankle fixation. I followed the good Sergeant, and when I got to the centre of activity, I saw that she hadn't been joking at all.

Dotted around the allotments, at about two-hundred-yard intervals, were galvanized steel water tanks, each about four feet square and two feet high; they were supplied by a network of underground pipes, the flow controlled by ballcocks. Two legs, bent at the knees over the edge, protruded from the one that was the epicentre of interest; as I approached it, I began to feel slightly unnerved, for the legs were clothed in light blue trousers which, unless I missed my guess, were of an indeterminate material.

Masson was standing by the water tank staring down into its depths and not, I surmised, because he had an abiding interest in freshwater flora and fauna. Sergeant Abelson and I joined him, one on either side. My suspicions were proved correct, for I found myself staring down at the corpulent entity who had been possessed, so recently, of feisty life. His arms floated freely at his sides, as if he was resting, or perhaps free-floating in the Apollo capsule. This isn't much of a metaphor, since he had stirred up the sediment a bit and there was a light covering of it on his pale bloated features; add to that the fact that the water tanks were home at the best of times to a bewildering variety of cold-water life – water fleas, water boatmen, worms, water beetles and many more I could not name – and his features were difficult to discern. Despite this, there was no doubt that I had been right in my initial identification; it was the irascible man Dad and I had seen accosting Mr Silsby and then, in turn, being accosted by Albert Stewart. Masson had his hands in his trouser pockets and, I was slightly distressed to discover, was smoking. I know little of forensics, but was fairly sure that this was not best practice.

He said not directly to anyone but to the company in general, 'They've just declared a drought, too.'

Photographs taken, the body had been removed from the tank and lay on a tarpaulin; a tent had been erected to provide some privacy, although the audience seemed disinclined to disperse. I performed a preliminary examination with Masson and Sergeant Abelson in attendance, the former exuding angry impatience, the latter interested detachment. There were signs of a struggle, but no more than I would have expected in the circumstances of someone holding someone else under the water until that final inhalation that must be so horrible. I have not seen many drowning victims but had read enough to expect extreme pallor, not a little pong and bloating of the flesh, but there was none of this. As there wasn't anything much bigger than an inch in size in the water tank, the lack of predation was no surprise, however.

'Well?'

I need not tell you that this came from the good Inspector. I told him my findings, not expecting congratulations and therefore not being disappointed. He took everything I had then enquired testily, as if I had missed the point, 'How long's he been in there?'

'Not long.'

He didn't snarl, but came close. 'What the bloody hell does that mean?'

I did the thing that years of medical training followed by even more years of medical practice have taught me. I talked bullshit. 'Less than six hours. Maybe only one or two.'

He was very good at staring was Inspector Masson; I know that because he seemed to do a lot of it at me. There was a stand-off between us until Sergeant Abelson said, 'That would fit with the time on the deceased's wristwatch, sir – five thirty-three.'

He continued doing his alpha-male thing for a few seconds more, then subsided with a grunted, 'Yes, I know.'

He then asked me, 'Is there anything more you can tell me at this juncture?'

I took a deep breath, that familiar feeling of being in the middle of an oral examination recurring. 'I can't see any evidence of a head injury, and there seems to be bruising around the neck, so my preliminary conclusion would be that he was killed by drowning and that he wasn't alone when it happened. I've checked his pockets, but they're empty.'

'OK.' I got the sense he was less than impressed with my forensic skills, which made two of us. He waited. I was just about to disappoint him and tell him that there was no more to be had from me, when I spotted something – a speck of dirt perhaps – at the corner of the dead man's mouth. I knelt down to look at it more carefully. It wouldn't come, because it was more than just a speck of dirt; it was attached to some-thing in his mouth. I had to prise the jaws apart – he was not many hours dead but the cold of the water had accelerated rigor in the facial muscles – but it wasn't too difficult. What I brought out was surprisingly large.

It was a frog.

Masson goggled, accompanied in this action by Sergeant Abelson and four uniformed officers who were looking on. After this, which was undertaken in perfect silence, he pulled himself together and called for an evidence bag so that I could be relieved of the amphibian. 'How did that get in his mouth?' he demanded, as if I had been guilty of a monstrous practical jape.

The Sergeant at least had a reasonable question to ask. 'Are there frogs in these tanks?'

'Possibly,' I replied.

'So it could have swum in there?'

'His mouth was closed. I can't see that happening.'

'Perhaps his mouth was open and, after it swam in there, rigor caused the mouth to close.'

She was doing her best, but Masson was less than impressed. He extracted another cigarette from his crumpled packet, applied his lighter to the end, drew in some carcinogens and then asked, 'How many drownings have you seen, Doctor?'

'A few,' I admitted cautiously and noncommittally.

'Remember any that had their mouths closed?'

Now he came to mention it, I couldn't; but then I couldn't remember any that had had their mouths open, in that I was new to the job and actually meant 'none' when I had said 'a few'. 'No,' I said in a sort of truthful way.

'No,' he repeated, for once mollified by my agreement. 'Which means I think that the frog was put into his mouth by his killer.'

Sergeant Abelson asked, 'Why would anyone do that?'

But Masson, having made this monumental deduction, had come to a halt in the detection stakes.

Jean pointed out, 'It would help if we knew his identity.'

'Have you organized the house-to-house search? Someone in Mayfield Road may have seen something. Presumably he was taking the dog for an early morning walk.'

'It's under control,' she assured him.

As far as I was concerned, my job was done. I closed my case. 'Why don't you ask the school? They'll have his address.'

Has that ever happened to you? You say something that to you seems normal and reasonable, yet your audience treats the words you have said as if you have just come from central office and told them that they're all going to face the firing squad. Masson asked in a gravelly voice that was a good few octaves lower than even his normal growl, 'You what?'

I looked at the Sergeant, mainly because she represented a far finer view than her superior. She asked in a sweet and light and undeniably controlled tone, 'Do you know who this is, Lance?'

'I don't know his name,' I said, sensing wolves gathering.

Masson growled then in a tone that was almost too low for my hearing (I've had dogs who did that, usually when they were just about to try to separate you from your sweetmeats), 'But you recognize him?'

'I saw him for the first time a day or two ago.' Why did I feel guilty?

'At a school? At Bensham Manor School?'

'That's right.' I felt that I had to justify myself and felt simultaneously that I should not have to. It was only my imagination that he was imperceptibly moving towards me, much as a hyena might do when the prey is dying but not yet completely defenceless. 'He was having some sort of argument with the headmaster, Mr Silsby.'

'What about?'

'I don't know.' While Masson looked incredulous at this, Sergeant Abelson looked only intrigued. I attempted elucidation. 'Dad and I were in the car. It was early Friday morning.'

Masson looked meaningfully at his sergeant, who nodded and scribbled in her notebook. He then said with a degree of irony that would have thudded to the ground on the Moon, 'Anything else you'd like to tell us, Dr Elliot?'

I was about to shake my head vigorously, temporarily overcome with a desperate need to be no longer a naughty boy, but then my brain started functioning again. 'He also seemed to have a bit of a row with someone else. It was outside the school grounds, just afterwards.'

'"Seemed to have"?'

'We were a hundred yards distant.'

This, it appeared, was little excuse. 'Do you know who this row was with?'

It was with some desperation that I fought down the urge to correct his grammar; it was made slightly easier because I suddenly recalled the photo in Albert Stewart's living room. I didn't know what it meant, but I knew it meant something.

TWENTY-EIGHT

Max and I were to have dinner that night at my father's house and it was going to be a jolly ménage-à-quatre because Ada was coming too. I hoped, but did not expect, the evening would be easy-going and relaxed, without any embarrassment on the part of anyone. When Dad had suggested it to us yesterday morning, neither of us had been able to raise a particular intense level of enthusiasm but, equally, neither of us wanted to let him down. As Max had pointed out, it would at least provide an opportunity for us to learn a little bit more about my impending stepmother and – more importantly to me – about her apparently testosterone-fuelled son. This was our thinking as we feigned joy-filled acceptance.

As Max was called out at the last moment to attend to a sick gerbil, we agreed that we would make our separate ways to Pollard's Hill, the leafy suburban glade in which Dad lived, as she would be about half an hour late. I rang the doorbell, looking up at the sky and wondering if the storm clouds meant anything, both meteorologically and metaphorically. It was Ada who answered the door, a happenstance that I found unsettling whilst telling myself sternly that I was being silly; she was going to be married to Dad all too soon, and then she would be greeting visitors on a regular basis and a very proper thing it would be, too. Unfortunately, until the nuptials were all done and dusted, it struck me as slightly forward. She had a glass of sherry in her hand as she said through her nose, 'Ah, Lance. How lovely to see you.'

She proffered her cheek for me to kiss and that sense that I was in the presence of someone who had not only found a safe berth but one who had, in very short order, changed the sheets, redecorated the walls and had taken charge of all the keys. I bent down and conformed to social norms by returning her gesture. 'Come in,' she said.

We went to the kitchen where the scents of Dad's cooking were working some serious magic on my cerebral hunger centres. He was wearing a plastic-coated apron on which was a cartoon of a curvy, topless female body; looking at Dad's hirsute visage above this made me feel slightly giddy, much as a member of the audience of Victorian freak shows would probably have felt, because fundamental laws of biology seemed to be broken by the spectacle. 'Hello, Lance,' he greeted me over a loud sizzle of frying onions. 'Tired?'

'Not bad. It was quite an easy night. Hardly anything until early this morning.'

'Lucky chap.' He turned to Ada, who had taken a seat at the kitchen table, nice and close to a bottle of sherry. 'Lance was on call for the police last night.'

'Did you have anything to do with Mr Gillman?' she asked excitedly.

That, as far as I was concerned, was a moot point; maybe I had and maybe I hadn't. It was difficult to be exact on the point, since I didn't know who Mr Gillman was. I conveyed this lack of intelligence to the assembled company. 'He was a teacher,' she explained. 'Apparently he's been done in, just like those lesbians.' It didn't take much in the way of perspicacity to spot that, from the way she pronounced the last word, she was not of a socially liberal persuasion.

'Oh, the art teacher . . .'

She looked at me scornfully. 'Art teacher? Where did you get that idea?'

I glanced at Dad, but he was clearly at a tricky stage in the cooking, since he was looking at the onions with a degree of concentration I have previously only seen on the faces of neurosurgeons when they're hacking around in someone's basal ganglia. 'I can't think,' I said to her.

'No, Jeremy Gillman was a biology teacher,' she explained, clearly concluding that I was a simpleton.

Whilst this came as a surprise – given the man's flamboyant, not to say criminally mistaken, dress sense – there was the oddity of the frog in his mouth, which suddenly seemed to make ominous sense, given what had been happening to the teaching staff of Bensham Manor. 'Was he really?' I asked.

Dad came out of his trance over the onions, saying as he opened a tin of tomatoes, 'Ada says that there's been a right kerfuffle at the school.' He stirred the cooking, turned the gas down a notch and went to the fridge to fetch two beers – a refill for him, a new one for me. I looked at the label suspiciously, afraid for my intestines; Dolly's Toe-Curler was its *appellation*, although I doubt it was in any way *contrôlée*. There was a colour cartoon of a buxom long-haired, big-lipped blonde on the label, leading me to suspect that I was not about to follow in the footsteps of Escoffier.

'How strong is this stuff?' I asked, sniffing the bouquet and getting hints of creosote and rose fertilizer.

'Not sure,' said my father airily, which was his way of dealing with – that is to say, ignoring – that which did not bother him. I vowed to go careful for the sake of the pedestrians I would encounter on my way home. Ada had helped herself to another dollop of Harvey's Bristol Cream and was impatient to tell me what she had to say.

'The police turned up at about eight thirty, just as a group of the children were assembling for their Cycling Proficiency course. They made a right fuss and caused no end of trouble for Mr Silsby. The girls and I had a really good view because the back of the kitchens look out over the front playground.' The use of the term 'girls' was, I had no doubt, a tad euphemistic in its implication that the average age of the Bensham Manor kitchen staff was only just beyond adolescence. 'He was marching around trying to keep the children in order whilst being chased by that funny little policeman.' I knew what she meant by her use of the adjective 'funny', but I still thought it slightly ill-chosen. She continued, 'Poor Mr Silsby's been having a torrid time of it recently, what with losing teachers left, right and centre, and I'm sure he didn't need this.'

'Did he get on with Mr Gillman?'

'Ah,' Dad exclaimed. 'That's exactly my line of thinking. I asked you that, didn't I, Ada?'

'You did, Ben.' There was a sense of conspiracy between them which, in its way, was quite comforting.

'And what's the answer?'

'Well,' she said, her voice dropping in volume, 'there have been rumours . . .'

I waited, but did so in vain. At last I enquired, 'About what?'

'People used to say that there was a lot of animosity between them.'

'Does anyone know why?'

She did not answer this question, saying instead, 'Mind you, he doesn't get on with many people. Bit of a marionette, is Mr Silsby.' I opened my mouth to correct this malapropism, but then decided against it out of a sense of diplomacy; Dad didn't seem to have heard it. She sailed on, by now clearly well lubricated by sherry. 'I'm surprised he didn't stop what was going on between Miss Mangon and Miss Jeffries.'

'Did they make it so obvious?'

Salaciousness came from every pore of Ada, like too thickly applied cosmetic. 'Well, no one knew for sure, but it was pretty *obvious*.' Dad added some minced meat to the onions and said over his shoulder, 'Ada says they were like a right old married couple, especially lately. There was a lot of arguing in corridors, all that sort of thing.'

'At the end, they could hardly talk to each other; it was most embarrassing.' The idea of Ada being embarrassed was difficult for me to envisage, but discretion was the better part of my valour.

The doorbell sounded. I went in answer to it, assuming it to be Max, and I was not disappointed. She was very upset and had clearly been crying. 'Max? What's wrong?' I bent to kiss her, but she barely made contact with me. 'What's wrong?' I repeated.

She shook her head. 'I still don't believe it.'

'Believe what?'

It took her a moment to pull herself back from tears. I waited, trying to be as patient as possible. I just knew that it had something to do with Tristan.

'When I got into the surgery, there was a letter waiting for me.'

'Who from?' I knew the answer, but asked anyway.

She ignored the question. In fact, she was crying again. I was the epitome of tolerance and cuddled her whilst she sobbed. Eventually she calmed down enough to fish in her handbag and pull out a piece of paper. It was lined and had been torn from a notebook; it was written in ballpoint and the pen had leaked here and there. It was from Albert Stewart and addressed to 'the girl vet'. It was short and the writing was irregular and untidy, making it difficult to read, but it didn't take too long to decipher.

I killed your rabbit. I'm sorry. I shouldn't have done it, but was overcome because of Major's death. I thought you were responsible. I'm sorry.

I breathed out slowly; in my head the words 'oh, shit' were sounding.

Max said, 'How could he do that?'

I explained tiredly, 'He's a very disturbed man, Max. Not entirely right in the head.'

'You can say that again,' she hissed through angry tears.

'What will you do?'

'Nothing yet. We've got our dinner to enjoy.'

'Are you sure? I could say you're not feeling well. It wouldn't be far beyond the truth.'

She shook her head firmly. 'No. We can't let your father down.'

I sighed. 'If you say so.'

'I do,' she insisted, at which point we were called impatiently through to the kitchen by Dad and we had to play our parts in the occasion.

TWENTY-NINE

Max coped very well, although I noticed Dad throwing the odd puzzled glance at her. During the course of the meal, we learned that Ada liked *Starsky and Hutch* but was not particularly enamoured of *Survivors*, that she sang in the choir at St Jude's Church and that she had once auditioned for *The Black and White Minstrel Show* – we were left to assume that she hadn't been successful, but didn't like to ask. These were amongst what she told us, her garrulousness increasing as first the sherry, then the wine, ebbed. What she didn't say, but what became obvious, was that she looked on my father as a trophy, one that she intended to display in a prominent position in her life. She had already paraded him around her workmates – 'the girls' – and around the congregation at St Jude's, as well as (less successfully) around her family. She had plans, did Ada; big ones. Plans that involved my father's money. She had found her sweetshop and was at the stage where she was still looking around, still trying to work out which particular item of confectionery to stuff between her ill-fitting dentures first. From Dad's point of view, he was thoroughly enjoying being the centre of attention, even if that attention came from a circling leech. There was no one else to blame but me; I had always assumed that he was happy with his crackpot obsessions, his allotment and his photographs of Mum, and I had always assumed that because it suited me to. As I watched the two of them, I was struck by the fact that they were both after something, and that they each had what the other craved. *Is that so bad*, I got to wondering. *Is that really so bad?*

Then I thought that it probably was because, overcome with wine both fortified and unfortified, Ada looked around the dining room and said, 'I've got such plans for this old place.'

There was a sudden silence in the room, one that she didn't seem to appreciate. Dad was looking at his chilli con carne as if one of the kidney beans had started mouthing obscenities at him, and even Max, despite her distress, looked astounded. I asked him, 'Did you manage to rescue the vegetables?'

'Oh, yes . . . Yes. No harm done.'

Another pause, then Max tried, 'How are your grandchildren, Ada?'

'They're absolutely fine, thank you, dear.'

'Lance said that Joanna hasn't been well.'

'She was a bit out of sorts, yes.' Her speech was never particularly clear, something I put down to a certain degree of looseness of the dentures, so that her teeth seemed to have something of a lag about them. Now that she was becoming noticeably sozzled, this lack of synchronization was becoming more pronounced, giving me an eerie feeling as she talked, as if a spirit were talking through her mouth. It didn't help the clarity of her diction much either.

'And David?'

'He's been very badly behaved of late,' she confessed.

Dad added, 'He's been teasing his sister a lot.'

'And he was truanting last term.'

'Truanting?' I said, without thinking.

Dad looked surprised, too. 'I thought you said he'd been unwell,' he said to his beloved.

She was taken aback. 'Did I?'

'Yes, you did.'

She looked at him, then shrugged and took another swig of wine. 'He has been unwell . . . but he's also been truanting.' Dad's expression showed his confusion but he didn't press the point. In any case, Ada hadn't finished. 'He's always been a wild lad. I blame his father.'

Max and I exchanged surprised glances; this was completely out of character. All the evidence theretofore had suggested that Ada viewed her son as something of a gift to the world; if she was going to blame anyone for the lapses of her grandchildren, I would have put hefty money on Tricia the daughter-in-law being held responsible. Dad, too, seemed baffled and, accordingly, the remark earned a perplexed silence; not that Ada was listening to anything other than her own thoughts. She said without obvious awareness of the atmosphere she had created, 'I've never met him.'

More puzzlement. Max asked, 'Who?'

She said through her wine, 'David's father.'

Dad sought some elucidation. 'Isn't Mike his father?'

'Goodness gracious, no!' She either thought the concept funny or disgusting; it was tricky to tell which because of her blood alcohol level. 'Tricia was married before.'

'You never told me,' complained Dad.

'You never asked,' she replied waspishly.

'So Michael is David's stepfather?' asked Max, presumably just to make sure that she had things straight now.

'And Tricia is Joanna's stepmother.' She spoke as if she had suddenly found herself among the mentally challenged.

Dad opened his mouth, clearly of a mind to speak but something – presumably recent experience – held him back.

There was another pause in the conversation, although the sound of wine slurping over Ada's top plate ensured that there was no silence.

'And how is Mike?' I enquired. 'Fighting fit?' I couldn't stop some bitterness seeping into this question, although Ada was too far gone to notice.

'He's been working very hard. I'm quite worried about him.'

'Perhaps he's worried about losing a mother and forgetting he's going to gain a stepfather.' It suddenly occurred to me that maybe, like Ada, my tongue was becoming a little unregulated; I had had only one bottle of Toe-Curler, but maybe that was one too many and I decided not to drink any more.

Ada looked at me sharply while Dad did a bit of glaring. His beloved said in a starch-stiff voice, 'Mike's very happy about the wedding.'

Dad added quickly, 'Ada says it was just a bit of a shock to him.'

Another one of those silences ensued. Max enquired, 'Have you set the date yet?'

Dad looked at Ada, a clear sign of the way the relationship worked. She said, 'Not exactly. I was thinking next month, though.'

If she had been thinking that, it was patent that my father hadn't; no way, no how, not never. He looked as if he had just been bitten in the nether regions and, you know, perhaps he had (in a metaphorical sense). 'Were you?' he asked faintly. I could see that it was an effort to hang on to his cutlery.

We made our goodbyes at about ten thirty and I walked Max to her car; this was the first occasion I had to resume our earlier conversation. 'How are you?

She was intensely thoughtful for a moment. 'You say that Albert Stewart isn't well?'

We were holding hands and I pulled her to a stop, then looked around to make sure that there was no possibility we were going to be overheard while I broke one of the big rules, the one about medical confidence. 'Mentally, he's in a bad way. He's epileptic and insomniac, disturbed by his military experiences.'

'I see.'

'And I didn't tell you that.'

She nodded. 'No, of course not.'

We walked on. As we reached her car, I asked, 'What are you going to do?'

She paused in the act of opening her door. 'I ought to tell the police about the note.'

'Yes,' I agreed, but I hope I succeeded in conveying my doubts about doing just that.

'It won't bring back Twinkle, though, will it?'

'Nothing can do that.'

She considered some more. 'There doesn't seem much point, then.'

I admit that I was relieved. I bent down to kiss her but as we pulled apart she said softly, 'There he is again.'

She was looking over my shoulder; when I turned, there was no one there. 'There who is again?'

'Just some chap I think I saw earlier. I came out of the surgery, and as I went to my car I saw this man in the shadows across the road. I couldn't think of a good reason why he should be just standing there, so I went across to ask him what he wanted.'

I all but staggered. Max was, generally speaking, a good inducer of staggering on my part. 'Are you sure that was a good idea?'

'Why shouldn't it be?'

'What did he do?'

'He walked away before I got there.'

'And you've just seen him again?'

'Just for a moment. At least I think it was the same man.'

I had a sinking feeling in my stomach that was probably only second to that felt by Captain Smith just after his ship had been introduced to its first and last iceberg. 'What did he look like?'

Her answer did little in the cause of settling my collywobbles.

'Um . . . Fairly tall with long, straggly looking ginger hair. He was dressed in denim.'

I closed my eyes in despair. *Tristan.* I had thought it such a good idea to go and confront him, yet all I had done was draw his attention to Max. She looked at me. 'Was that Tristan?'

I stretched a smile that felt like a knife wound across my face. 'Yes.'

She understood. 'He's watching me.'

'Looks like it.'

Ever ready to look on the bright side, she suggested, 'Perhaps he's just trying to scare me. I think he's the kind of man who enjoys frightening people, from what you said.' I wasn't going to argue with that, and said nothing. She appeared to come to a decision about Tristan. 'People like that back off when they're confronted. After all, that's what he did this evening.'

'Max, this isn't the playground. Tristan Charlton isn't a school bully and we're not in *Tom Brown's School Days.* Tristan's just your average, run-of-the-mill paranoid schizo-phrenic, with an obsession about his dead sister, and an unpleasant habit of parking his not inconsiderable intellect whilst he uses his not inconsiderable muscles. He won't respond to you standing up to him because it's not that he's trying to scare you; he's just plotting how to hurt you.'

She was about to argue, but, having taken a long breath to calm myself, I said, 'I think you should come back to my house. It's not safe for you to be on your own.'

'Don't be silly . . .'

'Max, Tristan Charlton is quite literally certifiable, and he's got a track record of hurting my girlfriends. Just do as you're told, for once.'

'But we've got two cars.'

'That's easily dealt with. We'll drive in your car to your place, pick up some clothes, then come back here and go in convoy to my house.'

'There's no need for all that. I'll pop home on my own . . .'

'No! No way.'

I think I got through to her and she reluctantly agreed. I got in the passenger seat of her car and we pulled away from the kerb. 'And if you should see him again, please don't approach him. Get to a phone and call me.' A thought occurred. 'Or Sergeant Abelson.'

'Why should I call her?'

'She said that she'd do her best to deal with Tristan.'

Max looked less than impressed with this reassurance.

THIRTY

I have two partners in the practice – Brian Goodell and Jack Thorpe, two people of such different character that I have often wondered how much DNA they have in common. Brian is quiet and easy-going, and so relaxed I often speculate about how he manages to sit upright, let alone do number twos; Jack is combative and sparky, ever ready to see the worst in everyone. They represent extreme archetypes of the way doctors evolve during the course of their careers and, to be objective and brutal about it, neither of them is perfect for the patients, but who am I to judge?

It was our custom after morning surgery to sit and gather our thoughts in the small back room on the first floor of the surgery that serves as our staff room, enjoying coffee and biscuits (if we were lucky, creams; if we were very lucky, chocolate creams) and relaxing. This was not just a time and a place to relax, it was also a time to confer – albeit in a very informal way – about our patients, to make sure that we were each up to speed about their latest problems and successes, so that we would reduce the risk of being taken by surprise when we were on call. It was not a perfect system – especially now that we shared our on-call with another practice whose patients were as strangers to us – but in those days of less structured health-care, it was a fairly good system. Often, Jane would join us, something that cheered us all up, even Brian who seemed to be incapable of anything other than gloom, and Jack who was terminally caustic and disparaging.

'How's your bit of totty, Lance?'

It was Jack's idea of a witticism to refer to Max – actually, to refer to any of my girlfriends – in this way. He seemed to want to create the impression that I was some sort of 'love machine'. Jane, reading the *Nursing Times*, looked up at that. 'Dr Thorpe . . .' she offered in a lightly scolding manner.

Brian chuckled to himself. Brian was close to retirement, but then he had been close to retirement for all the time I had known him. I said, 'Max's fine thanks, Jack.'

In all the many years that I had known Brian, I had never known him to eat *all* of a biscuit; usually he got ninety-eight per cent of one, but there was always some of it that went AWOL, generally on his waistcoat, although a small and clearly ill-coordinated rump was often left clinging to the sheer precipice below his lower lip. Today was no exception; he was partially encrusted in custard cream as he opined, 'Nice girl that, Lance. You should hang on to her.'

Jack, who despite being a very acute and caring clinician inhabited the same world as Kenneth Williams, snorted into his powdered Maxwell House, earning himself a look of reproof from our nurse come carer. A police siren sailed past the opened sash window as Jack said, 'I bumped into your pathologist friend yesterday at the hospital – Mark Bentham.'

'Did you? I'm not surprised, he's having to spend a lot of time around here at present.'

'He was quite chatty. He was telling me about your reputation amongst the police.'

'What reputation?'

Jack winked at Brian. 'The "Elliot curse". "All those who enter here beware, for this is the land of the Elliots, and you may well not survive".' He was within an inch of splitting his sides, so hilarious did he consider this.

'Ha-bloody-ha.'

A phone began to ring downstairs, probably in the receptionists' area. It rang three times before it was picked up. Jack said, 'He asked me to tell you that Jeremy Gillman was drowned, although he had been half strangled first.'

Brian winced. I had often noticed a touch of squeamishness in Brian, which struck me as odd in a man who claimed to have had a promising career in ophthalmic surgery before it had been foreshortened by tuberculosis, now thankfully vanquished. The intercom sounded. Jane, because she was nearest and not because it was her job as a woman, answered it. 'Yes?'

Our intercom system was not of the highest quality; it was made of the type of plastic that I remember my Christmas-stocking toys being made of, and the various components had suffered a variety of intermittent assaults over the years, so that often the buttons refused to work and the sound quality suggested that you were talking to someone with tentacles for vocal cords that lived on the far side of Neptune. However, we were used to its foibles and we were able to penetrate the distorted, unceasing white noise to discern that Sheila was talking and that the London Road surgery was on the phone. Brian rose from his comfy chair to go downstairs to take the call. We had been expecting a call since one of their four doctors had been on call last night and this would be to update us on any of our patients with significant problems.

Brian returned a few moments later.

'Well?' demanded Jack. 'Anything we should know about?'

'Mrs Wilson died.' Ethel Wilson had been close to succumbing to her womb cancer for close to six months now, so that this came as no surprise, although no less sad for that. 'A case of appendicitis in Queenswood Avenue, and an over-dose in Ross Road.'

'Was it successful?' I asked, not out of prurience but because it had practical implications.

He shook his head as he reached across to snaffle another biscuit from the tin. 'He swallowed half a bottle of paracetamol some time in the night. His wife found him first thing this morning. He's in Mayday now. He's apparently in a bad way.'

'Who was it?'

'Arthur Silsby.' He paused, a Rich Tea held halfway to his mouth, and I could sense that it was in an agony of indecision about its fate. 'I wouldn't have thought he was the type to do something like that.'

Sergeant Abelson lived in a pleasant semi-detached, pre-war house in Croham Road, not far from South Croydon Station. It took her a moment to respond to the doorbell and when she did, she looked flustered. 'Come in,' she said, and immediately turned away. I did as I was bade and was immediately assailed in the olfactory sense, by something unexpected; the smell of a baby. I had come to know this particular perfume well since, although having no children of my own, I had attended at (indeed, assisted at) the entry of numerous small citizens into this vale of tears; I had also done a six-month paediatric attachment at Queen Mary's Carshalton, probably the most heart-rending and depressing half-year of my life. I made my way through the dark hallway past a bicycle propped up against a radiator, into the small kitchen whither she had gone. She was at an ancient electric stove prodding with large wooden tongs at the contents of a huge cast-iron stewing pan, one with two handles. She was dressed in black slacks with the then-fashionable but surely totally impractical bell-bottoms; her T-shirt was a bright and multi-coloured tie-dyed thing.

I stood just inside the door as I said, 'I'm sorry to bother you at home, Sergeant.' I had tried to contact her throughout the day to discuss what Max had told me about Tristan, but without success until she had rung back only an hour before to suggest I come to here to talk about it.

She stopped her prodding and looked at me with a welcoming smile. 'Don't be daft. Police officers are always on duty. I learned that the first day out of training college.' Another prod, this one slightly more violent. 'And, please, call me Jean.'

I bowed and nodded once my acquiescence. 'You look busy.'

'Oh. I'm not too bad. I'm alone in the house for once, which has given me a breathing space to do this.' She indicated the pan. I realized then that this was not her supper but a nappy wash. To realize that not only was she not single, but that she had a child as well, left me with a feeling that I couldn't analyse properly. She was an attractive woman, with a charming personality and, patently, a good intelligence; of course she had a husband and a baby. She wore no wedding band on her thin fingers, but that was quite probably for professional reasons; anyway, it was entirely possible that she wasn't formally married. Although at that time such an arrangement was still novel and yet to become almost the norm, we were passing out of a post-war society that automatically condemned such an arrangement (except when it had been done discreetly by the upper classes). 'Coffee?'

'Please.'

'Milk? Sugar?'

'Just milk.'

She made me sit in the back room on a tatty blue sofa whence I could see through French windows that the garden was long and thin and parched; it was untended and bore in its basic wildness and air of abandonment an astonishing resemblance to mine. With me in the room were a wooden high chair and a variety of baby-type toys. On a folded-away dining table was a wicker washing basket in which there was a tottering pile of unironed but clean Terylene nappies; next to it was a collapsed ironing board that leaned against the wall. She brought in two mugs of instant coffee and set one down on the dining table next to me; the other she held in her hands as she sat in the only other comfy chair in the room; it was upholstered in red velour material and was clearly genetically unrelated to the sofa. 'Sorry about the mess. These murders are playing havoc with my domestic schedule and I've barely got time to do the essentials, let alone things like tidying.'

'How old is your baby?'

'He'll be eight months tomorrow.'

'Where is he now?'

There was a clock on the wall that proclaimed more or less truthfully that it was seven-twenty. She glanced at it and then said, 'With his father. I managed to persuade him to pick him up from my mother's and look after him for a while.'

The pause that followed was awkward and I own that it was my fault. I didn't want to appear nosy, but her answer – as well as her manner of answering – suggested that matters were not as I had at first thought. She looked at me with a neutral expression, perhaps waiting. When I didn't say anything, she resuscitated the conversation by explaining, 'I thought his father was serious about the relationship but, as is often the way in my ethnic group, he has other imperatives. Afro-Caribbean men tend to have a more relaxed attitude to commitment.'

'Oh . . .' I thought about this and fought to overcome my discomfort at such candidness. 'So, you're bringing him up on his own? That must be hard, especially doing the job you're doing.'

'It's harder being black and doing the job I'm doing,' she said flatly.

'Yes,' I hastened to agree. 'I'm sure it must be . . .'

She took a sip of coffee. 'My mother does most of the care for me; she's only too happy to, thank God. Otherwise, it's friends and neighbours and anyone who's stupid enough to volunteer.'

This whole conversation made me acutely aware that the last thing she needed was someone bringing work into her home life. 'I shouldn't have bothered you, Sergeant. I'm sorry—'

'Jean, remember?' she interrupted. 'And yes, you should have bothered me. I'm only sorry that I haven't been able to do more about your problem; it's not that I don't want to, it's just that the heat is really on us at the moment. The Inspector is under a great deal of pressure to stop the killings.'

'Has he made any progress?'

She smiled sadly. 'He thinks he has.'

'But you disagree?'

'Who cares what I think? I'm the token ethnic officer, only here so that the service looks good in the eyes of the black community.'

'Whoa,' I protested. 'I'm on your side.'

She looked at me over her coffee mug; her hands were clasped around it and I appreciated how long her fingers were. 'Are you?' she enquired. It wasn't a particularly suspicious tone she used, more of a wary one, if you see what I mean.

'Why wouldn't I be?'

She gestured with her head around her. 'Because all this has come as a surprise to you, I think.'

'Yes, I suppose it has,' I admitted.

'An unmarried black mother. I bet there are all sorts of things going through your head now, all sorts of assumptions being rewritten.'

'You're being unfair.' A defiant, slightly dismissive shrug met this; this said that it didn't matter to her what I was thinking. I wanted to tell her that I was telling the truth, that my parents, and later my father alone, had instilled into me

the overriding importance of never judging without knowing
as many of the data as were accessible. I wanted to, but I
suspected that – as is true so often in life and as is so hard to
enact – less was better. 'What does the Inspector think is going
on, then?'

'He latched on to your sighting of Albert Stewart arguing
with Gillman. We did a bit of digging and discovered that
Albert Stewart is a very troubled individual. Two tours of
Ulster have left him pretty mixed up. He served with some
distinction in the Parachute Regiment as a sergeant, but then
there was an incident in which a Roman Catholic civilian was
shot and killed; a court of enquiry found him responsible as
the patrol leader, although he didn't fire the shot. He was given
a dishonourable discharge.'

'A bit harsh.'

'Someone always has to carry the can. Presumably there
were no blacks to blame.' I didn't say anything, which was
probably the best thing I could have done, for she apologized
almost immediately. 'I'm sorry. That was unfair of me.'

Manfully and diplomatically continuing my silence on her
feelings of prejudice, I asked, 'Why would he go about slaugh-
tering the teaching staff of Bensham Manor?'

'He was born in Talbot Road, not far from Crystal Palace
football stadium; from nineteen fifty-seven until nineteen
sixty-two he was a pupil at the school. He was a wild boy,
too. They had a lot of trouble with him; in fact the police
had a lot of trouble with him. He was in juvenile court seven
times for vandalism and antisocial behaviour. I understand
the magistrates eventually gave him the ultimatum of joining
the army or going to borstal.'

Although I hadn't known the details, she wasn't surprising
me. 'Has Stewart been arrested?'

She nodded. 'We're sweating him, but he hasn't said
anything yet. Certainly, he hasn't confessed.' It was with something of a lost smile that she added, 'Stewart's seen and done
a lot in his life; I don't think there's going to be much that
we can do to scare him, anyway.'

'Do I get the impression you're not altogether convinced of
his guilt?'

She snorted softly and drained her coffee. 'I've been doing this job just long enough not to be surprised and not to be disappointed.'

'You do know what's happened to Arthur Silsby?' I asked.

'No,' she said, her voice low and questioning, as if she were about to hear something she wouldn't like, but it was with increasing interest that she listened to my account of his suicide attempt. 'He's all right, though?' she asked. 'He'll pull through?'

I could not be totally reassuring. 'If you want to take pills as a cry for help, paracetamol isn't the drug of choice. It produces immediate effects that, depending on dose, may or may not kill you, depending on the quality of emergency care you get; if you recover, within a short while, you'll be all hunky-dory again, happy as Lawrence because you got some attention and maybe feeling slightly silly. Trouble is, paracetamol has rather longer-term effects on your liver, which tend to kick in after another few days or so; unless you're treated in time, the liver cells literally die in large numbers.'

'Has he been treated in time?'

I had talked that day with the consultant looking after him; in his opinion, it was still in the balance. 'Too early to say,' I said.

She put her coffee mug down on the carpet next to her, frowning, and asked herself, 'What does this mean? Is it connected? If so, how?'

The doorbell sounded, breaking her out of her consternation. She got up and went to answer it, closing the door to the room so that I couldn't hear what was going on. There was a wait of some minutes during which I occupied the time by leaning back with my eyes closed. Something was nagging at me.

She came back in with a bundle of blankets in her arms. 'Sorry to leave you so long. That was Michael's father bringing him back.'

'May I see?'

She came over and crouched down beside me. Michael was asleep; Michael was beautiful, and I have a tendency to look on babies and children as nothing but a source of trouble and pain, especially for doctors. I said as much. 'Thank you.' She looked at him, then whispered, 'I think so.'

Even I could tell that it was time for my departure. 'I'd better go.'

She first of all put Michael in his cot in the nursery upstairs, then re-joined me in the hallway. I had one more thing to raise; I told her what Max had said about Albert Stewart's confession regarding Twinkle.

'But you said it was Tristan Charlton.'

'I thought it was.'

'Is she going to press charges?'

'I don't think that would be in anyone's best interests. Max agrees.'

She didn't look impressed. 'So it was pointless for me to go to Springfield Hospital.'

'Sorry.' She didn't say anything more, but then she didn't need to. For just a brief moment I thought I was really in trouble and that she would arrest me for wasting police time. I hastened to add, 'But I think I might have woken the sleeping dragon.'

Her face as I went on to tell her about Max's encounter with Tristan said it all; by the end of it, her eyes were closed and her face was raised to the heavens. 'Sorry,' I mumbled.

'We can't do anything more as it stands,' she sighed. 'Unless he actually touches her, threatens her or is persistent in his attention, he is beyond my reach.'

'I know,' I said, because I did. It wasn't what I wanted to hear, though.

She showed me out. On the step I tried one last time. 'Whatever you can do, Jean. Please.'

She smiled and agreed to do what she could. We both knew it was precious little.

I didn't tell Max that I had been to see Jean Abelson; I didn't like deceiving Max but then, I knew that if I told her, she'd be incandescent. On my way back to a dinner that Max was cooking, I wondered idly why she had taken against the police sergeant, but to no avail; it was just a personality thing, I supposed. Over pork chops, boiled potatoes and carrots, I brought Max up to speed regarding the murders, deciding not to go into details how I knew; Max assumed that it was Masson who had been my informant, and I did not disabuse her. To my surprise, she agreed with Masson's thinking. 'Anyone who could do that to a poor, innocent rabbit is clearly mad and capable of anything.'

I knew I would be on dodgy ground if I argued; even suggesting that homicide and lepicide weren't exactly equivalent would, I strongly suspected, be interpreted as heterodoxy of a dangerous, subversive kind. 'Be that as it may,' I replied cautiously, 'I still don't see that he's got a motive for killing Marlene Jeffries. She was too young to have taught him.'

'But she was living with Yvette Mangon; that's the connection.'

'If his interest is to kill teachers against whom he has a grudge, then killing Marlene Jeffries, just because her social arrangements brought her into contact with one of them, doesn't make sense.'

'Perhaps he doesn't like lesbians either.'

'That would give him a second, entirely different motive.' Max saw nothing wrong with that. I pointed out, 'And Marlene was the first to die. That's a bit odd, isn't it?'

I think she might have seen some sense in what I was saying, but Max could only see that Albert Stewart was a self-confessed rabbit-killer and therefore, by definition, beyond the Pale. 'I expect there's a good reason why he killed them in that order. You wait and see.'

I didn't say any more but as we sat and watched Gordon Honeycombe reading the *News at Ten*, his bald pate adding an air of authority to what was happening in the world, I tried to chase down what had begun to nag me when I was sitting in Jean Abelson's house. I fell asleep on Max's shoulder, and she had to wake me by gently shaking me at just before eleven. We went to bed and I was no nearer to catching and dissecting what was bothering me . . .

In the middle of the night, though, I was suddenly awake. There it was, in my mind, the reason for my psychic discomfort. It wasn't much, though. Probably nothing. Certainly not worth making a fuss about it; not until I had had a chance to cogitate a bit. I turned over and closed my eyes, thinking about it. It was obvious, I decided.

THIRTY-ONE

Perhaps you can imagine my delight to arrive at the surgery next morning to discover that in the small 'doctors only' car park in front was an interloping vehicle, and that in that interloping vehicle was one small, choleric inspector of Her Majesty's Constabulary. He was accompanied by Sergeant Abelson, but she had on her official face which, although not in any way unpleasant to feast upon, was distinctly unresponsive in that way that I have often found with those who, even metaphorically, wear the Queen's blue uniform. As soon as I got out of the car, I was accosted, as I knew I would be. He had been smoking and the faint tendrils of blue-grey smoke that drifted around him as he emerged into the foetid early morning air gave him faintly the image of a malevolent daemon summoned into the corporeal realm without his permission.

'Can I have a word, Doctor?'

If ever there was a needless question, that was it. I carried on walking and said as I passed, 'I haven't got long before morning surgery.'

He followed, taking my reply as consent to his question; it occurred to me that this small exchange had succinctly encapsulated our relationship; I was ahead of Masson when we went into my room, but in every other way – spiritually, legally and psychologically – it was Masson who was the leader. I sat behind my desk and he sat in the patient's chair, Sergeant Abelson on the only other one in the room, the one that is meant for mothers when they bring in little Johnny after he's spent the night projectile-vomiting. 'What do you want?'

'Arthur Silsby is a patient of this practice.'

He had me there, bang to rights. Since this was not obviously uttered in an interrogative manner, I didn't respond. He said after a short pause, 'I'm given to understand that he's attempted suicide.'

'He's in hospital being treated for an overdose of paracetamol, yes.'

I was treated to an owlish stare. 'Why do you put it like
that? Do you know something we don't?' His voice was so
suspicious I felt that he was ready to slap the handcuffs on.

'No. I just prefer to not to make premature assumptions.
That's all.'

He was doing the thing that he always did when he was
barred from playing a game of 'dare' with the lung-cancer
fairy, which was to fiddle with something in his jacket pocket;
presumably his cigarette packet or lighter. His shirt-collar
button was undone and his tie at half mast; somehow, Jean
Abelson was remaining apparently unaffected by the already
rising environmental temperature. He said, 'We've checked
with his wife. She was in the house all the night and heard
nothing. They sleep in separate rooms, so she had no idea
until the morning that he had done anything like it. The house
is secure and they had no visitors. He did it himself, all right.'

'But that doesn't necessarily make it suicide.'

'The doctors looking after him tell me that, to judge from
the blood levels reached, he took at least forty tablets. Difficult
to see that as an accident.'

'Maybe para-suicide?'

'Which is what?'

'A cry for help; an attempt at taking one's life that is meant
to draw some attention to the individual rather than result in
death.'

'If that was his plan, he's in for a shock. The quacks didn't
get to him in time to save his liver; they say he's going to die
a rather unpleasant death in about a week.'

I ignored the derogatory nomenclature for my usually so
well-regarded profession. 'Is he conscious?'

'Yes.' He sounded bitter. He added, 'And he's saying nothing
of any use, other than that he's ashamed of showing such
weakness. Apparently, it's not something that a proper man
should do.'

That sounded like Arthur Silsby, all right. I asked, 'So?'

'His wife says that that's typical of the man. Would you
agree with that assessment?'

'Absolutely. Arthur Silsby is the archetype of morality, decency and any old-fashioned Christian value you'd care to mention. He would see suicide as a mortal sin, and not the kind of thing a man of honour should do.'

He squinted at me, one hand fiddling in his jacket pocket while his teeth seemed to do a bit of grinding. There was a bit of heavy breathing – as if he were working himself up to tossing the caber or a bit of 'clean and jerk' in the gymnasium – then he asked in a voice that suggested much restraint of passion and little hope, 'I'm not going to ask you to betray medical confidences because I know I'd be wasting my breath, but do you have any reason to believe that he is in any way involved in this business?'

I could never resist baiting Inspector Masson and I pondered the possibility of what deeply seated psychological urge drove me to poke this feral law-enforcement officer so relentlessly as I replied, 'Please, Inspector, you know I couldn't possibly give away any confidential information, even if it's to aid the police in a murder enquiry . . .'

He exploded and turned to his sergeant at the same time. 'You see! I told you this would be a waste of time.'

Which changed things. Had I known that it was Jean Abelson's idea to talk to me, I might have been a little less aggravating. I raised my voice through his bluster and continued, '*However*, I don't wish to appear deliberately unhelpful.' And that made him turn back to me.

'What does that mean?' he enquired, his voice subsonic with suspicion.

'I see no reason why I shouldn't tell you the negatives. Arthur Silsby has not been to see us for over a year. That visit was, I can assure you, for a reason that can possibly have no bearing on this case. He has since made no contact with the surgery.'

He digested this, although to judge from his expression, it was more an act of indigestion. Eventually he shook his head, 'Why on earth has he done it, then?' he asked. 'He must know something, Doctor.'

'Have you got any solid evidence for that assertion?'

It was Jean Abelson who replied, however. She looked up from the notebook in which she had been scribing and said, 'His wife tells us that he's been under a lot of strain these last few days. Acting very strangely and refusing to tell her what's wrong.'

'That doesn't surprise me. His school – and believe me, he thinks of it as most definitely *his* school – has been beset by scandal and murder. I should think that to someone like Mr Silsby, that's about as bad as it gets. Losing three of his teachers in such circumstances would be bad enough, but finding out that two of them were lesbians was probably overwhelming for him.'

He considered this but he had already made up his mind. 'No, he's hiding something.'

I knew that there would be no budging him, so I changed the subject to what had been bothering me, what had awoken me in the night. 'Have you considered the possibility that there might be more than one killer?'

His head jerked up and for once his expression was neutral. 'Go on,' he invited in a voice full to overbrimming with curiosity.

'The first two murders – those of Miss Jeffries and Miss Mangon – were frenzied. They had the mark of a murderer who hated them.'

Masson asked curiously, 'Don't most murderers hate their victims?' This took me aback somewhat.

'I think you know what I mean.' He acknowledged this with a curt nod and a faint smile; Inspector Masson's smile was a fragile and rare thing and I was reminded of those jungle plants that flower only once every century. I continued, 'Whoever it was who killed them didn't just want them dead, he wanted them completely obliterated.'

'You have a way with words, Doctor.'

I was emboldened to continue. 'The murder of Jeremy Gillman was different, though. No blood, and not even much of a display of anger. Almost an afterthought, you might say.'

He was listening to all appearances quite intently; so was Jean. He opined, 'So, two MOs, therefore two killers.'

'Yes.'

'Someone searched both houses,' he said thoughtfully; actually, I was rather pleased to think that he said it as if he was looking at things anew.

'Yes,' I conceded. 'But quite conceivably Jeremy Gillman's

killer was an opportunist thief who saw him out walking the
dog, killed him, then burgled his house.' He seemed quite
taken with this idea, so I sallied forth. (Did I think that this
detecting lark was easy? You bet I did.) 'Was anything taken?'

He took a long breath in, a long one out, then stood up.
'Thank you for that, Doctor.'

He was out of the room before I could react, leaving me
looking at Jean. 'What's going on?'

She smiled tiredly. 'I think there are times when you underestimate my boss, Lance.' She stood up and followed Masson
out of my surgery. At the doorway she turned and said,
'Gillman left his house locked, as he always did. He had five
hundred pounds in one of the drawers of his kitchen dresser
– he was something of a horse-racing man, apparently – the
drawer had been left carelessly open and it was obvious to
anyone in the room that the money was there, but it wasn't
taken. OK?'

It was to an empty room that I said after a while, 'Oh . . .'

THIRTY-TWO

They had put Arthur Silsby in a side room not because
of his social status, but because they knew he was going
to die; it afforded him some privacy, and it also saved
everyone else from the agony of being reminded a hundred
times a day of his doom. I had a spare hour before my first
afternoon visit and I popped into Mayday Hospital to see him,
partly because he was a long-standing patient of the practice,
partly because I was very intrigued as to why he had done
something so out of character. I could not bring myself to
believe Masson's theory that he knew something about the
recent killings, but I could not conceive of what his motive
had been.

It wasn't yet visiting hours, but that was not a problem both
because of his fate and because of who I was. Having checked
in with the sister in charge for the sake of politeness, I made

my way to his room. I knocked gently but received no answer; looking through the square window in the door, I could see that he was asleep, so I quietly went in and stood at the end of the bed. He had a dextrose-saline drip feeding a Venflon in his left elbow and he was attached to a heart monitor that did its annoying beeping thing in the background. He didn't look well; not well at all; was there already a hint of jaundice, I wondered? As usual with me, having got there, I didn't know what to do; I thought about waking him, then thought perhaps it would be best just to let him sleep a while, so sank quietly into one of those over-padded, high-backed chairs that are only found in NHS institutions.

My excuse is that it was warm and I wasn't used to sitting down in the middle of the day; had I kept on the go I know that I wouldn't have fallen asleep, but this was not to be. Even in one of the most diabolical items of furniture that mankind has ever devised, my eyes closed and my hold on consciousness relaxed. Doubtless the intrusive yet curiously mesmeric beep of the monitor contributed; doubtless, too, the airlessness of the room played its part.

After a period of uncertain length, I came back from my light, dreamless sleep without obvious or abrupt transition; I opened my eyes and looked directly at Mr Silsby's. He seemed to be perfectly vigilant as his head lay on the pillow; in his eyes I saw what seemed to be awareness. We stared at each other for a moment that stretched into several bleeps of the medical machine to which he was attached; for myself, I was somewhat groggy, yet he seemed to be at once alert, even as he was inert.

He said then, and this quite succinctly, 'It is so good of you to come.'

At something of a loss, both because I was still slightly befuddled with sleep and because he spoke in an oddly affectionate tone, I said with some uncertainty, 'It's the least I could do.'

He nodded slightly, his head not rising from the pillow. 'I am so sorry, son.'

Which caught me slightly by surprise; he had been a regular although not frequent visitor to my work premises, and through all those years we had hardly got to know one another, except in a purely professional, detached kind of way, so that we had never until that moment got beyond the polite formalities. Certainly we had never reached the point of using forenames, let alone vernacular terms like that one.

'Are you?' I enquired pusillanimously.

'I taught you differently from this.'

I twigged. Arthur Silsby had had a son, an only child, who had been killed in the Korean War. I can only imagine how horrible that must have been for the Silsbys to experience, but neither of them had ever done any more than mention it in a purely informative, matter-of-fact way. They were, indeed, a stoical couple. 'Mr Silsby?' I said tentatively, hoping to disabuse him of his delusion.

It still seemed that he was looking directly at me, and doing so with perfect lucidity, although clearly he was seeing something else. 'I should have stamped it out . . .'

'Mr Silsby,' I repeated.

'I couldn't believe it, you see . . .' I began again to shake him from his delusion, then stopped, suddenly aware of what he had been saying. He shook his head and frowned before repeating the judgement. 'Absolutely disgusting . . .'

'What is?'

Unfortunately he was in transmission-only mode, with no incoming messages being processed. 'I've let you down, and I've let your mother down.'

'How?'

'They denied it, you see, and I was so shocked that it could be going on in my school, I chose to believe them. I was a fool.'

I leaned forward in the chair to be close to him, fairly sure that he would not suddenly see me for who I really was. 'Are you talking about Yvette Mangon and Marlene Jeffries?'

'Disgusting behaviour . . .'

'Lesbianism? Is that what you're talking about?'

'And then that snake came to see me. How did he find out? He wouldn't tell me. He just told me that unless I made him my deputy, he was going to go to the press and tell them that I had condoned it. He wouldn't listen. What could I do, son?'

'Who was the snake, Mr Silsby? Was it Gillman?'

'There was nothing else I could do. I had no other way out.'

A thought occurred to me. 'Did you kill Gillman?' I asked this urgently, my mind running through possibilities. Why was he muttering about how shocking the behaviour of two lesbians had been, if he had killed Gillman? Was it because he thought murder was OK? In any case, I didn't get a direct answer. In fact, I got no more from him; he closed his eyes and after a minute or two, I realized that he was silently crying.

THIRTY-THREE

I had kept in contact with Max as much as I could during the day; thankfully, she reported no further sightings of Tristan but I knew better than to relax too soon. She had another late surgery so, after a relatively lightly attended evening surgery of my own, I went over to Bensham Manor School; I knew that Dad would be there, because he had got his car fixed more quickly than he expected, and rather fancied he might want to chat about things. He was giving the weeds hell, pulling them out of the ground with vicious determination and hurling them into a wheelbarrow. He was so involved with this that he wasn't aware of my presence until I greeted him from only two yards' distance. He looked up, startled. 'Oh,' he said. 'Hello, son.'

Not a good sign, that. He hadn't used that epithet for years, and it had in the past heralded bad news. He would tell me in his own time, I knew, although I thought I could guess something of the problem. He carried on weeding for a while until I asked, 'How long will you be?'

Without stopping or even looking up he said, 'About fifteen minutes. I just want to get the lettuces clear. It's amazing how much better they do when you thin the weeds.'

'I'll go for a stroll,' I said and he didn't reply.

The gymnasium was probably only ten years old and already placed firmly in its architectural time, doomed to remain forever a sharp-angled, grey concrete mausoleum, always cold and always ugly. It was a bastard child of a school of building design that had been born in the post-war years and that had grown too fast, too quickly, becoming bloated and overbearing before the public woke up to the fact that 'modern' did not have to equate exactly with 'ugly', 'cold' and 'cheap'. It was showing its age in the way that the door and window fittings were soiled and stained, in the cracks high up under the eaves and in the rusting guttering. If ever a building were going to be improved by graffiti, this was it, and graffiti had failed; it still looked like defacement, even if it was defacing something that should never have existed. It was still an outrage to my eye, something that had no intrinsic value – be it as an 'art' or a means of 'expression' – and that could have no justification. I could imagine that to a man such as Arthur Silsby, such graffiti would have been a pain almost too much to bear, that he would have waged war on it with extreme vigour, and indeed, there was evidence to suggest this, for it was obvious that the daubing and writing had been in the past expunged, producing a general background of smeared colour. This had been to no lasting effect; the graffiti-mongers had returned. Here, on the back wall of the gym, it was isolated from the rest of the school, and in the dark it would have been the perfect place to begin again whatever nefarious scrawling might come to mind.

If one had to grade graffiti, I suppose one would say that in amongst the chaos there was a small subset of well-executed designs, often abstract; most of it, though, just consisted of cartoons either of human faces or human pudenda, done in a crude, talentless style. Where there was writing, it was what you would expect; mostly insults, a lot of obscenities, and a fair number of messages telling the world about who loved whom. At the back of my mind there formed the question of whether anyone had chosen to hint at the liaison between Yvette Mangon and Marlene Jeffries. I scanned the wall, finding nothing and wondering how Arthur Silsby had found out about it; perhaps it had been fairly common knowledge and he had been bound to discover it sooner or later. To judge from the wall, there was an awful lot of speculation about a

variety of liaisons in the area. I counted over fifty announce-
ments of love, almost as if this were a public display board
where matches (but not, as far as I could see, hatches and
dispatches) could be announced; over the years, there must
have been hundreds, I guessed; they would probably have been
erased every few months at Mr Silsby's order, only to provide
a tabula rasa for yet more messages. It seemed as if every
possible combination of names and initials was there.

As I thought this, I saw 'YM', partially hidden by a down-
pipe. It was perfectly possible, of course, that there was another
teacher or pupil with those initials, but it evoked in me that
damnable mistress that is curiosity; I looked more closely. It
was not in the most recent application of paint and had been
treated grievously by Mr Silsby's cleaning brigade (of which
presumably George Cotterill had been chief among their
number), so that it was smeared and faint and, as I say, partially
obscured, both by the pipe and by subsequent additions to
what appeared to be a communal archive of sorts, but once
seen it was quite easy to make out and to read the rest of it.
YM loves MJ. It was followed by the exclamation, *YUKKKKK!!!!*
Clearly the author of this datum did not approve. There it was
then; almost certainly, Mr Silsby had seen that, ordered it
removed probably, and at the same time it had caused him to
question them concerning the veracity of what was written on
the back of the gym. It had been denied and he, ever the
gentleman, had accepted their word. The subsequent discovery
of their house and home life – surely to such a man, grotesque
and unforgiveable – had been a hard blow, but Jeremy
Gillman's overtures had been the final straw. He saw himself
as having failed and having been tainted with something he
considered, no doubt, disgusting. He had taken an overdose.

That part of the mystery suddenly made sense to me. It
didn't throw light on who had killed the three teachers, but it
explained Mr Silsby's ramblings and it suggested to me a
strong motive for his actions. I returned to Dad, who had
finished the weeding and was sitting on a campstool just outside
the shed, drinking from a Thermos flask. He had poured something into two tin mugs, one of which he held out to me as I
approached. Not wishing to sound ungrateful, but aware that

sometimes my father mixed strange combinations for his liquid refreshment, I asked, 'What is it?' It looked like lemon squash, but you could never tell.

'Lemon squash,' was the reply. 'I put some ice in it to keep it nice and cold.' I raised it to my lips and took a swallow of the cooling draught, then caught my breath as strong alcoholic vapour went straight up my nose. 'I put a splash of vodka in the ice cubes,' he added, looking at me curiously, as if my reaction was most odd.

I put the cup down and, whilst clearing my throat, I thanked him for it most heartily.

Dad wasn't really listening, though. He said ruminatively, 'After you'd gone the other night, Mike came and picked Ada up.'

'Oh, yes?'

He made the kind of face that people make when they are completely foxed about something, and think it's jolly unfair. 'Whilst she was in the loo, we had a chat in the kitchen.'

'What kind of chat?' I asked nervously. He didn't look as though he had been the victim of GBH, but who knew what wounds lay under his outer garments?

His lips were pursed and remained so for some time. Then, 'I think Ada's been putting a bit of a gloss on his attitude to our communion.'

'He's not happy?' I suggested, thinking about the tête-à-tête I had enjoyed not long before with Ada's one and only. I didn't put my hand to my jaw but I was perfectly aware of it nonetheless.

'He's very protective of his mother . . .' *Tell me about it*, was my thought, although I kept shtum. 'Which is, of course, a good thing.' I must admit that I wondered if he was entirely sincere as he said this.

'Dad . . .'

'Yes?'

It was difficult to know how to phrase the question, but I reckoned it had to be asked. 'He didn't *threaten* you, did he?'

A lot of consideration went into his reply; that and a good swig of doctored lemon squash. 'He *warned* me,' he decided judiciously and charitably. 'As he put it himself when he was waving his finger in my face, he thought it necessary to make his views on the subject of my relationship with his mother quite plain and beyond dispute.'

I sighed. 'I'm sorry, Dad . . .' And I was; I should have warned him when Mike Clarke had taken a pop at me that he was a little bit on the angry side, but I hadn't wanted to spoil his friendship with Ada.

'He's extraordinarily jealous, you know, Lance. I should have realized that a few months ago when she told me that he discovered that Joanna was seeing a boy, one of her class-mates. I don't think it was anything too serious from what Ada says, but Mike apparently took exception to it.'

'What did he do?'

'He went berserk – not at Joanna, but at the boy when he came to pick her up to go to the cinema.' It didn't sound too bad. At least no violence had been perpetrated, I thought, but Dad had yet to finish. 'A couple of days later, the boy was set upon after dark. Quite badly beaten – ended up in Mayday with a broken nose and cracked ribs. No one knows who did it.'

The last sentence was one of those that I think can only exist in English – what are they called? – when the meaning is the exact opposite of the words. This news caused me to swig some more lemon squash, despite my earlier resolution not to touch any more. Dad said. 'Michael told me in quite strong and fruity language that he would never see his family hurt, and that he didn't look kindly on my intrusion.'

'Ouch,' I winced.

He looked at me. 'Yes, it wasn't very pleasant.'

'You should have told me straightaway.'

'Thanks, but he didn't hurt me or anything; I was just taken a bit by surprise. I'd known he was difficult but, as I told you, Ada felt sure she could bring him round. Now, I'm not so sure.'

'No,' I concurred. 'That does seem to be the case.'

He sighed but remained for a few moments silent. Some sparrows bathed themselves in dust among the beetroots. After a while he said in an almost pained voice, 'Was it me, or was Ada slightly "over the top" the other night?'

I held my breath; my father was always asking me questions like that, ones that required a lot of thought before I could answer them in a suitably anodyne manner; and even then I felt in constant danger of upsetting him. I replied after a pause, 'A bit.'

He nodded, took another sip.

Some starlings descended on the grass by the running track.

Turning to me, he said incredulously, 'Do you know, she told me that I should get a new car? She said that it was noisy and uncomfortable, and too unreliable.'

'Golly.'

He snorted. 'Exactly. The woman's clearly off her head. A damn close-run thing, I think.'

Half an hour later, and on the outside of rather more lemon squash than was entirely good for my driving skills, I left him because I was starting to get itchy feet to be back with Max. I passed the spot where the graffiti message about the 'YM' and 'MJ' had been written and then partially expunged. My eyes were automatically drawn to it, then they flicked down beneath it, as if not under my control. Another, partially erased message was some feet below it and slightly to the right. It was largely overwritten and very difficult to make out, but once seen quite clear.

MJ loves JG.

THIRTY-FOUR

'I don't really see the relevance of this, and I'm pretty sure that the Inspector won't be very impressed, either.'

'That's why I'm telling you first.'

Jean Abelson was sitting with me in my garden. We were drinking (unadulterated) fizzy lemonade and the day was overcast, the atmosphere sullen and brooding. It was the next morning; I had booked it as a day's annual leave a couple of weeks before, intending to set to and start decorating the downstairs cloakroom, but events had intervened; mind you, events always seemed to intervene when the prospect of decorating hove into view. I had told her not only of my discovery on the gymnasium wall, but also of Arthur Silsby's confession.

She went through it again. 'This piece of graffiti . . .'

'Graffito, is the technically correct term,' I intervened. It was not appreciated.

'This *graffito* states that MJ loves JG.'

'Yes.'

'And you think that JG refers to Jeremy Gillman. That MJ and JG were having a love affair?'

'Exactly. Now that gives you a motive for Marlene Jeffries's murder, and a suspect, too.' I had been doing a lot of thinking about this and had formulated some pretty red-hot theories.

'Yvette Mangon?'

'She found out the Marlene Jeffries was two-timing her and killed her.'

'So who killed Yvette Mangon?'

I thought that for a trained police detective she was being a bit obtuse but said patiently, 'Jeremy Gillman. When he found out what she had done to his lover.'

'So who killed him?' It was a simple and inevitable question, and one that had given me a bit of a mental tussle. One, unfortunately, that I had not quite overcome. 'Someone else. Hence the difference in MO,' I said weakly.

'That would give us three murderers in all, then.'

'Well, yes, I suppose it would.'

'It wasn't so long ago – just after George Cotterill had died – that you were scoffing at my suggestion that he might have murdered Marlene Jeffries and someone else might have killed Yvette Mangon. Now, you can't seem to stop coming with theories involving any number of murderers.'

'Yes, well . . .' I dropped my head.

'And all this is based on a piece of graffiti . . .' She saw me open my mouth and corrected herself. 'Graffito, written in spray paint on the back of the school gymnasium.'

'And what Arthur Silsby said.'

'Who is seriously ill, and unconscious half the time; and who said it to you, without anyone else present.'

I saw where she was coming from. 'I can see that it wouldn't stand up in court, but it's a starting point, isn't it?'

'Do you mind awfully if I don't tell the Inspector this?'

It was a blow, it has to be said. 'You don't think much of it, then?'

She smiled just enough to reveal perfectly white, perfectly regular teeth. 'Let me tell you what we already know.'

'Fair enough. Would you like some more lemonade?' She said yes and I fetched some more. Then she began to tell me the progress they had made. She did it in a careful, thoughtful way, keen to leave nothing out.

'The killing of Marlene Jeffries took place sometime between nine o'clock and midnight on the evening of the day before she was found; that was the same evening in which the school was open to parents. The pathologist is fairly sure she was battered viciously using the dumb-bells found on the scene, and then hoisted up on the rope; he also thinks she might have been still alive when that last bit happened. We have no witnesses and no forensic evidence to suggest anyone; in fact, we've got too much, because of the number of people who passed through the gymnasium and who had contact with Miss Jeffries.

'We fairly soon discovered her connection with Yvette Mangon and she was interviewed very quickly. She did not tell us the precise nature of their relationship and we didn't ask because at that time we didn't know. Mr Silsby gave us no clue.'

'He wouldn't have been happy about doing that, but I suppose it was a difficult subject for him to discuss,' I interrupted.

'Very probably. Anyway, Yvette Mangon allowed us into what she said was her lodger's bedroom – the box room – and everything seemed to be entirely normal. I thought at the time that the room seemed a bit sterile, but took it no further. She wasn't keen to let us poke around the other rooms and we didn't press the point.'

'No surprise there.'

'We were left with very little to go on; we had neither the manpower nor the resources to even begin to work out who amongst all the people in the school that night might have had a motive to batter her to death; the house-to-house enquiries led nowhere, and investigation of her previous life gave no indication of anyone who might have meant her harm. It looked as if it was going to be long, slow investigation, and then Yvette Mangon was killed in quite a spectacular fashion. That they lived in the same house was clearly a strong link; that they lived in the way that they did, an even more suggestive one. As you've pointed out, both were frenzied attacks, which suggests that we might be dealing with some form of homophobic attacker. Yet Yvette Mangon's house showed evidence of having been searched. Was that some sort of bluff, intended to give the impression that it was the act of a burglar?'

'I suppose it could be,' I chimed in, hoping to sound intelligent.

I failed, as became clear when she ignored my contribution completely and continued in a dust-dry voice, 'Nothing was taken as far as we can tell, though. Certainly the cheque book was there, and her purse was only emptied on to the floor, spilling twenty-three pounds that were just left behind.'

'Oh.'

'And then there was interesting coincidence: both had been attacked with the instruments of their work; dumb-bells in the case of Marlene Jeffries, a drawing compass in that of Yvette Mangon. Yet even that wasn't quite right; Miss Jeffries had been killed by the dumb-bells, Miss Mangon merely mutilated.'

'Tricky to kill someone with drawing compasses,' I put in.

'That's what we concluded. There was definitely a message, though. Someone appeared to be killing teachers because of what they did, and yet that couldn't be all of it. Why these two? Someone who has it in only for homosexual teachers? They worked at the same school and they lived together, and we have yet to find any other connection. Their lives never crossed before Marlene Jeffries moved to Thornton Heath from Bromley six years ago.'

'How did the murderer get into the house?'

'Nothing subtle. As you recall, the house is end of terrace; he climbed the fence from the side alley, broke the glass in the back door, unlocked it and just went in. She was presumably up by then because she was dressed; she had been off sick since the murder of her partner, so wasn't going to go to work. As far as we can tell, he charged in and surprised her where she was later found in the sitting room.'

'Who found her?'

'The window-cleaner. He was so shaken up, he had to spend the night in hospital, but he's clearly not in the frame for killing her as he has an alibi for Dr Bentham's estimated time of death.'

I didn't tell her my own personal opinion of how much weight she should place on such an estimate. She had finished her lemonade but assented when I asked her if she wanted yet more. When I returned she was lying back taking in the sun, her suit jacket on the chair beside her. She looked a little feline in the degree of contentment she seemed to exude.

'And so to Jeremy Gillman's death. You're right that it fits the pattern and yet, in important ways, doesn't. He is a teacher, but he is male. The murder wasn't particularly frenzied, but there was a frog in his mouth – one that Dr Bentham says couldn't possibly have got there without the killer, or someone else, inserting it after Mr Gillman was dead. It looked as if someone was deliberately trying to make it look as if the motive was to kill teachers – and perhaps it was.'

I snorted. 'Not a particularly good job. A slightly tenuous connection, wouldn't you say?'

She was looking closely at me, her expression neutral. She said simply, 'Except that Jeremy Gillman was a practising homosexual.' Surprised – nay, bloody staggered – I found nothing to say. She continued, 'He wasn't living with anyone, but we have found and interviewed his boyfriend – a bank manager in Addiscombe. He has an alibi – from his wife – for the time of the death and we do not consider him a suspect.'

I was still uncharacteristically quiet. She said, 'So, you see, it's difficult to take the *graffito* seriously.'

All I could say (and that in a rather embarrassed tone) was, 'Of course.'

'But we are left with three teachers at the same school, all of them associated in their deaths in some way with a symbol of their speciality, all of them non-heterosexual. That's starting to sound like quite a compelling link.' I didn't think any argument on my part would be either welcomed or valuable. She added, 'As for Mr Silsby's ramblings, I would say there probably is some truth in what he says. Gillman was a very frustrated man, eager for advancement, and according to his surviving colleagues, intensely envious of Mr Silsby. I don't see how it's relevant, though.'

I would have agreed with her, except that the front door opened and then closed. Max's voice called out, 'I'm home.'

I stood up and went to the back door to kiss her; this we did, but it was cut abruptly short when she caught site of Jean Abelson. Max's face took on a dark and dangerous expression. 'What's *she* doing here?' she hissed, none too quietly.

'We were discussing the murders and about what Mr Silsby said and . . .'

'Were you really?' Her eyes were alive with anger. She seemed to swell up slightly, to shake, to become somehow inflamed, but with one last venomous look at the Sergeant, she pulled away from me and stalked out of the kitchen, saying over her shoulder, 'I've got to get back to work.'

'But you've only just got in,' I pointed out, following her.

I got to the front door just as it was slammed in my face. I stared at it for a few seconds, trying to make sense of it all as Jean Abelson came into the hall behind me. She said in a quiet voice, 'I think I'd better get back to work, too. I'm really sorry.'

THIRTY-FIVE

Well, I was sorry, too, although I didn't quite know why. During the course of the next hour I repeatedly rang the vets' surgery but apparently Max was having a busy time of it resuscitating guinea pigs and whatnot, so couldn't come to the phone. When I insisted that I absolutely had to speak to her, the receptionist went away and this time there was a pause of five minutes before she came back on the line to tell me (and in a voice that was noticeably embarrassed) that Max was going to go back to her own house that evening, and that she would be grateful if I would leave her alone. It was to no avail that I remonstrated.

Max was being stupid but there was nothing I could do about it. Her refusal to speak to me was childish and potentially was going to be disastrous; she was leaving herself unprotected when Tristan was out there and stalking her. In desperation, I went immediately around to the vets' practice, which was located in Beulah Road, but I was told that she had left for the day, feeling unwell. I went to her house, in Whitehorse Lane, but there was no answer; inevitably I looked around for Tristan and, equally inevitably, saw no one. Perhaps she had gone to her parents'. I wondered and thought about ringing them, then thought again. We were not on particularly amiable terms (they thought the age gap too great) and I didn't especially want to have them intruding any more than was absolutely necessary into the private lives of Max and me. Frustrated and worried, I sat in the car for a while, wondering what to do; the only thing I knew for certain was that I wasn't going to start decorating the bloody downstairs cloakroom any time soon.

My journey back home took me past Bensham Manor School; it was, I suppose, some sort of displacement activity that had me driving in, almost on automatic pilot. It was a quarter to four. As I parked in one of the visitors' spaces – still unadorned by any local government dignitaries, I noted – and got out. I went around the main building to the back of the gymnasium. Why had I come? Well, I suppose part of me wondered if I would catch Dad there so that I could chinwag with him, and part of me wanted to look at that wall again.

Dad wasn't there; the vegetable plot was deserted, save for a black-and-white cat of scrawny appearance who was doing his business in between the parsnips. I turned my attention to the wall. As I approached it, I had the distinct feeling that the graffiti had been supplemented; presumably some self-proclaimed 'artist' had been at play whilst Mr Silsby languished in Mayday Hospital, his liver slowly turning to mush. Try as

I might, however, I couldn't identify what had changed. I went to the drainpipe, searching again for the graffito, finding it fairly easily. There it was – *MJ loves JG*. What did it mean? The simplest explanation was that *MJ* and *JG* weren't Marlene Jeffries and Jeremy Gillman, but two other teachers or pupils at the school. It seemed odd that the conjunction should be scribed just beneath the announcement that *YM loves MJ*; surely that must have been referring to the two teachers . . .

In which case, who was JG?

I looked at it more closely, gradually seeing something odd about it. I backed away from the gymnasium, keeping my gaze fastened to that area; the drain pipe was a problem, and the efforts to erase the graffiti followed by the efforts to re-establish its existence made it difficult to make things out . . .

'Cooey!' I was startled by the sound, looking around: even as I did so, I knew what I would see. 'Hello, Lance. Fancy seeing you here.'

It was Ada, about ten yards distant but closing rapidly. Her step-granddaughter was in tow, looking discontented. 'Hello, Ada,' I said, hoping that my smile appeared full of genuine pleasure, although my heart was unable at that precise moment to locate any of that commodity anywhere.

'I was looking for Ben, but he's not here.'

I could not argue with this statement regarding the absence of Bens, my father included. Accordingly, I replied, 'No.'

'I wonder where he is.'

'I'm afraid I don't know.'

'We need to start planning the wedding.' I smiled, feeling unable to comment; clearly Dad had yet to discuss the future with her. She seemed suddenly struck by curiosity. 'What are *you* doing here, Lance? Taking your turn in weeding and watering? I keep reminding the boys and girls to keep at it, don't I, dear?' It occurred to me that she used my first name like a nail gun, pinning me to her family.

She turned to her granddaughter, who was looking around in that bored way that only modern teenagers seem able to manufacture. She received no reply but didn't seem to mind, so turned back to me. 'How are you, Lance?'

I failed to respond immediately, taken as I was by

her granddaughter: she was heavily made up but slim and attractive, her skirt very short. She was chewing, but even this did not seem to make her ugly. She was holding a brightly coloured, extravagantly decorated, gaudily coloured file folder. There were all sorts of patterns and lettering scrawled on it in felt-tip pen, clearly done during numerous afternoons of stultifying boredom. As I looked at it, I saw that she had attempted a fairly good reproduction of the classic optical trick, the drawing that one moment looks like a young woman's figure, the next like a crone's face in profile.

Ada said, 'Lance?'

I pulled myself back to her grandmother, aware that I was perhaps appearing to behave peculiarly. 'Not too bad, thank you.'

She looked at me oddly. 'Are you all right?'

But I wasn't and when I looked back at the folder and then at the gymnasium to our right, I became even less well. 'I'm fine,' I lied.

She peered at me. 'Are you sure, Lance?'

I had to pull myself back once again. 'Yes, yes.' I was enthusiastic, positive, reassuring: I did not add that I wanted her very much to go.

After doing some more peering at me – she was very good at peering, was Ada – she became at ease with my subterfuge. A curt nod suggested that she was satisfied (but only just) and then she relaxed a little. 'We have to get back home, don't we, dear?'

Her reward wasn't a word, nor was it even a nod; it was merely a spin on the heels of some outrageously shod feet and some footsteps towards the main gates. Once more, Ada was completely devoid of nonplussment. 'Goodbye, Lance,' she said. 'See you soon, no doubt.'

'No doubt.'

You will never know how hard it was not to make that sound horrified.

Alone at last, I returned to the wall, my head filled with a new perspective. It was so easy to see things in all that chaos of writing, removal, rewriting, smearing and yet more rewriting; in fact, it was too easy. It was easy to see things that were there, and easy to see things that weren't. To see what had really been written required a different perspective, and it was one I now had.

THIRTY-SIX

own that I was in a bit of tizzy after that. As far as I could see, I had three immediate problems, of varying importance. The first was that Dad seemed to be AWOL, but I suspected that this was of his own volition and an Ada-related avoidance strategy; the unkind might call this cowardly, but I could sympathize with him, even if he was merely postponing the tricky conversation that was his unavoidable fate. The second was the radio silence of Max; for whatever reason she seemed to be pissed off with me, which in itself was worrying enough, but in the context of a predatory, not to say completely-off-his-trolley Tristan, it was seriously terrifying. The third was my new theory regarding the sequence of teacher-related murdering that had lately afflicted Bensham Manor School; I didn't have everything clear in my mind, and I didn't have any proof, but this time I *knew* I was right. Trouble was, I suspected that Sergeant Abelson would be tricky to persuade, and I had no doubt at all that Inspector Masson would find my hypothesis only marginally less amusing than last year's *Morecambe and Wise Christmas Special*.

Max, though, was the most important problem. I phoned her house and, receiving no response, I took a deep breath and phoned her parents. The receiver was picked up by her father, Henry: Henry was a barrister. Need I say more?

'Hello? Who is this?' He always answered the phone like that, as if whoever had dared to ring the Christy household was clearly potentially an oik and was going to be treated like one until their bona fides had been established. I had never asked him outright, but I suspected that a few Masonic code words would have worked wondrous miracles at this point.

All I had to give him was, 'Hello, Mr Christy. It's Lance.'

'Oh.' Then, lest this should appear somewhat too rude, 'How are you?' Notice, none of the usual niceties, just straight in with the probing questions. But I was equal to him.

'Is Max with you?'

'Max?'

'Yes.' I decided that he wasn't suffering from some sort of dyspraxia and therefore didn't give him a brief description of the person in question. A silence ensued.

'Yes,' he conceded eventually. 'Yes, she is.'

'May I speak to her?'

Another silence. In my mind, at the other end of the phone line there was during this lacuna a silent charade, with lots of gesturing going on between Henry, Max and Henrietta, Max's mother (yes, really). 'It's not very convenient at the moment.'

At least he didn't tell me she was washing her hair, or was having a nap. There were times when I was first courting that I had conversations like this with a girlfriend's parents; I didn't much enjoy repeating the experience. I knew he was lying; he knew he was lying; he knew I knew he was lying; and I knew he knew I knew he was lying. Just thinking about it made me vertiginous. 'Could you get her to call me when it is "convenient"?' I tried not to sound cynical and maybe I even succeeded.

'I'll tell her.' He didn't sound any too keen.

'Would you also tell her that I love her?'

Maybe he found that one a little difficult, a little too close to the emotional bone, because his response was reluctant. 'Of course,' he lied.

THIRTY-SEVEN

Whatever the reasons for Dad's absence from the scene, I had at some point to warn him that I had just unearthed another potential reason why he should stay at a barge-pole's length from Ada. He didn't have an answering machine, so I was temporarily stymied in that direction. I therefore sought first to apprise the plod of my suspicions.

Unfortunately, no sooner was I sitting in an office with Jean Abelson, wondering how to begin the explanation of my latest brain-straining theory, than Masson walked in. He did so without knocking, but then it was his office, so I could hardly raise strong objections. It brought him up short, though; Jean Abelson got up from behind the desk – his desk, I now appreciated – and went to a much smaller one in the corner of the room. He said nothing for ten long seconds while continuing to stare at me as he sat in the chair so recently occupied by his sergeant; only then did he ask, 'What are you doing here?'

If outlining my theory was going to be tricky when the aural recipient of my wisdom was Sergeant Abelson, the thought of pouring my sweet nothings into the hairy lugholes of Inspector Masson was a daunting one indeed. I hesitated and he took advantage of this to produce a cigarette packet, shake one of its occupants loose, then place it between his lips. He eyed me with an amalgamation of curiosity, distaste and smouldering resentment as he lit it with a match taken from a box that proclaimed it was 'England's Glory'. Then, through a lungful of fume-laden air that he expelled with much satisfaction – as if he came from a planet with a distinctly smokier atmosphere and felt liable to continual asphyxiation if there was too much oxygen in the air – he pressed me for an answer. 'Well?'

Prevarication was no longer an option, I realized. I found that I could not look directly at him as I spoke for I knew that his expression (of impatient disdain) would put me off; I thus had to look at the wall behind his head – it had a photograph of the Queen hanging upon it – as I sallied forth into my story.

'I think I know who killed Marlene Jeffries.' With which, nothing at all happened. Neither of them reacted, not even to scoff, or to laugh or even to sit back in amazement. The silence, as they say, sat heavily upon the three of us as they both continued to look at me until I asked, 'Do you want to know who?'

Masson sucked as only Masson could; then he tapped the cigarette to dislodge some ash into an ashtray; one, I noticed, that was made of glass and was a present from Blackpool. I wondered how he had come by it; it was difficult to see Masson paddling in the sea replete with knotted handkerchief on his head and rolled-up trousers. He said, 'Why not?'

'A man called Mike Clarke. One of the parents at the school.'

I noticed that Jean had scribbled something down; presumably she was making a note of the name, although I suppose she could have been writing something rude about me. Masson enquired, 'Why do you think he's our killer?'

As I led him through my reasoning, my misinterpretation of what had been written on the gymnasium wall and how this suggested to me a potential motive for at least one of the murders, I glanced at Jean; she had her head bowed as if she could not bear to witness the tableau, as if she were a sensitive soul and did not care to stare heartlessly at self-immolation. I came to an end; it was much as T. S. Eliot had said, with a lot more of the whimper than the bang about it.

There was silence during which I brought my gaze back to the Inspector's grizzled, not to say grisly, visage. As usual, it had upon it a look of impending anger, meaning I could not tell what he was actually thinking. He had finished his cigarette but, fear not, he had already captured and activated another.

'That's quite a theory.'

'Not so much a theory, more of a hypothesis. I wouldn't put it any more strongly than that.'

He waved this modesty impatiently away with a hand that held the cigarette. 'Whatever you call it,' he conceded, 'it's quite ingenious.' In case I should accidentally mistake his comment for praise, he went on, 'For which you have not a single piece of evidence.'

'Not direct evidence.'

'Not any kind of evidence.'

'I think it's quite plausible,' I protested.

He enlisted Jean, a tactic which I think to this day was unfair; of course she was going to agree with him, wasn't she? 'What do you think, Sergeant Abelson?'

She surprised him, however. 'It would explain some things about her murder. The extreme frenzy that seems to have been used, for instance.'

Masson stared at her for a moment, as if contemplating the

sentence for such insubordination. Then he turned back to me. 'Yes, it would. How did Mr Clarke find out that his daughter was being seduced by Marlene Jeffries? Did he see this graffiti? The one that says *MJ loves JC?*'

I didn't for one second entertain the notion that I should correct his use of the Italian. 'I don't know.'

'And how do you know that *JC* refers to Joanna Clarke?'

Well, I didn't know, did I? It wasn't a fully formed explanation, just a moment of inspiration, albeit one that I was sure was right. 'I don't know,' I was forced to repeat.

'And why did Yvette Mangon get sliced to death?'

'I don't know that either.'

'And what about Mr Gillman? Did he have something to do with deflowering Mr Clarke's daughter?'

I had hoped not to be in the position of petitioning the Inspector without first persuading Jean Abelson to support my cause; this was exactly what I had foreseen would happen if I waded straight in on the redoubtable senior plod person. I told myself that it was no use getting impatient with him, or reacting to his over-the-top sarcasm. 'I rather thought you might work out the details of the theory.'

'Hypothesis,' he butted in quickly and, I thought, with undue nastiness.

'Yes,' I conceded. '. . . Hypothesis.' Out of the corner my eye I caught once again Jean looking upon the spectacle doubtless in much the same way as members of the audience had once watched heretics arguing their case with the Spanish Inquisition; there was a definite touch of 'I told you so'.

'Perhaps Yvette Mangon and Marlene Jeffries raped her.'

'Possibly,' I agreed, and immediately regretted my enthusiasm.

'And what? Gillman watched? Or did he join in as well?'

I stayed silent on that one, my sensitive nose for these things telling me that he was being facetious. There was a pause which can be most accurately described as 'brooding', before he asked, 'And you think I should investigate this possibility?'

Well, yes, I did, so I said, 'I'm sure you'd be discreet about it.'

'I'd bloody have to be, wouldn't I? I could upset a lot of people, Dr Elliot.'

'Isn't that an occupational risk?'

I could see him running that reply through his sarcasm detector; fortunately he seemed to find it bereft thereof. He changed tack, 'Do you use green ink, Doctor?'

This was a right Chinaman googly and it left me standing at the crease wondering what had just happened. 'Not habitually,' I admitted cautiously, just in case he was seeking to make me incriminate myself.

'Every time there's a murder, we get a fair few letters written with the stuff. Some of them are in capitals, some of them are so poorly written they're almost indecipherable, and all of them are anonymous.' I was beginning to see what he was getting at but he wasn't going to let me break in to his little diatribe. 'And every single one of them has a theory about the murder.' He looked at Sergeant Abelson. 'They make quite amusing reading, don't they?'

She nodded dutifully. 'They can be quite extraordinary.'

'A lot of them are just people attempting to make trouble, either for us or for the people they're accusing. Another large proportion is from crackpots – people who insist that they have incontrovertible proof that the killing was done by Jack the Ripper, or Martians, or the KGB, or even the devil himself. Not a few are from clairvoyants, in contact with the deceased. They all have some common characteristics – most of them demand a reward (whether or not one has been offered) and all are completely unproven.'

'Well, I'm not claiming a reward . . . and by definition I'm not anonymous.'

He gnawed at his teeth for a bit, the cigarette idly turning to ash and smoke as his forefinger tapped the desk blotter. 'No, you're not, are you?'

I didn't know what I was to say at that so, in line with a strategy that I have generally found the most successful in these situations, I said nothing. Jean was looking on with pity in her eyes. Masson stood up. 'You have privileges, Dr Elliot. Unlike most members of the public, you are allowed into my office and I can't just screw up your "hypothesis" and throw

it in the round filing cabinet in the corner. I find myself sitting
here and listening to you.'

I shrugged and smiled; I didn't mean to annoy him but
somehow it always seemed to take him the wrong way, as
it did now. It was with a display of great forbearance that
he said, 'The only problem that I have, Doctor, is that at
present I don't have a better theory, and I'm starting to get
desperate, and there are people upstairs who are starting to
get desperate, too'

I saw Jean's eyes widen slightly as he admitted this.

I enquired of him, 'What about Albert Stewart? Is there
anything to link him with any of the deaths?'

'He and Gillman weren't the best of friends is about the
best it gets. Stewart blames Gillman for persecuting him when
he was in his class; apparently barely a week went by when
Gillman wasn't giving him detention, or even caning his hand,
so he definitely bore him a grudge, but we can't find any such
link with Yvette Mangon, and Marlene Jeffries wasn't around
when Stewart was at school.'

'How does he feel about lesbians and homosexuals?'

He grunted. 'The psychiatrist tells me that Stewart isn't too
fond of poofs – says it's to do with his military training – but
he's not too worked up over lesbians.'

'No motive there, then.'

'Not if you believe psychiatrists.' He sounded as if he
didn't, particularly. He chewed for a while, perhaps on a
rubber band, perhaps on his own tongue, perhaps on a wasp,
then he declared, 'You're almost certainly wrong, but should
you be right and I am found to have ignored you, I won't
just be for the high jump, I'll be hung, drawn and quartered
by the powers that be.' He sounded bitter; once again, it
seemed that I was making trouble for him. He turned to his
sergeant. 'Go with the doctor and check out the graffiti,
Sergeant, and then do some background checks – but do them
quietly. Then, when we have put the good doctor's mind at
rest, we can get on with solving this case.'

THIRTY-EIGHT

J ean said nothing for a long time after we had driven out of the station car park at Norbury in my car. The silence was painful; she just stared straight ahead, lips firmly closed, eyes unblinking, whilst I drove with due care and attention. In a temporal and spatial sense, it was a short journey; in the sense of interpersonal relationships, it was a voyage around the world. I gave in, of course. 'Are you pissed off with me?'

She turned her head to me at once for a brief moment, then back to the oncoming road; her stare had been painfully intense, though. She said, 'Inspector Masson warned me about you.'

'Did he?' I was, I confess, surprised.

'Oh, yes. As soon as he spotted you in the gymnasium he told me what you're like.'

I felt a touch of affront. 'What am I like?'

Now that was always going to be a dangerous question, but, alas, also an irresistible one, you will doubtless have realized. She said dispassionately, 'He said you're probably a very good GP but, as far as he was concerned, you're a constant irritant; he added that you cannot resist trespassing where you're not wanted and that your interference in police procedure, no matter how well intentioned, verges on the criminal.'

'Oh . . .'

But she had yet to finish. 'He added that your father's even worse, although at least he has the excuse of senility.'

All this seemed a bit of a turnaround on the part of her attitude towards the Elliots, especially the junior branch. 'Oh . . .'

The journey was completed in silence. The evening was cooling as we walked through the playground to the back area of the school; the buildings sheltered the worst of the traffic noise, and so there was a hint of the rural about the scene. It seemed to soften her somewhat. 'Where is this clue?' she asked, her voice mocking but gently so.

I took her over to the spot and drew her attention to what

had been scrawled. She contemplated it for a long time, tilting her head on occasion, even going so far as to screw up her darkly hazel eyes. Then she relaxed, as if holding her breath was all part of the 'police procedures' in which I apparently interfered. 'You've got a thing about graffiti, haven't you?'

'Not so as you'd notice.'

She scanned the entire wall. 'This is like finding the face of the Virgin Mary in the froth of an emptied beer glass. You could make out anything in this chaos.'

'But you see, don't you? It looks like *JG* because of the upstroke of the *h* beneath it, the one from the word *shit*. It turns a *C* into a *G*.'

'If you say so.'

I gave in. 'OK. Thanks for taking a look, anyway.'

She must have felt a bit sorry for me for it was with a slight smile that she said, 'You should have told me your theory first.'

'I was going to.'

As we walked back to the car, I told her what had happened between me and Max. 'I'm worried about her,' I said.

'I'm sure you're exaggerating the threat from Tristan.' Everyone seemed to think that; even I could occasionally be persuaded to that point of view, although there were times in the middle of the night when I awoke from a dream in which he was stamping on my fingers; rather painfully this was a dream based on memory and not fantasy. She added reassuringly, 'I've no doubt her parents will look after her until she calms down a bit.'

'I still don't understand why she's reacted like this.'

She stopped abruptly, looking at me with an expression that at first I thought was concerned, then I realized was pitying. 'No,' she agreed. 'You don't, do you?'

Another long, quiet journey then ensued. As we arrived back at the station, Masson was just hurrying down the steps of the front entrance. He sailed past the front of the car as we both got out. Jean called out, 'Sir? What's going on?'

He turned at her call. 'There's been some sort of incident in Kingswood Avenue. A man's been stabbed.'

Ever eager to help, I called, 'Do you need me?'

He swung his gaze around upon me and, even for Masson,

it was malevolent, quite possibly unto the point of loathing. 'There's an ambulance in attendance and I'm sure they will be able to cope so no, Doctor, I don't need you.'

'Is it a domestic?' asked Jean as she went to join him.

He was still staring at me; I momentarily wondered if unbeknownst to me I'd sprouted some sort of appendage out of the back of my head, so fascinated was he with me. 'Sort of,' he replied. 'The casualty's name is Mike Clarke.'

THIRTY-NINE

Of course I tagged along, didn't I? And much as the good Inspector might not have wanted me there, he could hardly refuse, could he? I'm glad I did, too, because it was a proper carnival of entertainment. There were two ambulances, three police cars, at least a dozen members of the constabulary fraternity and a crowd of perhaps twenty on-lookers.

Oh, and my father's car.

Uttering a silent but still potent fricative, I pushed through to the front gate where I was stopped by a burly policeman who wasn't interested in who I was, what I did for a living or the fact that my father's car was parked nearby and he might well be inside the house. Jean and Masson had disappeared and it was clear that this stolid example of blue-uniformed, decerebrate intransigence was not going to be swayed by anything I might say; also, the Thornton Heath citizenry – or at least those of them who were present – were becoming restive at our duologue and were muttering things like 'Prat' and 'What a tosser'. Frustrated, both physically and emotionally, I was about to leave hoi polloi to their sport and try to gain access another way, when Jean came out of the house.

'Jean?' She looked less than elated to catch sight of yours truly, which saddened me somewhat. 'Is Dad in there? Is he all right?' She hesitated, then came down the garden path. I said quickly, 'Can I see him?'

She came to a quick decision which, thankfully, was the one I wanted; I was allowed admittance, much to the disgust of the good burghers of our fair town. 'Where is he?' I asked. 'Has he been hurt?'

She said tersely, 'No, he's fine.'

I was relieved, of course. I asked, 'What's happened, then?'

'We don't know yet. Give us a chance.'

'But it's to do with the murders. It must be . . .'

She turned on me at that one. 'Look, Lance. I'm letting you in here as a favour; the Inspector will probably rip me up into tiny pieces for doing it, but . . .' She paused, as if she had lost her thread. When she carried on, it was in a pained sort of voice. 'I suppose I like you . . .' and another pause, followed by, 'And you have a sort of right to be here, especially in view of your father's presence. But please just be quiet and just keep your father company. OK?'

I nodded meekly and followed her into the house.

She led me through the house past the closed doors of the front and rear sitting rooms out through the galley-style kitchen. Dad was sitting in the garden with Ada at a green plastic table on which were two empty tea cups; they were overseen by a woman police constable who stood behind them, her back to the house. She glanced over as I hove into view but was given the nod by Jean and did not spring into action; she was of a fairly stocky build and I was seriously afraid that she would have done me no little harm. Dad was justifiably surprised to see me come out of the back door. 'Lance!' he said at once, then looked at Ada and I appreciated for the first time that she was in a bad way. She had been weeping and doing so, it seemed to me, copiously. She had got to that stage which rarely afflicts those beyond childhood; the one in which the weeper starts to gulp and hiccup. She held to her nose a small lace handkerchief but, alas, it was totally inadequate for the task it had been given; it was, to put it bluntly, sodden. Dad was up and out of his chair at once, but not before I had detected a degree of awkwardness 'twixt the pair.

He came over and took my elbow, asking in a quiet tone,

'Nothing's happened, has it? Mike's –' he glanced over at Ada who was staring at us – 'all right, isn't he?'

'He's not good, Dad.' In fact Mike Clarke was receiving medical attention in one of the ambulances; according to Jean, his wound was deep and there was a large amount of internal bleeding. He would require emergency surgery, but the ambulance crew were afraid to move him even the short distance to Mayday Hospital without first making some effort at stabilizing him. David Clarke was in the other ambulance, apparently bruised and battered, but not in a serious condition.

'Oh, dear,' he said gravely and kept glancing over at Ada. Jean had slipped back into the house. 'I did what I could.'

'What's happened?'

He deliberately turned his back on Ada, presumably afraid that amongst her undeclared talents was one for accurate lip-reading. 'I finally plucked up the courage to tell her I thought things weren't going to work out between us . . .' He whispered, using that strange enunciation that people think stops the sound of their voice dead at about two feet. He halted, thought about what he had said and what I might be thinking, and added suddenly, 'Not that I was unkind, or anything . . . but there's no easy way, is there? I mean, however it was said, it was . . .'

'Dad, I don't mean what happened between the two of you: I mean what's gone on here? Who stabbed Mike Clarke?'

'Tricia.' He barely made any sound at all when he said the name.

'Good Lord!' This earned me a solemn nod. I asked, not unreasonably, 'Why?'

He took me further away from Ada, who was again crying piteously and now being comforted by her police escort. 'I called over here about an hour ago. I'd done a lot of thinking and decided it was only fair to tell her how matters stood. I knew that she'd been waiting at school for Joanna, so I knew she'd be a bit later than normal. Anyway, I arrived, knocked on the door and Ada let me in. She made me a cup of tea and we came to sit out here; Mike was asleep before going to work this evening, and she didn't want to disturb him. I had just got to the meat of the matter when there was a kerfuffle from inside the house. Well, naturally, Ada went to see what was going on, and I followed, because I didn't want her put in harm's way.'

'And what was going on?'

'Mike and David were having an argument in David's bedroom.' He reconsidered this. 'No, actually, they were having a fight. Mike had his stepson by the lapels and was shaking him, screaming at him. I don't mind telling you he was using language that was most unsuitable for a lady like Ada. Mind you, David was being none too restrained. He was spitting in Mike's face.' He stopped in recollection. 'Funny thing was, he was laughing.'

'Laughing? Was he enjoying it, do you think?'

'I had the impression that what he was enjoying was riling his stepfather. Ada's always been a bit reticent about the family dynamics, but I have my suspicions that things can get a little tense at times, especially between those two.'

I supposed that living with a man of Mike's atavistic tendencies might make for an atmosphere that was less than chilled.

'What was the row about?'

Dad's demeanour became even more secretive. After another covert glance at Ada, he said, 'That's the funny thing.'

'Yes . . .?'

'Mike kept shouting that David had "gone too far this time".'

'Is that all?'

'David just said that he didn't know what Mike was talking about – he calls him "Mike" just to infuriate him, I think.' From what I had seen, David would enjoy doing that. Dad continued, 'Mike said that he wasn't a puppet and that David was . . . well, he used some fairly unparliamentary language . . . and he seemed to drop him, then brandish his fist at him.'

'His fist?' I said, even as I considered that the word 'brandish' was such a lovely word.

'David said something along the lines that he thought Mike was a lunatic, although by now his language was none too delicate either – I'm not sure Ada has ever heard such words, because she looked stricken. She kept calling up to them to stop it. By now Tricia had joined us at the bottom of the stairs; she'd been sewing curtains in the front room. She started to go up, but Ada pulled her back.

'David kept saying he knew nothing about it – whatever "it" was – but I could tell from his voice that he was really enjoying getting his stepfather going; getting under his skin, if you know what I mean.' From the few moments I had spent in David's company, I could see exactly what Dad meant. 'Anyway, there suddenly came a titanic crash as Mike picked David up and almost threw him out of his bedroom across the upstairs landing. As he did so, he shouted, "These!"'

'That was when Tricia finally got involved. She shook herself loose from Ada and pushed and rushed upstairs, shouting at her husband to stop it. It was difficult to make out exactly what happened then because we only had an obstructed view.' He said this last in a tone of some disappointment, as if he had been sold duff tickets for the Cup Final. 'She still had a pair of scissors in her hand, I recall. There was some sort of scuffle and she must have stabbed him.'

My appreciation of Tricia shot skywards; here was a woman not to be trifled with, I surmised. In the face of a marauding Mike Clark, I thought it unlikely that I would have made a gesture as aggressive as that one; in fact, I was fairly sure I'd have been moving backwards at a fairly rapid rate.

'You don't know what "these" were?'

'Haven't the foggiest. By this time the next-door neighbours had rung the police because of the noise. I tried to do what I could for Mike – putting pressure on the wound and making him comfortable – and got Ada to phone for an ambulance. When she got back from doing that I went over to David to see if he was all right; his mother was cradling him and he obviously wasn't too badly injured, although I should think he was a bit concussed and shocked.'

A thought occurred to me. 'Where's Joanna?'

'With a neighbour, I think.'

'You've had a quite a day, then.'

He laughed bitterly; I could see that he was worried that he might not have done enough to save Mike Clarke, and he was reproving himself; I thought he was doing so unfairly and told him so. He smiled briefly, then a deep frown replaced it. 'He's a funny lad, that David.' I wasn't going to argue with him; even amongst the Clarke menagerie, David seemed something special. He said thoughtfully, 'Even after he'd been thrown against the wall and was clearly dazed and in some pain, he had a satisfied smile on his face, as if he'd achieved something special.'

FORTY

With Dad going back to comfort Ada, I wandered back into the house. Upstairs, at the precise scene of the stabbing – readily identified by the blood stains on the carpet and the wall and the newel post – two people from the police laboratory were taking samples. I stood at the bottom of the stairs wondering if they'd mind if I pushed past them into David's bedroom to nose around, but decided they probably would, and very much so, too. The door to the back sitting room opened and a woman police constable came out, pushing past me a tad rudely to go out of the front door; I could see beyond her that the curtains were closed, the lights were on and Masson was sitting – to all appearances uncomfortably, as if he were perched on a Space Hopper – on a bright red chair in the modern style; it had a back that was no more than a foot in height, no arms and was covered in an artificial fabric that seemed to be uniquely frictionless. He was staring at someone or something out of my line of sight – presumably Tricia. I couldn't see Jean, but I guessed she was in there, too.

Suddenly the front door burst open and the police woman returned. She pushed back past me, only now it was totally bereft of any semblance of politeness. She rushed into the back room, shouting, 'Inspector? There's something wrong.'

Masson stood up at once. I heard him say, 'You two stay here.' With that he was doing a bit of pushing-rudely-past-me of his own (accompanied by a surprised glare that I was once again in the neighbourhood), and was gone. I followed, of course.

Masson made his way to an ambulance; I say 'an ambulance',

although it was by now the only one in the vicinity, the one with David Clarke having departed. He hefted himself into the back, there was a pause of about fifteen seconds and then his head appeared. 'Get over here,' he shouted at me over the heads of the audience; ever obedient, I hurried over and he stepped down to let me in.

One of the two ambulance men was pumping on Mike Clarke's chest, another had clamped a green rubber mask over his face with one hand and was squeezing a black rubber bellows with the other. There were two drips up, clear fluid running rapidly into his veins; the dressing on his upper abdomen was sodden to overflowing with blood. One of the ambulance crew recognized me and let me assess him. It didn't take long; he had exsanguinated and all the fluid they were pushing into his circulatory system was just running out into his abdominal cavity within seconds.

He was dead.

As soon as I had informed Masson of this incontrovertible and irreversible fact, he stormed back into the house, having let out his breath in a kind of long, low growl that was not only menacing but, I would imagine, brought up a fair amount of phlegm. I did the formalities in the back of the ambulance and was about to get back down when I spotted that Michael Clarke still held in his hand two pieces of paper.

It was less than five minutes before Masson re-emerged, this time leading Tricia Clarke; she was handcuffed to the woman police constable and Jean was holding her other arm; the newly widowed Mrs Clarke did not look particularly upset but perhaps she had yet to be informed of her new legal status. I tried to attract some attention but, what with the murmuring, gasping and occasional jeer from the crowd, I couldn't make myself heard. I sighed and murmured, 'Oh, well.'

I reckoned it could wait.

They let Dad go about an hour later, after his and Ada's statements had been taken. The crowd had dispersed, Mike Clarke's body been taken to the mortuary at Mayday Hospital, and all the police had vanished; the insubstantial pageant had faded, leaving not a rack behind.

All except two bloodstained pieces of paper.

'Are you all right?' I asked.

'Oh, yes,' he assured me, although he sounded slightly shaky.

I walked with him over to his execrable yet somehow adorable car. 'You know,' he said as he put his key into the door lock, 'I really did love Ada.'

'Did?'

He accepted my correction at once. 'You're right,' he admitted. 'Maybe I've been fooling myself for a while.'

'Ada's a very nice person. I'm not sure I can say the same about her family, though.'

He took a while to answer. 'To be frank with you, Lance, I think I would have regretted marrying just one member of the Clarke clan, let alone the whole brood of them.'

He got into the car and started the engine, in the process waking every sleeping babe within a mile radius of Kingswood Avenue, then drove home.

And I was left with those bloodstained pieces of paper.

I went home myself, feeling tired and frustrated; no one would listen to me. Even when I rang the police station to try yet again to get someone to listen to me, I was told that I would be rung back; no one did, of course, because they never do. I went to bed, reassuring myself that it could wait until the morning.

The phone went at three in the morning; in my groggy state I even wondered if it might be Jean or Masson ringing me back, but I should really learn not to be so naive. It was Max, and she was scared.

'Lance? Is that you?'

I didn't need to ask why she was ringing me at the hour, and why she sounded terrified, but I asked anyway. 'What's wrong, Max?'

'He's outside! I can see him in the back garden.'

'I'm going to put the phone down. As soon as I do, dial 999. I'll be right over.'

'Please come quickly.'

'I will.'

I put the receiver down and was dressed and in the car within ten minutes. It's about an hour's drive to Max's parents' house but I managed it in forty. When I arrived, there were two police cars parked outside; all of the lights were on and the front door was open. I ran up the path and met two policemen; between them was Tristan, grinning; behind them in the doorway was Max being all but asphyxiated by her mother, her father standing protective guard. I stood aside to let Tristan and his friends past; as they did so, Tristan winked at me; he mouthed something too, and although I could not decipher what, I had the impression it was lewd. I then hurried on into the house.

'Is everything all right?' I asked.

Her father opened his mouth, drew in some breath and, as far as I could tell (and I *am* a doctor), looked about to speak, but he never got the chance, because Jean Abelson emerged from the front room on his left. She looked at me with a completely neutral expression and walked straight past me. By now utterly confused, I looked at Max, for which all I got was a venomous look from her mother and no look at all from her.

FORTY-ONE

Everyone has days on which one's paid occupation just doesn't do it. No matter how hard one tries, one can't engage; not even Mrs Potter, who had held me in thrall on regular occasions by regaling me of tales of her torrid battles with *tinea pedis*, could keep me interested that morning. I had tried to contact first Max, then Jean, first thing, with a completely equal lack of success in both ventures; consequently, I felt not a little frustrated.

It was during my morning digestive (so to speak) that Sheila came to tell me that Sergeant Abelson was on the phone.

'You wanted to talk to me,' she said without any of the usual preliminaries; her voice was worrying impersonal.

'I wanted to thank you.'

'For what?'

Which found me momentarily nonplussed. 'For what you did last night. For helping protect Max. I still don't quite know how you did it, but thanks anyway.'

'I said that I'd do what I could,' she pointed out.

'Yes, I know that . . . but I appreciate how busy you are, what with the murders and everything.'

There was a hint of tired amusement as she said, 'I wasn't personally standing guard over Miss Christy. I called in a few favours at the local station. She didn't have a twenty-four-hour bodyguard, but as soon as the 999 call came in, there was a car only two minutes away.'

'But when I got to the house, you were there, too.'

'They let me know at once. I was still at work – as you've just pointed out, we're slightly busy at the moment, especially with what happened yesterday.'

Which brought me neatly to my next point. 'About that, Jean . . .'

There was a long pause, and then she sighed deeply; it was a sound that I think was full of exasperation but tinged also at the edges with something else; I sort of hope it wasn't just anger. Then, she said, 'You were right, OK, Lance? Well done. Mike Clarke was the murderer.'

But that wasn't what I was trying to say, as I now started to tell her. 'I think there's more to the story than any of us know.'

'Look, Lance. We appreciate your help – even the Inspector, although he might not ever say that – but the case is over. Tricia's told us everything.'

But I had those pieces of paper, and I knew that it wasn't quite everything. It was my turn to take a deep breath. 'I bet she hasn't.'

'What do you mean by that?'

'I need to speak to you and Masson, but I've got a house call to make first. Can we meet in, say, a couple of hours?'

She asked cautiously, 'Is this going to be relevant?'

'Definitely,' I said confidently.
'You'll come to the station?'
At which I had to demur. 'No.'
'Where, then?'
'At the Clarkes' house.'

FORTY-TWO

M asson was small, irascible, impatient and quite frankly, horrible; he was always a bit – quite a lot, actually – like that, but when we met that day, he was like it with golden knobs and no returns. I still managed to have a lot of time for him, though. I'd always had some empathy with his incredulous attitude to the vicissitudes of life, to the way that he had to endure constant irritants. Perhaps, though, this was at least partly because I seemed to be one of the largest irritants that constantly beset him; he was, I think, the Job of the Croydon Constabulary establishment, and I suspect I was one of his largest boils.

How Jean Abelson managed to persuade him to turn up was one of those questions that cannot be answered, at least not by me, but turn up he did. I met him outside the Clarkes' house in Kingswood Avenue; I was slightly late, which probably didn't improve his temper. He was restrained, I'll give him that, but restrained as in Big Boy and Little Boy were restrained until they had fallen to about nineteen hundred feet above ground level. 'Why am I here, Doctor?' he asked at once. 'Sergeant Abelson tells me you have something that may be relevant to the case; the normal practice would be to hand it in at the police station.'

'I haven't done too badly in this case so far, have I? I mean, considering I'm a constant irritant.'

He looked from me to Jean Abelson sharply, his eyes narrowed to hostile slits; when he looked back at me, Jean's glance at me would have withered a witch. 'I am a busy man, Doctor. What is it that you have that may be relevant?'

'Can we go inside the house?'

We did as I wanted, Masson clearly doing so at great cost to his systolic blood pressure. The house was empty, of course; David was still in hospital, Joanne was in the care of the social services and Tricia was in the care of HMP. We sat in the back living room; it was as chintzy and over-ornate as I had suspected from my brief, blinkered look the day before; there were a pale brown shag-pile carpet, a three-piece suite of the most lurid red hue, a chandelier and a reproduction of the Green Lady; as my mother would have said, it was all very 'red hat, no knickers'.

'What is Tricia Clarke's story?'

Jean answered. 'You were right. Joanna had a crush on Marlene Jeffries. That would have been OK, except that Miss Jeffries took advantage of her. It got more and more intense, possibly even physical; certainly when her father found out about it, he imagined the worse. According to Tricia Clarke, he was a violent and repressive man, especially so when it came to Joanna. She says that there is a history of violence in the family; that she has been attacked on many occasions, and the assault on David wasn't the first either. Clarke, it seems, was not able to control his temper. The thought that his daughter might have been seduced like that was too much. He lost control and battered her to death, as we know.'

'And why then kill Yvette Mangon?'

'He then learned from Joanna that there were letters she had sent to Miss Jeffries. They were fairly explicit and Mike Clarke realized that unless they were destroyed, they could potentially implicate him. He paid a visit to the house in the early morning, on his way back from work. We don't know the details, but Tricia Clarke says that he had become desperate to get hold of the letters, so we can surmise that he was probably pretty aggressive. We don't actually know if Yvette Mangon even knew about the relationship, let alone about any letters. We think, though, that her denials probably just inflamed Clarke even more; he lost his temper and . . . well, attacked her. It was a kitchen knife – we found it in the back garden.'

I asked, 'Why the drawing compass in the eye?'

Masson spoke for the first time. 'I would guess that after he'd lost it again and killed another teacher, he decided to try a bit of misdirection. He'd killed one teacher with the instruments of her profession, so to speak; he decided to leave a similar symbol after killing Miss Mangon.'

I nodded. It was plausible. 'All of which brings us to Jeremy Gillman. Where does he come in to this?'

Jean continued. 'According to his widow, Clarke didn't find the letters at Yvette Mangon's house, for which there was a good reason. She didn't have them; Gillman did.'

'How did he get hold of them?'

'We've yet to establish that precisely, although it would seem that Gillman and Mangon were fairly close. They'd been colleagues for years.'

'And Gillman blackmailed him?' I guessed.

'He sent Mike Clarke a note demanding a thousand pounds.'

'Not a huge amount considering Clarke is on a printer's salary,' I pointed out.

Masson explained testily, 'It was a first demand; one to test the water. The next one would have been ten times that, probably.'

'Except that Clarke charged straight round there and drowned him.'

'Yes.' Masson, I think, began to suspect that all was not as he had previously thought.

I said, 'I wonder how he found out who the blackmailer was.'

Masson looked at his sergeant for a moment, then said, 'We haven't found out as yet.'

'Perhaps the note gave a clue,' I suggested.

It was Jean who said, 'Not as far as we can see.'

'You've got the note, then?'

She admitted that they had.

I have now to confess that I like a dramatic effect, and on this occasion I felt I did pretty well. I reached into my pocket and brought out the pieces of paper I had found in Mike Clarke's hand. 'Is it anything like these?' I asked.

*   *   *

Masson went through an astonishing range of facial coloration; everything from deep purple to the palest of rose whites, with a few hints of yellow in between. His vocalizations were no less varied – although without obvious sense being conveyed – as he looked at my exhibit for the prosecution. Eventually, he spluttered, 'Where did you get these?'

I came clean and he was not impressed. 'Why the bloody shining hell didn't you tell anyone?'

'I tried,' I said. 'Several times. No one was interested much.'

There was a long pause until he said in a very low voice, 'That's no excuse.'

'Nevertheless, it's true.'

'As evidence, it's now completely useless.'

I thought about this. 'Not entirely,' I decided

At which point I think, in terms of my previous image, Inspector Masson dropped below nineteen hundred feet. He went off, and he did so big time, in a blast of atomic strength. He ranted; he raved; he did a fair amount of profaning; and he threatened.

Only eventually did he subside.

It was Jean who calmed him down. She did so by asking a very pertinent question in one of the short pauses that he was forced to employ whilst breathing. 'What do we make of these notes, sir?'

'What does that mean?' he asked; my medical instincts suggested to me that he was becoming slightly hysterical. 'It's two more blackmail demands.'

'They're almost identical to the one we were given by Tricia Clarke,' she pointed out.

'So?'

'Where did Clarke get hold of them?'

Masson embraced the beauty of silence for the first time for about three minutes; it was a very good question. She pressed home her point. 'I'd say that these look almost like practice attempts.'

I put in then, 'I think they are.'

I took them upstairs to David's bedroom.

*   *   *

It was archetypal of a teenage boy's bedroom. On the walls were posters of Status Quo, Led Zeppelin and a young lady in soft light who played tennis in a distinctly free and easy style. There was a pile of *Melody Maker* papers in the corner; I didn't check, but I would have laid a fair sum of money down that somewhere in the vicinity was a copy or two of *Mayfair* or *Knave*. The walls were covered in woodchip paper that was emulsioned a repulsively deep shade of orange; there was a black coverlet pulled up over the bed, although the bedclothes beneath were patently still rucked up. In front of the window was a desk on which were piles of textbooks, exercise books, pens, paper and an electronic calculator.

'What are we doing in here?' growled Masson.

I went over to the desk and started searching through the items thereon. It wasn't long before I found what I was looking for – David's biology exercise book. It was A4 in size and the cover was deep pink. David was not a tidy worker; many of his diagrams of stamens and carpels (I hurried past those of the sexual organs of a mammalian intimate nature) were, I am afraid to say, shoddy; clearly Jeremy Gillman had thought so too, for he had written a far from few acerbic comments on them; these, together with his commentary on the persistently poor test scores, provided a good sample of his handwriting.

I showed Masson. 'So?' he demanded.

It was Jean who answered, although she did so in a questioning, wondering manner. 'You're saying that David wrote the notes?'

I nodded. 'I think David stage-managed everything. Every single murder.'

FORTY-THREE

'This is a deeply dysfunctional family. Both parents had been married before, and none too happily. Both of them brought a child from those marriages. Mike Clarke was a man of violent tendencies with little ability to control them; Tricia was equally combative, especially when it came to her son, David. Mike's relationship to his mother, Ada, and to his daughter, Joanna, verged on the paranoid. Clearly there was – or at least had been – some sort of bond of affection between Tricia and Mike, but between David and his stepfather there was very rapidly marked antipathy. At best, Mike ignored him; at worst, he looked for every opportunity to make him suffer. Often, I think, physically. Not surprisingly, it was the source of a lot of resentment between Tricia and Mike.'

'How the hell do you know all this?'

Jean suggested, 'Your father?'

'Yes,' I said. 'And I saw them in action, too.' Both of which were the truth, just not all of it.

Masson grunted. 'Sounds like another fairy story, Doctor.'

Despite this less than glowing review of my performance up to that point, I continued. 'And then Joanna developed a schoolgirl crush on Marlene Jeffries; one which, moreover, was reciprocated. There was no way that it wasn't going to become the subject for a lot of rumours around the school, which meant that David got to hear about it; he in turn used it as a way of getting at both his stepsister and stepfather. I wonder if he found some letters that Marlene Jeffries had written to Joanna. He knew that Mike Clarke would find the concept of his daughter being involved in a lesbian relation-ship beyond his ability to bear so, of course, he at once told him. It was as cruel as killing a kitten, but it was done in a deliciously subtle way. He waited until they had returned home from the parents' evening at the school to show him the letters that Marlene Jeffries had written to his daughter. They had met Miss Jeffries just a couple of hours before, and she had appeared to be nothing more than a caring teacher; this decep-tion only magnified exponentially the effect. Mike Clarke was primed and ready to kill.'

'How did he know she'd still be at the school?' Masson sounded churlish, like a man who felt cuckolded.

I shrugged. 'I don't suppose he planned ahead. From my experience of Mike Clarke, he didn't think more than ten minutes into the future. He went to the school first and that

was where he found her. She was alone in the gym and he
let rip.'

'This is all speculation.'

'Some of it,' I admitted, but I wasn't about to feel cowed.
'Can you prove it's wrong?'

Which he couldn't.

Jean suggested gently, 'Why did he kill Yvette Mangon?'

'Because David Clarke pointed out that not only were there
letters from Marlene Jeffries to Joanna, there were also possibly
letters going in the opposite direction. He left his stepfather
to ponder the potential consequences. He manipulated him
into a state of paranoia about them.'

'And he just went around there and killed her for them?'

'I don't know, but I should think he went around there in a
state of extreme fear that Yvette Mangon had some evidence that
could give him a motive for a vicious murder. I imagine that he
lost his temper once again.'

Masson looked less than impressed. 'Have you got anything
to substantiate any of this?'

Jean was a little more accepting. 'Do you know if he found
the letters?' she asked.

'I haven't the foggiest,' I replied cheerfully because, as far
as I was concerned, it didn't matter. Apparently it did to the
good Inspector, for he made the kind of sound that people make
when they have something stuck to the roof of their mouth. I
continued, 'I would suspect that he didn't, because I can testify
he was a bit jumpy about that time.' The bruise on my jaw line
had faded, but there was still an ache in the mandible beneath.

Jean said thoughtfully, 'So, you think that David then forged
a blackmail note from Jeremy Gillman so that his stepfather
would seek him out and kill him?'

'David's always had problems at school. If you ask his
teachers, he's been something of a trial for a lot of them, but
especially for Yvette Mangon and Jeremy Gillman. Those two
he had real run-ins with. Those two hated him and he hated
them, and he had found the perfect weapon with which to get
his revenge. His stepfather was none too bright, and easy to
manipulate; David knew exactly which levers to pull, and he
pulled them.'

She asked, 'Where does Arthur Silsby fit into all this?'

'Nowhere. He's just punishing himself because he had been told what was going on between one of his pupils and a member of the teaching staff, and he didn't want to know; he allowed himself to be fobbed with Miss Jeffries' convincing denials. He feels worthless and ashamed; he believes he has betrayed a sacred trust.'

Jean's face was closed down, a frown twisting it, although not in an unattractive way. Masson had his eyes closed and when it came, his sigh could have inflated a bouncy castle but he said nothing. Both Jean and I were left waiting for his next withering comment or sarcastic question.

Neither of which came through.

In the end, he enquired of no one in particular, 'These notes –' he indicated the ones I had produced for his delectation – 'these are practice notes, right?'

'I think so. I think that David Clarke can be extremely conscientious when he wants to be.'

Suddenly it was Jean's turn to be the epitome of doubt. 'Are you really expecting us to accept this story without a single shred of physical evidence? There is no forensic evidence connecting Mike Clarke to the deaths, let alone providing some basis for the idea that he was in turn manipulated by his stepson.' What could I say? She was right. 'And how did Mike Clarke find out who had sent the note, and where he lived?'

To my surprise and, I think, Jean's, Masson got there first. 'David told him. Probably not in an obvious way, but done subtly, done so that Mike Clarke wouldn't know he was being used.' He spoke in a voice that sounded, if not totally convinced, at least not completely contemptuous.

'Yes,' I said, encouraged. Jean looked as if she had just discovered that her cocktail sausage was a piece of poodle poo.

He nodded in the deepest of deep consideration. 'If I were David Clarke – evil mastermind, perhaps the most manipulative teenager on God's green earth – I wouldn't have hung on to my practice attempts at the blackmail note. I'd have got rid of them pretty sharpish.'

'He thought that he had.'

He cocked his head at me, one eyebrow raised. 'But he hadn't?'

'He threw them away in the dustbin,' I said.

Jean scoffed. 'Mike Clarke made a habit of going through the bins, did he?'

I asked, 'Aren't you forgetting something . . . or someone?'

She looked at Masson, who looked at me and then said, 'Joanna Clarke.'

FORTY-FOUR

'Joanna's got no love for her stepfamily. In her way, she's as evil and scheming as David. I even wonder if she was tired of her fling with Marlene Jeffries and she wanted it all to end anyway. She had no love for the teaching staff, so their systematic slaughter hardly bothered her. I would like to believe that she had no idea what was going on until she found the practice notes. I hope that it was quite by chance – she was in David's bedroom, looking to pinch that week's issue of *Smash Hits* from him. She accidentally knocked over his wastepaper bin and had to put it all back in; amongst the rubbish were the practice notes. When she saw them, she realized everything; she's no fool, and she told her father.'

Jean asked, 'How do you know all this?'

For once I was in a room with Masson and somebody else, and I wasn't his least favourite person. 'Because he's talked to her,' he told her sourly.

I explained, 'I've just come from where she's been fostered. Considering what's happened, she's amazingly calm; I would almost say that she's happy. She's certainly quite chatty about what's been going on, and she's got nothing to hide. She hated her stepbrother and hated her stepfather even more, and I can't blame her. You should talk to her.'

As soon as I said that, I regretted it. Masson turned a

scorching glare on Jean, who in turn surveyed me with a gaze I swear shrivelled my testes. Masson said in a low but deadly way, 'Yes, perhaps we should.'

FORTY-FIVE

Aand so here I am, one month later, still being a GP in Thornton Heath, still having to look regularly at someone's stye, or tongue, or armpit (only we in the medical profession call it an 'axilla' just to make sure that the general public think we're intelligent) or perhaps, if it's a good day, their perineum (don't even ask). Jean Abelson won't talk to me, but I'm starting to see that it might be for the best. Unfortunately, Max still won't talk to me either, but she'll come round, I'm sure. I know that she still loves me, deep down.

Arthur Silsby has died a rather unpleasant and totally undeserved death.

Regarding the Clarkes: Tricia has been charged with manslaughter and has been released on bail; she is living with her son David in a flat provided by the social services. Joanna is living with Ada in Kingswood Avenue. As far as I can determine, no legal action is planned against David because of lack of evidence.

So, life goes on, and whilst it does, so will death.

I called in on Dad this morning. It was the first day that we've had serious rain and boy, was it good. He was sitting in his conservatory, grimacing over the *Daily Telegraph* crossword, something he has done on a daily basis since he retired. He was tutting a lot, something else that he has done on a daily basis since he retired. Try as hard as I could, I could not see Ada having let him do that; it was too idiosyncratic, too unhusbandly.

'Hello, Lance,' he said jovially. 'How's things?'

'Well . . . you know.'

'Still no contact?' he asked, solicitously.

'No.'

'Don't worry, she'll come round. She's a sensible girl.'

Was she, I wondered? Maybe that was the problem. I said only, 'I expect so.'

He put down the paper. 'I've got some news.'

Just four words but, oh my Lord, what words!

'Have you?' I cannot lie, I spoke warily.

'I had a call yesterday from one of my old pals.'

My sense of horror was rising exponentially. 'Which one?' Dad had a lot of old friends but there was only a small chance that it would be one of the non-loony ones.

'Bill Wotherspoon.'

Only the news of an asteroid going to hit Thornton Heath within the next ten minutes could have been worse. William Wotherspoon had been a fighter pilot in the Second World War; he had been brave and resourceful and a hero; unfortunately, thirty years on and he still lived the same life, except that now he couldn't fly Hurricanes and kill Jerry. Subsequently, he was into displacement activity, big time. 'How is he?'

'He's on top form.'

'That's good.'

'Isn't it? He's asked me to help him out.'

I smiled; I don't know how, but I did. 'Doing what?'

'Raising money for charity.'

I knew instantly that he didn't mean shaking tins at the entrance to Waitrose. 'How?' I asked, my voice a curiously husky thing.

Dad, in total contrast, was excited.

'He's come across this curious thing they do in Mexico. Apparently they've been doing it for thousands of years. It's great fun and he thinks we can raise thousands of pounds.'

'What is it?'

'Something called bungee-jumping. He says it's great fun.'